Emily's Beau

Allison Lane

A SIGNET BOOK

SIGNET
Published by New American Library, a division of
Penguin Group (USA) Inc., 375 Hudson Street,
New York, New York 10014, U.S.A.
Penguin Books Ltd, 80 Strand,
London WC2R 0RL, England
Penguin Books Australia Ltd, 250 Camberwell Road,
Camberwell, Victoria 3124, Australia
Penguin Books Canada Ltd, 10 Alcorn Avenue,
Toronto, Ontario, Canada M4V 3B2
Penguin Books (N.Z.) Ltd, Cnr Rosedale and Airborne Roads,
Albany, Auckland 1310, New Zealand

Penguin Books Ltd, Registered Offices:
80 Strand, London WC2R 0RL, England

First published by Signet, an imprint of New American Library,
a division of Penguin Group (USA) Inc.

First Printing, October 2003
10 9 8 7 6 5 4 3 2 1

Chapter One

*J*acob Winters, eleventh Earl of Hawthorne, cursed the memories suddenly swirling through his mind—heat, filth, betrayal, and the intense hatred that had marred his final months in Bombay. They battered the calm he cultivated so assiduously, reminding him that his heritage included more than a title and fortune. He glared at Lieutenant Stevens, whose unexpected arrival had pierced his defenses. Years in India had added a too-familiar languor to the man's movements and a singsong cadence to his speech.

Another wall cracked, releasing images he wanted to forget—officers biting back protests to orders that should not have been issued . . . his nurse lying dead on his sixth birthday . . . his mother cringing in terror at every unfamiliar sound. Dark faces, white faces, highborn and low. And the one harsh face that had controlled them all . . .

Feelings returned that he'd tried to forget—overwhelming grief for those who had died, searing pain at the reminder of his father's broken promises, horror over the murder of—

He swept the memories back into hiding and slammed the door. "I'm told you bear letters."

"They are for the earl, sir."

"I am Hawthorne." Jacob bit back another curse.

Stevens must want his father. Didn't the regiment know the man had been dead for nineteen years?

Stevens bowed, then proffered a sealed note. "The matter is urgent, my lord. I should have arrived a month ago, but storms off the Cape prolonged my voyage."

The words freed other memories. His own voyage had been remarked for reaching England at all. Pirates had attacked off Madagascar. Storms shattered the mainmast and damaged the rudder. Disease claimed half the crew, encouraging a poisoner to ply his trade.

He shook the images away and scowled. What calamity in Bombay warranted posting an officer halfway around the world to call on a man who had retired twenty years ago? Major Winters had severed all ties to the regiment the moment he'd acceded to the Hawthorne title.

But he said nothing. Accepting the letter, he cracked the seal. It was brief, with none of the perorations so beloved of solicitors.

14 October 1817

Lord Hawthorne,

> *I regret to inform you that Colonel and Mrs. Wentworth died of typhoid yesterday, leaving their daughter orphaned. You are now the girl's guardian. She will sail for England on a Company merchantman in early November, accompanied by a suitable companion.*

> > *Robert Berriton, Esq.*
> > *Solicitor*
> > *East India Company*

"I don't know Colonel Wentworth." Jacob set the missive aside.

"He was the regiment's commander until his untimely death. I understood he'd been a friend of Major Winters earlier in his career."

"My father left the regiment in 1798."

Stevens extended a packet of documents. "Perhaps it was his wife who knew the major. Wentworth married a widow shortly after arriving in 1799. Her first husband served under Major Winters."

Dread pooled in Jacob's stomach. "His name?"

"Captain Nichols, my lord."

"And the girl?"

"Miss Harriet Nichols, born six months after the captain's unfortunate death."

Jacob clenched his teeth as grief welled. Captain Nichols had been his father's antithesis—kind, caring, never too busy to listen to a boy's chatter. Nichols had been the best part of his childhood, a surrogate father who almost compensated for his real father's neglect. But everything had changed when he'd married.

Jacob's hatred resurfaced as the image of Mrs. Nichols hovered before him. She'd been unworthy of such a fine man. If not for her, Captain Nichols would still live. What evil fate had thrust her brat into his care?

Captain Nichols would expect you to help, whispered his conscience. *He did so much for you. Don't blame the child for its mother's transgressions.*

"The situation is urgent," continued Stevens, recalling Jacob to the library. "If Miss Nichols boarded the November merchantman, she could arrive at any moment."

Jacob nodded as he rang for a footman. "You are acquainted with the girl?"

"Of course. You must know how small the English enclave is."

"Just so." No matter how many common soldiers were posted abroad, the officers mingled only with one another and with the more important envoys of the East India Company.

The footman arrived.

"Refresh yourself," suggested Jacob. "When I have studied these documents, we will speak again. We eat in two hours," he added.

He waited until the door closed behind Stevens before releasing a string of curses. Not that it helped. Even a large glass of brandy couldn't melt the ice gripping his chest. He'd thought he'd put Mrs. Nichols behind him. Now she was back and doubtless laughing at his predicament.

Guardian. To the daughter of the brassiest jade in Christendom.

Sucking in a deep breath, he spread out the papers.

The first described the birth of Harriet Nichols to Captain George Nichols and Mrs. Beatrice Nichols on December 14, 1798.

He cringed, remembering again that fateful day in June when word of Captain Nichols's death had dashed his hopes for the man's safety, shattering his reliance on justice for all time. He had dedicated his adult life to obtaining justice for others, but he knew life's vagaries too well to ever again expect it for himself.

The next page was marriage lines for then-Captain Wentworth to the Widow Nichols on January 3, 1799. Another naïve fool. He must have wed her immediately on arrival.

Jacob's jaw clenched. But Wentworth was hardly the first to succumb to Mrs. Nichols's blandishments. If only Captain Nichols had known what marriage would bring . . .

Shoving the paper aside, he picked up a copy of Wentworth's will. Dated May of 1799, it proved that he had quickly discovered his wife's defects. Disdain and distrust permeated the document, which left everything to his brother, Sir Harold Wentworth—a note in the margin valued his estate at ten thousand guineas. Out of that, Sir Harold was to pay one hundred guineas per annum to Wentworth's wife as long as she remained unwed. If she left India for any reason, she forfeited further claim on his estate. If she died within a year of his own demise, Harriet would receive a dowry of five hundred guineas. Otherwise, she got nothing.

The insult to Mrs. Wentworth was no surprise to anyone who knew the woman. Nor was the minimal amount left to Harriet. The girl was not Wentworth's, after all. But Wentworth's antagonism meant that Jacob could not appeal to Sir Harold to take Harriet in.

The ideal solution would be to send Harriet to the Nichols family, but there wasn't one. Captain Nichols had been the last of the line after his father and brother died in a fire in 1796. To prevent its demise, he'd sent home for a bride—a fatal mistake.

Now Jacob must repair the damage.

Don't blame the girl, his conscience repeated. *She is innocent.*

Maybe. But her breeding made that doubtful.

Jacob was still brooding about breeding when he joined Lieutenant Stevens in the Oakhaven dining room for dinner.

Most families passed peculiarities from generation to generation. The Raeburns produced madcap daughters who often ran mad in adulthood. Caldwells were mostly cads. At least five Dougherty men suffered the distasteful fits of falling sickness. His own family curse was blind obsession. So he must assume that Miss Nichols had inherited her mother's selfishness. One could control a selfish miss only by trading something she wanted for her good behavior.

She would want a husband. A five-hundred-guinea dowry would attract a merchant or farmer, which was all her mother's blood could aspire to. But Nichols had been gentry, so if Jacob could offer her a younger son or a professional man, maybe even a squire or baronet . . .

"Tell me about Miss Nichols," he urged his guest. "If I am to look after her, I need information."

"She is striking," admitted Stevens, helping himself to the broccoli. "Dark hair is common in India, of course, but porcelain skin and blue eyes are not, so she drew attention. And her vivacity made her the sweetheart of the regiment once Wentworth allowed her into local society."

Jacob's fork paused midway to his mouth. "Then why is she unwed at nineteen?"

"Choice." He shrugged. "The offers she's received would keep her in India, but she hates the heat, dust, and fevers."

Jacob nodded, though her antipathy puzzled him. He could understand it in one who had lived elsewhere, but why would Harriet notice? Like him, she'd been born there. He'd heard others complain about the heat and dust, but their words had meant little, since he'd known nothing else. He'd not realized how different India was until he moved to England.

The first week in his homeland remained clear in memory—the damp chilliness so different from India's monsoons, the daylight that lasted seemingly forever, the fog . . . It hadn't taken him long to revel in the cool mornings and soft light. Hawthorne Park didn't reek with stupefying odors. Nor did it teem with voracious rats. And when he'd bitten into his first fresh beef loin, he'd found heaven—in India, beef arrived in barrels from England, salted.

But despite hearing about England since birth, he'd formed none of those impressions before leaving India.

Stevens hadn't noticed his abstraction. "Miss Nichols also hates the military," he was saying. "Mrs. Wentworth encouraged her by painting a distorted image of England. Since many wives echoed her sentiments, Miss Nichols is determined to reach England's shores."

It was true that such tales might act as a lure for the greedy, Jacob admitted. Homesick men often spoke of England's vast wealth, its glittering elegance, and the majesty that overshadowed the most wealthy raj. Thus he'd expected gold-paved streets, panniers so wide ladies must sidle through doors, powdered wigs a foot high . . .

In truth, fashion had not been much different from

what officers' wives wore in Bombay, for powder had disappeared under the weight of new taxes, hairstyles had shrunk to clusters of curls, and gowns had become diaphanous draperies that clung to shapely legs—not that he'd thought of it that way at age eleven. The opulent buildings that filled Mayfair had seemed dark and cold with their thick walls and narrow windows. The streets were mere stone cobbles. And while London society dressed in silk and satin, the styles had seemed subdued after watching brocaded, bejeweled rajas and other Indian notables gather with Company leaders for a banquet.

But once he accepted the difference in details between story and reality, adjustment had been easy. Each tale's essence was uniquely British—and nothing like Bombay.

Harriet might have a harder time adjusting, though. Life as the ward of an earl would bear little resemblance to her mother's childhood.

"She will likely be disappointed," he said aloud. "Mrs. Wentworth can't have many good memories to pass on. Her own experiences were hardly endearing."

Curiosity lit Stevens's eyes. "I didn't realize you knew her."

"Not well." Too well, but he needn't reveal that. "Nichols was a family friend and our nearest neighbor. When he sent home for a bride, the parish chose an orphan who had recently come under its care."

"A common situation, though you must have confused Mrs. Wentworth with someone else," said Stevens stiffly, making Jacob wonder if he'd been enamored with her. "She was never a parish orphan. Her father was a baron, you know."

Possibly, but Jacob had no interest in discussing her, so he turned the subject. "I need to understand Miss Nichols's training. Describe Bombay's social calendar. I was ten when we left India, so I was not included in most gatherings."

Stevens's accent broadened as he spoke of balls and teas and other entertainments, sending shivers along

Jacob's arms. Every word evoked new memories. Some were good—like his mother dressing for a Christmas ball. But most were painful. He didn't want to listen, didn't want to recall those years. But duty called. If the merchantman found favorable winds, it could dock any day. Wasting time on recriminations was pointless. Harriet was now his responsibility.

He had planned to return to London next week for a debate in Parliament. Now he must leave at dawn. Harriet would need a companion and a proper place to live. Keeping her at Hawthorne House for even a day would invite scandal. And sending her to Hawthorne Park would be worse. Though he'd not visited his seat in ten years, it remained home to his aunt, widow of the ninth earl. His mother had shared enough tales of Mrs. Nichols that his aunt would never welcome Harriet.

He signaled the footman to clear. His best course was to consult his closest friends. Lord Charles Beaumont was a charmer whose fortune and breeding drew every matchmaker in town. In contrast, Richard Hughes projected a lighthearted conventionality that hid a hellion curbed only by pinched pockets. Both had sisters making bows this Season. He'd already agreed to help escort them, easing the burden on their mothers. His friends would delight in returning the favor. The three of them should find Harriet a match in no time.

Housing her was a bigger problem. Charles's mother, Lady Inslip, would take her in, but living at Inslip House would reduce Harriet's chances of meeting a suitable husband. The Marquess of Inslip was so far above her station that she would receive different invitations, complicating everyone's schedules. And since Charles kept his own rooms, Jacob would never know if Harriet proved disruptive. His sister Sophie might complain, of course—she was outspoken enough—but she posed other problems. Having already enjoyed three Seasons, Sophie no longer needed the close supervision a green girl required. It wasn't fair to restrict her.

So Inslip House was impossible.

Hughes House might work, though. Lady Hughes's long illness had eased enough to allow travel, so Emily would finally have a London Season at the advanced age of four-and-twenty. Richard's strained purse meant he had to live at Hughes House even when his parents and sister were in residence, thus he could keep a close eye on Harriet and prevent trouble. Lord Hughes would welcome the allowance that would cover Harriet's keep. Both Emily and Harriet would be in their first Season, and their stations were closer so they would receive similar invitations.

It would do. He hadn't seen Emily for several years, but she had always been a levelheaded, intelligent girl. He could trust her to accept Harriet and polish any rough edges in the girl's training.

His butler removed the covers, set out a platter of cheese and sweets, then left the men to their port.

While Jacob considered the arguments that would win Lord Hughes's cooperation, he encouraged Stevens to discuss the changes he'd seen in India during his ten years posted there. Having partaken freely of the wine, Stevens willingly embarked on a monologue, unaware that his host was no longer listening.

Tomorrow Jacob would discuss his dilemma with Richard and Charles. If they agreed with his assessment, he would seek out Lord Hughes. The viscount had reached town a week earlier and was likely reeling at the expense of mounting Emily's come-out.

Richard and Charles could help compile a list of younger sons and cousins who might like Harriet. If she was anything like her mother, she would jump at the chance to better her station. And if Stevens's description was accurate, she could be off his hands in a week. *Sweetheart of the Regiment* sounded promising.

Emily Hughes wiggled into the carriage seat beside a mountain of packages. This third shopping expedition in as many days had been exhausting, but she'd finally amassed the essentials for her Season. Excitement surged through her veins, making it hard to sit still.

She'd waited seemingly forever for this moment. Four years to finish growing up. Six more interminable years because of her father's financial reverses and her mother's endless illnesses, which always worsened in the spring. Then heavy rains had postponed their departure until the roads were dry enough to let Lady Hughes travel in comfort, so the Season was already underway. But she was in London at last. Only one last wait remained—Jacob had stayed late at Oakhaven, overseeing the spring planting, but he would return next week.

Thoughts of the man she loved increased her excitement. Sunlight turned his eyes bluer than a summer sky. His silky hair seemed at odds with the rugged planes of his face, but touching it drove her fingers wild. He was tall enough to stand out in any crowd. She couldn't wait to again caress those powerful shoulders and mold his chiseled lips with her own.

It had been ten years since she'd last seen him. Ten years since he'd crushed her against his hard body, ravishing her mouth. Ten years since her heart had been her own.

She'd tried to reclaim it—after all, he'd insulted her brutally before abandoning the orchard that day. Yet she'd failed. She might have been barely fourteen, but his kiss had propelled her from the schoolroom into the world of adult passion. His rejection couldn't erase that, especially since she knew how much he'd wanted her. He'd figured prominently in her dreams ever since.

A week had passed before her anger had cooled enough to admit that he'd been right to leave. Fourteen was too young for marriage. She'd needed to grow up before they could be together.

Now the time had finally arrived.

The carriage bounced, feeding her excitement. She was the most fortunate of girls, for the Season held no terrors, no uncertainty, nothing to threaten her success. A fixed future had made it easy to be gracious when her father admitted that he could not afford even a small ball. Jacob would give her a ball the moment they were wed.

She knew how it would be, had dreamed of it over and over, the image growing clearer with each postponement of the moment. He would spot her as she entered her first ballroom. Brushing past the other guests as if they didn't exist, he would rush to her side, sweep her into a waltz, then propose on the spot.

She would wear the pale yellow Venetian gauze with its broad blond flounce edged in roses and pearls. Even her dull brown hair and muddy brown eyes seemed brighter when she wore yellow. The fan she'd bought this morning would be perfect—yellow silk painted with a pastoral scene. Her grandmother's pearls. And the yellow slippers with—

"We're here," said Huggins from beneath a pile of parcels.

"Of course." She pulled herself together. Not once in ten years had she revealed her love, and she wasn't about to slip now. She looked forward to everyone's surprise at her instant success almost as much as to her next meeting with Jacob. So she chattered gaily about the day's shopping even as her mind remained on *him*.

Jacob, whose dark hair was usually a little too long for fashion, whose laugh could send shivers down her spine that had nothing to do with cold, whose reputation—

She wouldn't think of that. All young men sowed wild oats.

He was one of her brother's best friends and had often visited Cherry Hill during his school days. As had Charles, for that matter. Now that the three lived in town, she had to glean information about Jacob from Richard—which meant listening to interminable tales of Charles, too. But singling Jacob out might raise questions that would reveal that kiss. Even ten years later, the incident could cause him trouble. Richard would be appalled, and her father—

Their footman lowered the steps and helped her down.

Richard wasn't her only source of news, of course. Jacob's aunt, widow of the ninth earl, lived at Hawthorne Park. Emily called often—unremarkable, for she called on all her neighbors. And she had no trouble hiding her interest in Jacob. Lady Hawthorne doted on him, sharing his letters with everyone.

Now her secrecy was nearly at an end. In another week he would claim her, letting her shout her love to the world. The next time she saw Hawthorne Park, it would be as Jacob's countess.

Leaving Huggins to deal with her packages, she skipped up the steps and into the hall . . . and bounced off a gentleman unaccountably standing inside the door.

"Oomph!" she grunted as his hand shot out to catch her.

"Steady, Miss Hughes. You must temper your exuberance. This isn't a racetrack."

Jacob.

Emily backed into the wall, her head shaking in disbelief. This was all wrong. He wasn't due until next week. She was wearing a faded walking dress two years old. Her bonnet—

Forcing air into her lungs, she curtsied, then managed, "My lord. How pleasant to see you again."

"And you." But his tone dismissed her as negligible.

She cringed. How could she meet the love of her life when she looked like a hoyden who'd been dragged through a hedge?

Without another word, he turned back to Richard. "Convey my appreciation to your father. He has my eternal gratitude. I'd no place else to turn."

"It's nothing," said Richard. "Even Mama seems pleased."

"About what?" Emily forgot her embarrassment, touching Jacob's arm so he had to look at her.

"Ask your mother, Tadpole. I'm pressed for time." His use of the despised childhood nickname threatening her with tears. "White's tonight?" he added to Richard.

"Charles will join us for dinner."

Jacob nodded, then left without another word.

"What was that all about?" Only fierce effort kept Emily's voice steady. Her hand burned where she'd touched him.

But Richard was as dismissive as Jacob. "Just a small favor, Em. Mama will explain." He headed for the study, leaving her to climb the stairs to the drawing room alone.

Something was up that neither man wanted to discuss—how often had they hidden secrets in just this way? Their capacity for ignoring questions had long infuriated her. It was one reason Jacob's openness that summer had been so precious. But what could he be hiding now?

Needing time to regain her composure—and not wanting her mother to spot the sheen in her eyes— she passed the drawing room and continued up to her bedroom.

"Stupid girl!" she cursed her reflection as she removed her bonnet. "Scrape the stars out of your eyes."

Footsteps in the hall snapped her mouth shut, but the oaths continued to bounce through her head. Jacob had been less than dazzled to see her.

She wanted to blame her appearance, but he'd seen her looking worse—like the day he'd fished her from the lake after a tree branch cracked, dumping her in. It had been the most frightening experience of her life—yet also exhilarating. He'd dragged her ashore, then held her until the shaking stopped, all the while murmuring soothing nonsense into her ears. His warmth had driven away her chills, replacing them with heat as sparks rampaged along her nerves.

The next afternoon had been that devastating kiss . . .

Idiot! He could hardly sweep you into his arms in front of an audience.

"True." He couldn't know that she still loved him— one of his charges had been that she was too young to know her mind. With Richard standing in the hall— to say nothing of the servants—he could only treat her as Richard's baby sister. They must talk privately before pledging their love in public. Perhaps his abrupt departure covered his struggle to remain aloof.

A weight lifted from her chest, restoring her excitement. Everything would be all right. She could wait. Hadn't she waited ten years already? Hadn't she expected a week more?

As Huggins pushed open the door, Emily smiled brightly, smoothed her skirts, and headed downstairs.

The drawing room hadn't been refurbished since her grandmother's tenure, but the staff kept the French furnishings impeccably clean. The red silk wallcoverings had long since faded to rose, but they still added warmth to the space. A new Grecian sofa covered the worn spot in the carpet and gave Lady Hughes a place to lie during the day.

"There you are, dear," she said as Emily entered. Her waxen cheeks were nearly transparent, confirming how difficult she'd found their recent journey. On days like this, Emily felt selfish for expecting a Season. Even stretching the two-day journey into four hadn't kept it from draining Lady Hughes's meager store of energy.

"You look tired, Mama," she said, pressing her hand before taking the nearest seat so Lady Hughes needn't raise her voice.

"A little, but I've wonderful news for you. Lord Hawthorne has asked us to take in his ward. It is a marvelous honor, and she will provide company for you."

"Why would she be in town?" asked Emily, frowning. "It would make more sense to send her and her governess to Hawthorne Park."

"Miss Nichols is past needing a governess. She is coming out, just as you are. The earl and Richard can chaperon you together, allowing me to rest. And I'm sure you will enjoy having a friend beside you at balls. I often wished there was someone with whom to share confidences during my own come-out. So many incidents require a stoic response in public when one would so much prefer to laugh."

Emily stared, the words buzzing loudly in her ears. Share her come-out with a stranger? Six postponements, only to be saddled with a green girl? And Jacob's ward to boot. Where the devil had he acquired a ward? Lady Hawthorne had said nothing of it, though they'd last spoken only a week ago.

She wanted to scream.

But it wasn't possible. Her mother would fall into a swoon at the first sign of unpleasantness. Triggering one of her spells would postpone this come-out yet again.

"Who is Miss Nichols?" Emily asked with credible calm.

"His ward," said Lady Hughes crossly. "I told you."

"But who is her family? I know nothing of any Nichols." She knew Jacob's family tree as well as her own. There wasn't a Nichols on it.

"As to that, he didn't say, though he mentioned India."

"Captain Nichols was a close friend of Jacob's father," said Richard, joining them. "His daughter Harriet is now nineteen. Her mother died last autumn, naming Hawthorne as her guardian. There is no other family. She will arrive from Bombay any day now, and he can hardly house her himself."

"True." Such an arrangement was too scandalous to contemplate. But she was reeling. Of all the times she and Jacob had talked, he had never once mentioned his life in India. Even in childhood, when he'd been back only a short time, he'd turned aside any questions. It was as if the first ten years of his life didn't exist.

She didn't recall his actual return, of course—she'd been in the nursery at the time—and though he'd met Richard shortly afterward, they'd not become close until Jacob started school the following year. Only then had he started spending more time at Cherry Hill than at Hawthorne Park. Richard had once remarked that the death of Jacob's parents had cast shadows over the park that Jacob couldn't forget.

Emily understood. She meant to erase those shadows once they were wed. Her success would boost his love even further and—

"This is a wonderful opportunity for all of us," repeated Lady Hughes. "Her housing allowance will let us expand your wardrobe, increasing your chances of drawing attention. Perhaps we can even afford a rout—I know we'd talked of holding one, but I didn't know how we could manage. Everything is so much more dear than I recalled. Your father was complaining only this morning—"

"You needn't fret about our finances," said Richard, patting her hand. "That is not your affair. If you want a rout, we will hold one, but do not schedule anything until you discover how wearying it would be. For now, have you finished the list of friends we must notify of your arrival?"

"Yes, but—"

Emily swallowed a snort. Lady Hughes would never manage a rout, which would keep her in a receiving line for hours. Nor did she know the first thing about expenses, having lost interest in the world twenty years ago after suffering a debilitating miscarriage. Ten years later, she'd turned her last duties over to her only daughter and taken permanently to her sofa, preferring to wallow in her fragility rather than oversee the staff.

Emily suppressed the suspicion that some of her relapses had been exaggerated to keep that daughter home until Richard was of an age to wed, allowing his wife to run the manor.

Richard again patted his mother's hand. "Hawthorne trusts us to take good care of Miss Nichols. She will likely be a trifle rustic, having never moved in the more exalted circles, so we must be ready to smooth her manners. Em and I will take care of that. You need only welcome her."

Emily nodded, but inside she was moaning. How could Jacob do this to her? Not only must she share her Season, but she must teach his ward how to go on in society, then accept the blame if the girl misbehaved.

Yet wasn't this proof of his love and trust? He must know how frail Lady Hughes was. Even a restricted social schedule would exhaust her, so Richard would be Emily's primary escort. If that frailty hadn't postponed her debut, she and Jacob would have long since wed, making Miss Nichols her responsibility. So who better to take charge of the girl?

Housing Miss Nichols at Hughes House would allow him to call often without raising eyebrows and to remain at her side every night.

Satisfied, she poured tea and let her mother chatter while her mind recalled today's glimpse of her beloved. Their collision had stolen her breath.

He had become an imposing man, adding breadth to the height he'd achieved at age twenty. His eyes still burned like sunlit sapphires. His hard body exuded a masculinity that recalled the feel of his lips on hers, his long fingers digging into her skin as he crushed her in his arms. His manhood had pressed against her stomach, igniting sensations that loomed large in many a dream. His tongue—

Heat pooled between her legs. Her fingers itched. The longing was more powerful than ever, though she couldn't explain what she wanted beyond Jacob himself. But the wait was unbearable. Heat made her want to rip off her clothes. She might have run for miles as far as her body was concerned.

To hide the breathing that refused to stay even, she excused herself to change for dinner.

Tomorrow she would attend the Penleigh ball, where Jacob would sweep her into his arms forever . . .

Chapter Two

*J*acob's heartbeat had yet to slow when he reached Hawthorne House ten minutes after leaving Hughes House. Slamming his study door did little to lessen his shock. He felt like he'd been kicked.

Emily had grown into a stunning lady. Not a diamond in the conventional sense, for she lacked the peaches-and-cream beauty that was currently popular. But her honey-brown hair and golden eyes would turn heads. And her natural manner felt refreshing after years of fending off determined flirtation.

He hated being a matrimonial prize. Girls stalked him, following him into gardens and private rooms, accosting him on the street, interrupting conversations. Yet none cared about him, coveting only his title and wealth. They would betray him as easily as breathe.

But Emily remained a friend, thank God. She had never tried to attach him, making her the only female he could trust. Even Charles's sister Sophie was flirtatious enough to raise alarms. That niggling fear that she was holding out for his offer grew stronger every time she passed another Season without encouraging anyone in her court.

He'd feared that his stupidity ten years ago had irrevocably shattered his friendship with Emily, but she had seemingly put the incident behind her. Or so he hoped; wariness had flashed in her eyes when she'd identified him—and who could blame her? But she would soon realize he meant her no harm. He could finally set his grief aside.

For the first time in years, he allowed himself to recall their last summer together. He'd been twenty, home on long break, and frustrated because his requests to discuss the earldom that would soon be his had fallen on deaf ears. His trustees had refused to answer his questions. Even the Hawthorne steward had ignored him.

He'd been furious. Did they expect him to magically transform into a knowledgeable owner overnight?

The answer had been *no*. They had expected the ignorant earl to retain them as his advisers and administrators, just as his father and uncle had done. After all, what did a greenling know about the vast Hawthorne estates and complex Hawthorne investments? He would need help, and who better to provide it than the men who had run the earldom for twenty years?

His uncle, the ninth earl, had ignored his inheritance, preferring the excitement of London to the tedium of business, so he'd left the men hired by the eighth earl in charge. Jacob's father had spent most of his brief tenure out of touch. He'd died six months after returning from India, having done little more than sign whatever people handed him. With Jacob only eleven at the time, the consortium of stewards, bankers, and trustees had continued in power. By the time he had come of age, they had treated the earldom as their personal fiefdom.

Thus he'd been helpless that last summer of his minority. His aunt understood his need to learn, but couldn't help. With even the tenants unwilling to speak to him, Jacob had spent his days at Cherry Hill talking to Richard, for Lord Hughes had groomed him in estate management from birth.

That was the year Emily had changed from pest to friend.

Since the day she'd left leading strings, she'd followed the boys relentlessly, insisting that they include

her in their adventures. It had been cute when she
was six, but his tolerance had rapidly waned, though
for Richard's sake, he hadn't complained.

Jacob shook his head. That year had been different.

Emily at fourteen had been a sympathetic listener
willing to endure his rants. And he'd had plenty to
rant about—Hawthorne Park, his trustees, his steward,
his London banker, tutors at school . . . Once he realized that she never repeated his confidences—not even
to Richard—he'd said plenty. In retrospect, some of
his tirades made him cringe. He must have sounded
mad at the world and everyone in it. But Emily had
merely smiled. Sometimes she shook her head. Fre-
quently she offered amazingly sensible advice.

As a result, he'd sought her out often. He could tell
her things he couldn't tell Richard lest he seem to rub
his fortune in Richard's face. Even Charles didn't
know some of the things he'd told Emily. Talking to
her never failed to ease his mind and brighten his day.

It was probably her sense that had made her seem
older than her years. When he'd mentioned that Hawthorne Park would benefit from adopting new agricul-
tural methods, she'd agreed but warned him that
tenants were often suspicious, so he should be careful
how he introduced change. She'd described agitators
who played on ignorance and fear to foment rebellion
against machinery, then urged him to educate his dependents so they could judge ideas for themselves.

He'd taken her advice to heart and included everyone in his discussions, down to the last field hand. As
a result, Hawthorne Park had been spared trouble
four years later when General Ludd and his frame-
breakers urged everyone to riot.

He and Emily had become friends that summer,
though few would think it possible. And though they
never arranged meetings, they ran into each other
three or four times a week. She'd still been a child,
so he'd not feared compromising her. She was safe.

Thus he'd searched her out the day before he returned to Oxford, to thank her for her advice and bid her farewell. Another summer gone. A frustrating period survived. By his next term break, he would be of age and able to act.

He still didn't know how it had happened. They had wandered through an orchard heavy with ripening apples, talking lightly as always. She had wished him well with his studies. He had compared them to her pianoforte lessons, which she hated. When they returned to his horse, he'd placed a friendly good-bye kiss on her cheek. . . .

The next thing he knew, he was devouring her mouth, pulling her tightly against his heavy arousal, reaching for the ties that would bare her half-formed breasts to his hands. Her nails dug into his back. Her cries clogged his throat, muffling his moans.

Appalled—she was barely fourteen and his best friend's sister—he'd shoved her away, ignoring her shock, her pain, and even the stumble that pitched her to the ground.

"Go back to the schoolroom, Tadpole," he'd snapped. "If you want to be a courtesan, I know a brothel that specializes in young country misses. But I doubt you'd like it. Take my advice and grow up before tangling with men."

Without waiting for a response, he'd leaped onto his horse and sped away, leaving her sprawled in a pile of old leaves, her lips still wet from his kisses.

Shocked that he could entertain lascivious thoughts about a girl who was little more than a child—he despised men who frequented such brothels—he had viciously suppressed the incident and concentrated on school. He couldn't afford to think of it, even to castigate himself for his stupidity. If Richard ever discovered how close Jacob had come to defiling his sister . . .

Gaining control of his inheritance had finally distracted him, for it entailed hours of study, numerous confrontations, and close supervision of his new employees. By the time he had everything under control, the incident in the orchard had been locked away with other ancient memories.

But it had exerted a profound influence on his life, he admitted now. He had never returned to Hawthorne Park, not even during the transition period. He'd let his new man of business turn off the old steward, then make the annual inspection tours to see that all was well. He'd thrown his own energy into Parliament, splitting his time between his Grosvenor Square house and the small estate of Oakhaven in Surrey. Gloucestershire was too far from town.

The incident had been a warning. Too many of his ancestors had lost control by letting untidy emotions rule their lives. In his family, emotion quickly became obsession, leading to bad decisions, lost chances, and lifelong regret. He'd nearly fallen into the same trap with Emily.

Ever since that slip, he'd kept emotion locked away with his unwanted memories. The only way to protect himself was to remain aloof, especially from women. So he avoided society ladies, refused to keep a mistress, and rarely bedded any courtesan twice.

Jacob poured brandy, then settled into his favorite chair. Notes for an upcoming debate in Lords sat at his elbow, but for once, he ignored them.

He could no longer deny that he'd drifted into an infatuation for Emily that summer. Luckily, school and his inheritance had drawn him away before it had gone too far. But today's reaction proved that he remained vulnerable. Her womanly curves made her more desirable than ever—which meant that housing Harriet with her family was a serious mistake. The Winters obsession lurked in every Winters breast, a curse waiting to strike him as it had done others before.

Only the entail had kept Hawthorne Park intact after his great-grandfather sank everything and then some into the South Seas Bubble. Loan payments had kept his son in poverty for years afterward.

Then there was his father's cousin, who had fallen in love while attending a friend's wedding. Unfortunately, his inamorata had been the bride. Ignoring custom, honor, and even common sense, he'd taken insane risks to be with her, ultimately perishing in a duel when her husband discovered the affair. Her first child had the felicity of being female, for it was obviously a Winters.

The tales would fill several thick tomes. Every generation. Nearly every male and many of the females. Greed, dishonor, recklessness, and more, all the result of obsession. The Winters blood was passionate, driving the family to its doom. Jacob was determined to avoid adding new scandal to the family legend. His narrow escape with Emily had shown him how vulnerable he was.

He was more susceptible than the worst of his ancestors, for he had inherited dishonorable blood from his mother, too. His only hope for a reputable life was to avoid caring for anyone or anything. As for an heir, he would eventually wed someone unlikable who would welcome living apart once she completed her duty.

But not Emily. She was too enticing. It was good that she remained wary of him.

Yet that wariness hurt, he admitted. Did she think him caddish enough to reveal their kiss, tarnishing her reputation at the very moment she was entering society?

"Damn it, Em!" he growled. "Don't you know me better than that?"

Unfortunately, she did. She was more perspicacious than even his friends and might recognize the latent violence seething inside him. News of Harriet's imminent arrival had stripped some of his defenses, bringing that violence closer to the surface.

He badly needed to concentrate on Parliament. Its ponderous deliberations always brought his temper under control. Unfortunately, he had agreed to escort Emily and Sophie this Season. With Harriet due soon, he could not renege.

But Harriet must wed quickly—keeping her at Hughes House would force him into Emily's company too often for comfort. While Harriet worked on finding favor with London gentlemen, he would compile a list of country suitors—farmers, squires, merchants—in case anything went wrong.

Relaxing, he drained his brandy, then picked up his notes.

Emily checked Harriet's room. It was small, having originally been meant for a governess or tutor, but it was the best they could provide. Hughes House had never been large, and a tight budget meant Richard could not afford his own rooms despite his advanced age of nine-and-twenty.

That hadn't been a problem until now, for her parents had last visited London fifteen years ago. But having the run of the town house since leaving school must make sharing onerous for him. She'd overheard enough from the servants to know he was accustomed to holding parties that included courtesans. And while he'd never kept his own mistress—money again—he had a reputation for enjoying the favors of many a bored matron. Their parents might accept his angelic façade, but she knew his true nature.

Shaking away truths she wasn't supposed to understand, she smiled at Molly and Rose.

"Well done," she told the maids. "It looks every bit as nice as my room. I'm sure Miss Nichols will be pleased."

They blushed and curtsied, then hurried away.

The moment they were gone, Emily's face slipped into a frown. Everything was ready for Harriet's arrival. The real question was whether Harriet would be ready for London.

Over breakfast, Richard had regaled her with everything Jacob knew about Harriet. She had apparently been the regiment's diamond, basking in attention from all and sundry—which sounded good, except that parties in remote military outposts had little in common with society gatherings. Harriet would be rustic at best.

Emily foresaw tense discussions as she tried to cram years of lessons into a few days, starting with an explanation of how Harriet's background would affect her reception. Few military wives hailed from the aristocracy, so it was doubtful that she would understand the nuances of society manners.

Girls relied on breeding, beauty, and behavior to attract a husband. Exquisite beauty could overcome marginal breeding if the behavior was impeccable. But Harriet's beauty might be merely average. Her success in Bombay could as easily have arisen from her stepfather's position or the scarcity of English girls in the area.

She turned when the footman rapped on the door-jamb.

"Lady Hughes requests your presence in the drawing room, Miss Emily. Lord Hawthorne and Miss Nichols have arrived."

So soon? But her heart raced at this chance to see Jacob when she was clad in one of her new gowns. Pausing before a pier glass, she smoothed her skirts and tucked a wayward strand of hair behind one ear. This time, he would encounter a poised, gracious lady capable of handling any task he gave her.

Emily recoiled from the tension crackling through the drawing room. A tableau of three statues and a flame stopped her just inside the doorway.

Lady Hughes lay on her couch, clutching her vinaigrette to ward off a swoon.

Richard stood with his back to the window, his jaw open and his tongue hanging out. He hadn't looked that stunned since the day his pony had kicked his thigh, narrowly missing more vulnerable parts.

Jacob stood by the fireplace, looking every inch a powerful, wealthy lord in a wine coat trimmed in black velvet to match his hair. Gray pantaloons outlined his muscular thighs. His boots gleamed.

The focus of everyone's attention was the girl clinging to his arm in a most unseemly fashion. She was violently alive, exuding a force that diminished everyone else. Emily felt instantly dowdy, like the ugly stepsisters in the fairy tale. If Richard's reaction was typical, Miss Nichols could start a riot by simply walking outside. She was an exotic, tropical flower transplanted into a barren field.

Jacob did not look pleased. "There you are, Miss Hughes," he said, catching Emily's eye. He made it sound as if he'd been waiting hours for her arrival. "I must again apologize for giving you so little warning."

"It is nothing, my lord," she said gravely.

He gestured to the girl pressed against his side. "My ward, Miss Harriet Nichols. Miss Emily Hughes. Pay close attention to her instructions," he added, stepping far enough away that Harriet could curtsy.

"Miss Nichols." Emily inclined her head, but inside, she was quaking. Her initial impression seemed truer every moment. Harriet was a Siren—striking black hair that made her blue eyes seem mysteriously transparent, a very red mouth that pouted provocatively, exaggerated curves readily apparent under a scandalous gown of the thinnest cotton she'd ever seen. Its neckline plunged so low it barely covered the shadowy circles of her nipples, clearly visible even in moderate light because Harriet wore no corset. And possibly no shift! The gown clung to every generous curve. Her languid motion as she swayed against Jacob demanded attention.

Richard took an involuntary step forward, his tight-fitting pantaloons revealing his reaction to anyone with eyes. The very air thickened as he studied her bosom.

Harriet was Trouble. This was no English miss. And Jacob didn't treat her as one. He made no attempt to seat her, no objection when she practically crawled inside his coat, and his eyes seemed frankly appraising whenever they touched her.

Emily drew in a shaky breath. She had never

watched a pair of rakes size up a potential conquest before, but she had no doubt about their current thoughts. Jacob might have better control—his manhood was barely stirring—but she could feel his awareness.

What was she to do with Harriet? She couldn't imagine Miss Nichols running an English household. Nor would a gentleman want a wife with such flagrant power to attract others. Every male in town would fall panting at her feet, for she was fully aware of her effect and basked in her power.

"Pay strict attention to Miss Hughes," Jacob repeated when Harriet laid a beseeching hand on his arm.

"Of course, my Jacob." Her voice had a lilt that enhanced her foreignness. She deepened her pout. "But it would be so much easier if you—"

"No. We've spoken of this already. It is important that you learn to go on in society, so you will stay here and study manners." He turned to Emily, who remained barely two steps from the door. "She has a ball gown, so I will return at eight to escort you to Lady Penleigh's. Order anything she needs. For now, I have a meeting I cannot postpone."

"Of cour—"

"You can't leave me here!" Harriet wailed, plastering herself against him. Her lashes were the longest Emily had ever seen.

"I know this will be difficult for you, but neither of us has a choice," he said firmly, gently forcing her into a chair. "Now behave yourself and pay attention. I will return this evening." Turning to Lady Hughes, he smiled. "Thank you for taking her in. I am forever in your debt. And yours," he added to Emily as he headed for the door. Beckoning Richard, he left the room.

Richard reluctantly followed, taking much of the tension with him.

Emily wanted to run after them and demand answers to the thousands of questions tumbling about her head. Jacob had paid her less heed than the furniture. Even her days as Richard's pesky sister had garnered her more notice.

But chasing him down would be impossibly gauche. And leaving her mother to deal with the too-exotic Harriet would be worse. Lady Hughes could never handle her. Emily feared she couldn't, either.

"Welcome, child." Lady Hughes said, covering Emily's indecision. "I hope you will tell me if you need anything. I can do little myself, but I will see that my staff makes you comfortable."

"You are kind." Harriet's tone belied her words.

"But ill," put in Emily with a pointed stare.

Harriet mouthed sympathy while Emily castigated herself for letting jealousy make her rude.

"You must be weary," she said in contrition. "You've doubtless had a grueling journey. To be thrown in with strangers at the end of it can be overwhelming."

"How very astute." Lady Hughes nodded. "Emily will show you to your room and discuss tonight's ball. It is very important to make the right impression. A bad one can color your entire Season."

"Of course." Emily led Harriet upstairs, understanding her mother's unspoken command. Given the unsuitability of her gown, Emily must discover the state of Harriet's wardrobe and find out if the girl's maid was up to London standards. A difficult job, for tonight would be her first London ball, too, so her own knowledge was sketchy. But if Harriet was to find a suitor instead of a protector, Emily must transform this exotic orchid into an English rose. In half a day.

"Have you a maid?" she asked when they reached Harriet's room.

"Mine refused to leave Bombay. I shared Mrs. Paine's maid on board ship—she accompanied me from India but has nothing to do with society. Jacob assured me that he would hire a new one."

"Good." She paused, but the lessons must start immediately. If Harriet had any hope of making a successful appearance tonight, it was impossible to wait until they were comfortable with each other. "London is very formal, Miss Nichols. Never use anyone's given name without permission, and even with permission, you can use it only in private. Your guardian is Lord Hawthorne. Never call him anything else when others are present."

"But—"

"Do you wish to be cut?"

"No."

"Then you must adhere to the rules. Even I, who have known him since childhood, call him Lord Hawthorne in public. I understand your father was the younger son of a vicar."

"So?"

"So your breeding is marginal by London standards. Lord Hawthorne's sponsorship will garner invitations to some events, but not all. And the hostesses will not forgive indiscretions. Poor manners will see you cut in a trice. We will do our best to bring you out properly, but there are limits to what we can accomplish. I presume Lord Hawthorne explained that already."

Harriet scowled. "I was the belle of the army and pursued by Company representatives and every gentleman who visited Bombay."

"I'm sure you were," said Emily, hiding exasperation. "You are lovely, as you must know. But men have very different standards in foreign ports than in London drawing rooms. The military's acceptance of deeds in lieu of breeding does not exist here. Never forget that society is controlled by ladies, not men, and the most powerful of those ladies are the Almack's patronesses. Beauty will not sway them, for they judge on breeding and behavior. Without their support, you are nothing. So show deference to everyone."

"Everyone?"

"That way you will make no mistakes. It is unlikely that you will meet many people below your own station. But enough of that. May I see your wardrobe? The gown you are wearing is lovely, but unsuited for daytime wear."

"Why?"

"The neckline is too low, and the fabric thin enough to freeze you."

"True. It is very cold. I should have worn a shawl."

"And a gown that covers your shoulders."

"Absurd!" Harriet scowled. "No one covers the shoulders."

"In India, perhaps, but fashion is different here. Your position does not allow you to flout accepted standards. This year's gowns bare the shoulders only at night."

Harriet's eyes flashed, but she closed her mouth and turned toward the wardrobe. The maids had already unpacked her trunks.

Emily said little while Harriet displayed her gowns. Keeping the girl out of trouble would be a bigger challenge than she'd expected. And while Jacob could help at night, Emily would have the entire responsibility during the crucial morning calls, where the dowagers formed their opinions.

The next months would be nothing like her dreams. Having an exotic flower constantly at her elbow would throw her into the shadows. Thank heaven her future was assured.

Already she disliked Harriet, who embodied all the arrogance of a diamond despite lacking the breeding of one. It was not a demeanor calculated to win society's approval. Hostesses and gossips expected deference, not a supercilious smirk.

When the last gown had been held up for examination, Emily sighed. "The blue will do for tonight—barely—and the green will make a suitable dinner gown for dining *en famille*. But the others need work." She pointed to three gowns of printed cotton. "Adding a lace fichu will make these acceptable as morning gowns, but they will not look *au courant* no matter what you do. This shawl is very nice, though, and will likely draw envious glances. And adding a flounce to the pink might produce an acceptable theater dress."

"What about the gold silk? It's my best gown."

"But five years out of date. The skirt is too slim and contains little ornamentation. We can recover some fabric by removing the demi-train, but not enough to add fullness. See mine? It is a simple morning gown, but the skirt is full enough to swirl as I move, and it ends in a deep flounce. Ball gowns need multiple rows of ornamentation to be au courant. And everything, day or evening, requires a corset and petticoats."

"But—"

"If your maid is talented, she might fashion the gold into an open robe over a contrasting slip. It is a style that is returning to favor, and I agree that the fabric is beautiful. As for this—" She pointed to a pale yellow with matching spencer. "Silk is not suited to walking dresses. Even wearing both spencer and shawl will leave you cold. The park requires a pelisse this early in the year. We will have to call on the dressmaker immediately. Lord Hawthorne's credit will speed things, but it will take a week to gather even a minimal wardrobe. This is the busiest time of the year."

Harriet's eyes lit up. "It will be fun to visit a dressmaker. Wentworth had nothing beyond his military pay, so we were always in debt and could rarely buy new gowns. Mama complained often that he had pretended to a comfortable income before marriage. It took her a year of begging before he would buy her that shawl."

Emily shook her head, but this explained why so many of Harriet's gowns were unsuited to her age. She was using her mother's clothing as well as her own.

Which raised new questions—such as the size of her dowry. Unless it was substantial, she was doomed. Beauty might draw eyes, but with marginal breeding and questionable manners, she needed a fortune if she was to make a successful match.

"Wentworth always hated me," continued Harriet.

"Why?"

"I wasn't his, of course. My real father was a talented and respected officer who would be a general by now had he lived. Everyone loved him. His death was a tragedy, but also glorious, for he sacrificed himself to save three of his men—Mama wept whenever she recalled his fate. She loved him dearly."

Emily started to speak, but Harriet swept on.

"The other officers hated Wentworth, calling him a brutal tyrant and worse. But his harsh treatment of subordinates was nothing compared to how he treated me. I was proof that his failure to produce a son was his fault. He kept me shut away for years, hiding my very existence. And he begrudged me every rupee. Even after he became a colonel, he refused to increase my pin money."

Emily wasn't sure what to say—or where to start pointing out the subjects no girl discussed.

"At least I had Mama," continued Harriet, stroking the brightly colored shawl. "She loved me very much. If she'd had funds of her own, we would have fled to England long ago. She talked about it often—the places we'd see, the people we'd meet. . . ."

"And now you're here."

"I know. It's a dream come true. And I'm so pleased that Jacob is not like Wentworth."

"Lord Hawthorne," Emily reminded her.

"Of course. He is the most wonderful man. I nearly expired in relief when he said to buy anything I need. I had no idea what to expect, you see. No one knew anything about him beyond that he was Papa's closest friend. I thought he'd be an old man. But it was really Jacob's father—Lord Hawthorne's father who was Papa's friend," she said, correcting herself. "Ja—this Lord Hawthorne was born in India, too, so he knows what it is like. And he knows how awful my voyage was. I was never so sick in my life. Even though Captain Hartwell assured me—"

Emily closed her ears to Harriet's chatter. Her worst

fears were being confirmed. Harriet bordered on vulgar and had little concept of what constituted genteel conversation. When they returned from the dressmaker's, they must start immediate lessons.

Jacob heaved a sigh of relief as he left Hughes House. After three hours in Harriet's company, he was ready to run, screaming, from London. He should have sent his man of business to collect her from the docks. But he'd thought the personal touch might settle her fears.

What it had done was knock his plans into chaos. Harriet was trouble. The suitable companion provided by the Company was a vulgar widow with no manners and no sense of propriety. Despite that it had been barely nine when he'd collected her, Harriet had donned a gown that would have shocked even a courtesan as unflappable as Harriette Wilson. What had they been thinking? Bombay wasn't *that* out of touch.

Thank God Emily had the sense and patience to deal with the girl.

Harriet's manners were even worse than her clothing. She had thrown a fit worthy of Siddons when she discovered that she would not stay at Hawthorne House. Her behavior had shifted from provocative Siren to haughty lady to petulant child, all in the time it took his footman to shift two trunks from the ship to his carriage.

She was as manipulative as her mother. Unless she controlled her tongue, she would be ostracized in a week.

On the other hand, her looks demanded attention from every man still breathing, and not only because of her beauty. Growing up in India had added an exotic air that gentlemen would covet. He must trust Emily to teach her manners while he dampened her flirting to something more suited to ladies than courtesans.

Part of her problem was nerves. She had to be terrified. Moving to a strange country was never easy. At least he'd had his parents with him. All she'd had was a camp follower.

Tonight, she would meet Charles and Sophie. Surely the five of them together could protect her and find her a match. Fast.

He needed to resume his usual activities.

Chapter Three

$\mathcal{E}$mily's heart soared as she descended the stairs that evening. Jacob waited in the hall, smiling in admiration, his eyes bluer than ever before. The yellow gown had definitely been the right choice.

It was the first time she'd seen him in evening dress. His blue coat and snowy linen suited his dark hair and softened the harsh planes of his face. The sapphire nestling in his cravat glinted like a third eye. He extended his hand—

Harriet rushed past, nearly knocking Emily over, and threw herself against him. As his arms closed around her, Emily's heart stopped.

"You're here! You're here!" trilled Harriet. "Thank heaven! The day seemed positively endless. I feared you had abandoned me."

Emily frowned. The way Harriet was carrying on, she might have just escaped the rack. But at least Jacob saw through her.

"What is this nonsense?" he chided, setting her aside. "I told you I would collect you at eight, and I always keep my word. Now behave yourself. Has Miss Hughes discussed society manners with you?"

"Of course. Not that it was necessary. I've been out for years."

"But not in London."

Harriet waved away his words, demanding, "How do like my new gown? We had to visit Madame Francine, as my ball gown is out of fashion." She twirled, brushing against him. "And I needed other things, too." She smoothed her gloves to draw attention to her long, slender arms. "The air is so cold here. I don't know how I'll stay/warm." She aimed an arch look at Jacob as she leaned against him.

Irritation flashed across his face. And no wonder. Harriet's gauche flirtation was making a poor impression, casting doubts on Emily's competence as a teacher and mentor. But what could he expect in so short a time?

The trip to the dressmaker had demonstrated how difficult this job would be. It had taken the combined efforts of Emily and Madame Francine to keep Harriet from dressing like a harlot—her tastes ran to low-cut bodices, high hems, and nearly transparent fabrics despite her complaints about the cold. Then she had fallen into hysterics when Madame Francine confirmed that it would be a week before she could deliver the first of Harriet's new gowns. Finally, to quiet her, Francine had given her a peach silk made up for another customer.

"You look lovely," agreed Jacob when Harriet again crowded him.

"So does Emily," said Richard from the stairs. Lady Hughes clung to his arm. "Yellow becomes you, Em."

"So it does." Jacob cast the briefest of glances in her direction before turning to Lady Hughes. "And you look quite your old self, my lady," he said warmly, guiding her down the last steps. "The card room will empty as men rush to gaze upon your loveliness."

While Lady Hughes blushed and protested his fustian, Emily's heart plummeted. He hadn't even noticed her. That earlier smile had been for Harriet, clattering down the steps behind her. As she'd feared, Harriet made everyone around her appear mousy. Even Jacob succumbed to her exotic looks.

"Shall we go?" asked Richard. "Since you have the roomier carriage, you can take the girls, Jacob. I'll escort Mother." He headed for the door.

"How exciting!" Harriet latched onto Jacob's arm, snuggling against his side. "My first London ball. You must stay close to keep me from making mistakes. I do so want to make a good impression." She laughed up at him.

"You will do fine. Watch the other girls and follow their lead. Above all, be gracious. That is the best way to become a success." He turned toward the door, leaving Emily behind.

Emily blinked away tears. This was not the way the evening should have gone. Where was the man who had crushed her against him, devouring her mouth as if he could never get enough? Where was the friend who—

"Miss Hughes?" Jacob glanced over his shoulder, extending his other arm.

Her fingers tingled when they touched his sleeve, the sparks biting sharper than yesterday. But instead of raising excitement, they now invoked dread. Including her had so obviously been an afterthought, done solely because Richard had asked. And probably because of propriety, she realized when he seated her next to Harriet. Even a guardian must protect appearances with a ward like this one.

Jacob sprawled across the opposite seat, igniting new fire in Emily's belly. He was well set up, those elegant clothes unable to hide his power, his precise manners at odds with the wildness lurking just beneath his surface.

She'd seen that wildness often as they raced across hills or climbed trees or set their horses at dangerous obstacles. It escaped in the form of a fierce temper and a penchant for dares, as if a demon lurked inside him that could only be tamed by taking risks.

Whatever risk he contemplated now had nothing to do with Emily, though. He ignored her, his attention focused on Harriet. Even understanding his duty to his ward did not lessen Emily's pain.

"There are very firm rules you must follow," he said

as the carriage jerked into motion. "The first is that you cannot waltz unless one of the patronesses gives you permission. That will not occur tonight."

"Why?" Harriet licked her lips, focusing so intently on Jacob that the temperature inside the carriage seemed to rise.

"Because your breeding is inferior," said Jacob bluntly. "Until people know you, you must be on your best behavior. And until they judge you worthy, you will not waltz. Also, no lady can dance more than twice with a particular gentleman. In your position, it would be best if you danced no more than once—this is part of endearing yourself to society," he added when she tried to protest. "Don't do anything that will raise brows. Every lady of consequence will be here tonight."

"All the patronesses," said Emily unnecessarily, hoping to draw at least an acknowledgment that she was present.

"Exactly." But his eyes never left Harriet. "Even those who do not receive vouchers to Almack's remain subject to their opinions, for they can make or break anyone. Some are sweet. Others are rigid. But all wield great power. So do the gossips."

"Lady Beatrice," murmured Emily, who had heard much about that formidable dowager from Richard.

"And Lady Debenham." Jacob shook his head. "They are more dangerous than the patronesses, for news reaches their ears from even humble abodes. If you are ever indiscreet, they will know."

"You must stay close." Harriet laid a hand on his knee. "I cannot remember everything without your help."

"For tonight, but hovering will do you much harm."

He continued the lecture, but Emily stopped listening. Jacob seemed no more aware of her than he'd been when she was six. He'd probably forgotten their last meeting entirely. Harriet filled his mind.

By the time they reached Lady Penleigh's door, she

was near tears. What should have been her triumphal Season had turned to ashes.

"Emily!" exclaimed a gentleman as a footman helped her down. "It's been years."

"Lord Charles!" She extended both hands. His smile was a balm to her lacerated sensibilities.

Richard, Jacob, and Charles had been closer than brothers since their school days, earning the sobriquet The Three Beaux for their exploits with the fair sex. They were fanatically loyal to one another. Even if wrong, any Beau could count on the others to stand by him in public—an argument with one was an argument with all. But they would unmercifully punish any transgression in private, even one brushed aside by society. The Beaux' code of honor was superior to other men's.

Their code had never included chastity, of course. She'd heard many tales of their exploits—Charles, whose charm left a broad trail of broken hearts in his wake, even in the demimonde; Richard, whose affinity for widows and wives kept husbands on their toes; Jacob, whose appetites had reportedly sampled every courtesan in town, but who never bedded anyone twice.

Charles examined her from head to toe, his green eyes sparkling in the torchlight. "My, but you do clean up well, Em. Who would have thought . . ."

"I wasn't *that* bad when last we met," she laughingly protested.

"Oh, worse. Much worse." Setting her hand on his arm, he turned toward the door. "I do believe I'd just fished you from a bog."

"How unchivalrous of you to recall." She was grateful for his teasing even as she wished for Jacob's admiration. "Though honesty compels me to mention that you are the one who tossed me in there."

He laughed. "Why would I do such a thing?"

"If you've forgotten, far be it from me to remind you. But I must say that you clean up rather well yourself. No one would mistake you for a stork these days." He'd filled out enough that his tailor no longer had to pad his coats. Or his legs. Not a particle of sawdust filled his stockings. And his hair had darkened from carrot to a rich auburn, adding a spark to his green eyes that had nothing to do with boyish pranks. "I hear you set hearts aflutter wherever you go."

"A few," he admitted, winking. "And grateful I am for the interest."

"You would be." She joined his laughter. "So were you waiting for us, or did you just happen to be passing by?"

"Neither." He gestured a gorgeous redhead closer. "I'm playing chaperon yet again. This is my sister, Lady Sophie Beaumont. You can call her Sophie. *Lady* is much too pretentious for the brat."

"Brothers!" snorted Lady Sophie.

"Sisters!" he replied in the same tone. "This is Emily, Soph. At last."

Emily opened her mouth.

Jacob swept past with Harriet on his arm. Richard and Lady Hughes followed, pausing only long enough for Richard to pinch Sophie's chin. "Save me the second set, Soph." And he was gone.

"Which gives Jacob the third," Charles told his sister, then scowled at Jacob's back. "Not even a greeting for us. He's being haughty tonight. I suppose that's Miss Nichols."

Emily closed her mouth, unable to keep up with the rapid shifts in conversation. Beside her, Charles fell silent, his eyes glued on Harriet's hips as she swayed up the steps. His expression was as startled as Richard's had been. Emily had no doubt the rest of him was reacting the same way, too.

"Welcome to London, Emily," said Sophie, ignoring her brother. "I've heard so much about you that I feel we've been friends for years."

"As have I." Richard often mentioned Sophie, usually applying the same descriptions he used for her—

pest, hoyden, and other epithets denoting little sisters. "I hear you are the most pestilential female in London."

"To be sure. Controlling my fits and starts keeps the poor Beaux from pursuing their own business—or so they claim."

"It doesn't seem to have slowed them down, if gossip is any indication."

"No. Their most important business takes place after midnight." She grinned.

Charles shook off his abstraction to lead the ladies up the steps. "If you have any questions about London, Emily, ask Sophie. She has much experience. This is her fourth Season."

"To Mama's despair." Sophie's smile invited Emily to share the joke. "I'm the family scandal, for I've turned down two offers—which everyone assured me were very good—and deflected several others. I'm quite the choosiest female in town."

"Or the most repugnant." Charles laughed.

"That's a horrible thing to say," gasped Emily, punching his arm. Sophie was beautiful, with the same rich auburn hair as her brother. Her eyes were softer, though, more mossy than his brilliant emerald. But they could shine with delight, as they were doing now.

Emily grinned at Sophie. "Are London's gentlemen unacceptable, then?"

Sophie laughed. "I knew I'd like you. No. Many are quite nice, and some have become good friends. But I am determined to wed for love. Besides, I'm having too much fun to settle down."

"Love does not guarantee happiness," said Charles with surprising perspicacity.

"Just because *you* don't believe in it—"

"Says who?"

"I heard what you told Jacob last month about love being a fantasy perpetrated by those trying to enslave others to their wills."

"A sneaking spy." He glared. "How dare—"

"No spy. If you are careless enough to divulge your

innermost secrets before checking a room for occupants—"

"What the devil were you doing in—"

Emily squeezed his arm. "Does London condone sibling squabbles in public?"

"Lord, no!" Sophie forced a smile back on her face and relaxed her fists.

Charles fought his irritation under control. "Have you had time for morning calls yet?" he asked Emily.

"No. We would have gone out today, but Miss Nichols needed new gowns."

"I don't envy you having to watch her," said Sophie, shaking her head. "She looks like trouble."

"Envy doesn't become you," snapped Charles. "Just because she's lovely—"

"Her looks have nothing to do with it," swore Sophie. "It is her attitude. Look at how she clings. That's a schemer if I ever saw one."

"Perhaps," agreed Emily. "But she only arrived this morning, so I am trying to make allowances." She wasn't about to admit her fears, especially to someone she'd just met. Instinct recognized that Sophie might well become a bosom beau, but it was too early to tell for sure. And too early to condemn Harriet. "She's only been ashore a few hours and has had no time to adjust to England, let alone society."

"Spoken like a true lady—and a diamond to boot," said Charles, again gifting her with an admiring smile. "That gown makes your eyes glow like antique gold. I've never seen a color as enticing."

Emily didn't believe a word of his flummery—he poured it over everyone, which accounted for his conquests—but it felt good, making it easier to face society's lionesses.

"Did Richard describe society's matrons?" asked Sophie as they entered the house.

"He mentioned names, but not much else. Jacob talked about some of them in the carriage. Now I must learn to identify them. It wouldn't do to discuss them when they are standing nearby."

"We'll help."

"Of course, we will," said Charles warmly. "The one greeting our hostess at the top of the stairs is Lady Beatrice."

"With the purple turban?"

"Right."

Emily shuddered. "I heard she knows everything."

Sophie nodded. "Rumor credits her with spies in every household."

Lady Beatrice didn't look dangerous. Though her back remained straight, a wrinkled face and swollen knuckles proclaimed her well into her seventies. Her gown was at least two Seasons out of date, hinting at pinched pockets—not that anyone would dare comment.

But when Lady Beatrice turned, Emily nearly gasped. There was nothing old or forgetful about that gaze. Her eyes were sharp and very black, instantly taking in every detail.

Emily bowed her head to acknowledge the lady's superior position, then turned back to Sophie. "Who else is here?"

"The pair in front of Jacob are Lady Cunningham and her latest daughter," said Charles. "Harmless, for the most part."

"The family is enormous," added Sophie. "Every year they fire off a new girl. This will be the sixth, I believe."

"Seventh," said Charles firmly. "With three more at home."

"Heavens!" Emily waved her fan.

"And all wonderful people. You'll love the third girl—Lady Renfrew now. They returned to town last week, as did the oldest sister, Lady Basil Chalmers. Lord Basil works at the Foreign Office with Charles." As the Cunninghams moved into the ballroom, Sophie glanced down the stairs. "Lady Debenham just arrived."

"The other gossip?"

"Everyone gossips, but she is trying to dethrone Lady Beatrice as the most powerful gossip."

"Which one is she?" Two ladies had entered together, both on the shady side of fifty, though not by much.

"Blue silk with matching plumes. The one in green is Lady Horseley—rigid and formidable."

"Ah."

"You need to step ahead of me, Em," murmured Charles. "Since this is your first outing, it is Richard's place to introduce you."

"Of course." Suddenly Jacob's monopolization of Harriet made sense. As Harriet's guardian, he had no choice.

Her relief carried her through the receiving line and into the ballroom. Only as they paused inside the door did she again turn to Sophie.

"What now?" Already the room contained a hundred guests with more crowding in every minute. For the first time, she truly understood the splendor of London, so different from her corner of Gloucestershire, where large gatherings might include thirty people, and the local assemblies took place in the dining room of the Dragon's Egg Inn.

Here, silver sconces holding dozens of wax candles tossed reflected light from mirrors and polished marble. Potted palms clustered in corners. A filigreed screen separated black-coated musicians from the guests.

Everywhere, colorful gowns swayed like flowers in a spring breeze—or like ribbons set dancing by the flutter of myriad fans. Scents ranged from delicate to bold. Voices uttered greetings, recounted gossip, and feigned shock over the latest scandal.

"We will mingle until the dancing starts," murmured Sophie. "Here comes Lord Wroxleigh. He was a bigger rake than Charles before his marriage."

"Is that possible?" asked Emily before she could think.

"Minx!" Charles shook his head. "Save me the third set. I can't wait to spar with that shockingly forward tongue." Grinning, he moved off before she could respond.

"You'll get Jacob for two, then," said Sophie. "The Beaux will take the first three sets at every ball you attend—and then they dare to complain that I've not found a suitor to my taste!"

"Brothers!" For the first time, she understood the tone Sophie had used earlier.

"Exactly. They will smother you, while assuring themselves that they are protecting you from harm. Now pay attention. We have only a moment before Wroxleigh gets here. Lady Jersey—dark-haired beauty in red by the first window, Almack's patroness."

"Who is she laughing at?"

"Laughing with. Lord Ingram. Thinks he's a dandy, though his legs belong to a stork."

"So did Charles's a dozen years ago."

Sophie giggled. "Ingram is too old to develop curves. He'll be in sawdust for life. Now concentrate. The battle-ax near the next window is Mrs. Drummond-Burrell. Another patroness. The silver-haired gentleman in the green coat is Lord Castlereagh. He is talking to Lady Marchgate and her son Lord Hartford."

"Who married my cousin," put in Wroxleigh as he joined them. "We must be playing Who's Who. My favorite game. Introduce me, Lady Sophie. Who's the new diamond you've brought us?"

Half an hour later, Emily's head was spinning. As the crowd grew, the Beaux closed ranks around their charges—Lady Hughes had retired to a chair. Emily wished she could join her. Despite Charles's teasing and Wroxleigh's compliments, she couldn't hold a candle to Sophie and Harriet. Sophie might complain about the Beaux driving off suitors, but she drew a large court. Harriet's exotic looks attracted gentlemen in droves, her foreign mannerisms and lilting voice keeping them enthralled. And the Beaux themselves were targets for a score of matchmaking mothers towing aspiring daughters. Even Richard was a prize, for he would one day be a lord. Emily felt invisible.

Worse, Harriet's flirtation bordered on vulgar. The elegant room had triggered a fey excitement, leading to coarse allusions and suggestive comments that might draw applause in a barracks, but not in London society. Yet Jacob did nothing.

Emily gritted her teeth. Jacob would blame her if anything happened, for she had accepted the job of keeping Harriet under control. The moment they returned home, she must deliver yet another lecture—not that she expected Harriet to listen. The girl had the bit between her teeth and had no intention of being reined in. Filling her card within moments of her arrival would make it hard to convince her that proper behavior mattered. That Emily's card still contained holes added to the difficulty.

Richard pulled her mind back to the ballroom.

"You must meet Lady Beatrice, Em," he said, drawing the gossip forward. "My sister, Miss Emily Hughes."

Emily uttered the expected greeting. Up close, the gossip was even more formidable, confidence and power shining from those dark eyes.

"Nice-looking gel." Lady Beatrice tilted her head as she studied Emily—she was clearly checking out new arrivals tonight. "A little long in the tooth, perhaps, but remarkably unspoiled. She should do well. Lady Sophie, on the other hand, is nearly on the shelf." Clucking her tongue, she turned a quelling glance on Charles's sister. "Inslip should put his foot down."

Sophie laughed. "He does, my lady. Quite regularly. Very demanding man. Why only last week he forced me to wear pattens while taking the air in the garden, and you know how much I hate pattens."

"Hmph! Saucy miss." But her eyes sparkled. "Are you going to shape up this Season? I've seen no evidence of it so far."

"I will try ever so hard. It pains me to disappoint you. But what can I do when the perfect gentleman refuses to fall at my feet?"

Sophie's response tugged at Lady Beatrice's lips. "What about Benning?" she suggested, examining Sophie's court, which had drawn back when Lady Beatrice appeared and now moved farther away.

"Far too spindly. I do love well-formed limbs."

"Gresham?"

"A weakling. I cannot accept anyone unable to carry me to safety should the need arise—without puffing. I swear Gresham is hard-pressed to haul himself up the stairs with any degree of finesse."

"Penfield?"

"Dull. My lids droop the moment he opens his mouth."

"Alders?"

"Haughty. He accepts only his own opinion, and he prefers blonde hair to auburn."

"You are hopeless," sighed Lady Beatrice, shaking her head.

"Very," agreed Emily, having enjoyed their sparring. "I'm surprised you don't expect your suitors to fly."

"What a lovely talent that would be!" exclaimed Sophie. "So many things lurk just out of reach. I must consider it."

Charles burst into laughter.

Lady Beatrice chuckled, letting Emily relax. What had possessed her to joke with the woman? If the gossip had taken the words wrong, Emily's Season might have ended before it began.

"You must be Hawthorne's ward," Lady Beatrice boomed.

Jacob nodded. "Miss Harriet Nichols, daughter of Captain Nichols."

"I don't recall a Captain Nichols."

"He died before I was born," said Harriet before Jacob could respond. "I never knew him, though ev-

eryone claims he was a great man. My mother next
married Colonel Wentworth. They succumbed to fever
last year."

Lady Beatrice turned to Jacob. "Breeding's tolerable. Introduce her to Sir Bertram." Without waiting
for a response, she headed for the next group.

"You did well," said Charles, sensing Emily's uncertainty. "Lady Beatrice loves anyone who will stand up
to her. As for you," he added to Sophie. "You'd best
expect a Season of similar observations. Four years
is enough."

"He's right," murmured Sophie when he turned
away. "I have to wed this year, but I think I'll manage.
I've been cultivating a gentleman for some time. He
should be ripe by now." Her eyes strayed to the door
where a man in stark black had just appeared. "Don't
mention it to Charles," she added. "If he meddles, he
will ruin everything."

Emily wanted details, but this wasn't the place, particularly if Sophie meant to keep her interest secret.
Before she could figure out how to arrange a moment
alone—or even how to learn the gentleman's name—
the musicians struck up a country dance, and Richard
swept her into the first set.

Jacob commandeered her for the second set, but
any hope that he considered it more than a duty dance
vanished with his first words.

"Harriet's manners are rougher than I feared. Is
everything all right?"

"So far," she said. Reporting Harriet's tantrum at
the modiste's would serve no purpose. And since calling her blue gown suitable for a ball had been an
exaggeration, demanding a new one—and paying extra
for the service—had been her only option.

"Good. She thinks your mother hates her, but I
can't believe it."

"How did she form that notion? Unless she misunderstood Mama's comment about the queen's Drawing Room."

He raised a brow.

"My presentation is tomorrow. She expected to accompany me."

"She actually expected to be presented?"

Emily sighed. "It was more a question of whether she could accompany us—she must know presentation is impossible. Mama said no, of course. Breeding aside, court gowns take weeks. In explaining, Mama also mentioned that she will not receive vouchers to Almack's. Her father's station simply isn't high enough."

"I told her that, but I will repeat it. It must be difficult to absorb so many rules at once." He fell to muttering as the music started. "Perhaps bringing her out was a mistake. But how else . . ."

The dance separated them, giving them no further chance to talk.

Emily hid her disappointment. Mistake or not, Harriet was now out. They would all have to deal with the consequences, one of which was Jacob's focus on duty.

At least he trusted her to help him.

Jacob berated himself as he moved through the dance. If he'd had more warning, he could have planned things better—might even have had a husband lined up before Harriet arrived.

No doubt about it. He'd rushed his fences. Studying her manners should have been his first step, even if that meant she had to miss a week or two of the Season once her ship arrived. Instead, he had assumed she would know the basics and understand the importance of remaining in the background until she had established her place. So he'd thrust her into society without knowing a thing about her—except that her mother was not a lady.

He grimaced as he spotted Harriet fluttering her lashes at a notorious rake in her set. Nervousness was pushing her into gauche behavior. And ignorance.

He hoped Emily could settle her nerves quickly. Harriet was clinging in a most unseemly fashion. He'd managed to put some physical distance between them, but merely hovering near her would draw comment if it continued.

Yet he couldn't abandon her. He recalled too clearly how frightening England had been that first week—and he'd had his mother to help him adjust. No matter how much the English abroad clung to their customs, living in India was nothing like living in England. Class distinctions blurred and manners softened. People who would not have spoken in London welcomed each other to dinner.

But he could do little beyond trust Emily and Lady Hughes to look after her.

He stifled a frown. Lady Hughes was far more frail than Richard had claimed. Within minutes of arriving, she'd retired to a corner, paying no heed even to Emily. Her color was bad and her eyes blurred, as if she'd taken laudanum. But if she was unable to watch even Em—

Perhaps he should hire a chaperon for Harriet. It wasn't fair to place the entire burden on Emily's shoulders. She was in town to seek her own match and had but one Season to do it, according to Richard.

When the set ended, he led Emily back to the Beaux' corner and glanced at her card. "Save me the supper dance, Em."

"Of course."

Engrossed in thought, he moved away. While a chaperon might work, he needed to consider the idea before broaching it to Richard. He could not afford another mistake. Nor could he afford to insult Emily. But with luck, he could reach a decision before supper.

Yet thinking proved difficult, even after seeking solitude. Too many questions remained, from mundane ones, such as whether Hughes House had room for another resident—a chaperon was not a servant, so needed decent quarters—to nebulous thoughts about Emily's reaction to this latest change of plans. He would have to discuss it with her and hope she didn't take offense.

He was returning for the supper dance when Harriet dragged him behind a palm. "You have to help me, Jacob," she demanded. "Miss Hughes won't talk to me."

"What now?"

She raised pleading eyes to meet his. "I heard that lady in blue tell her friend that she wears a different gown to every ball." She nodded toward Mrs. Camberly. "Is that usual?"

"For her. But few people command her fortune. Three or four gowns should suffice for a girl in your position. Most maids are adept at changing trim to keep appearances fresh."

"But that's my point! This is my only gown." She thrust her chest out.

"You told me you had a dozen gowns."

"But Miss Hughes won't let me wear them. She took me to a dressmaker, but the woman refuses to deliver anything until next week. I tried to talk to Miss Hughes about it before this last set, but she told me to be quiet."

"And rightly so. You should not discuss such things at a ball."

"But—" Her hand gripped his arm.

"Miss Nichols!" he snapped, shaking her loose. "There is no way you can hurry a dressmaker during the Season. You can either make do with what you have or stay home until your new gowns are ready."

"You can't expect—"

"I can, and I do. A smart girl would remain quiet until she understood the rules. She would study how others conduct themselves and accept her place. You must never forget that Captain Nichols was low gentry, so you have limited entrée to society. Thus your behavior must be perfect."

"You want me to become one of those insipid misses who never dance," she wailed, drawing eyes as she clutched his arm.

"Of course not. You are attractive enough to draw attention, but you must behave. Beauty will never compensate for a crass tongue. So cease this childish display this instant. No one has ever been cut for being too proper, but plenty have been cut for breaking rules. Don't annoy Miss Hughes with demands she cannot grant or complaints that have no place being uttered in public."

She sputtered and objected, even trying tears when he ignored her wheedling. It took half of the set to settle her. And by the time he could find her partner, the music had ended. All he could do was lead Emily into the supper room.

Emily was understandably annoyed to have been abandoned. And they were so surrounded by people that he could not broach the subject of Harriet's chaperonage.

All in all, it had not been a good evening.

Chapter Four

*E*mily could barely keep her eyes open as she climbed the stairs to her room, but she knew that sleep would come slowly, if at all.

Lady Penleigh's ball had gone well from everyone's perspective but hers. Richard was happy because she'd danced every set—there were always more ladies than men in ballrooms, a situation worsened by twenty years of warfare and by the penchant of so many men to retire to the card room the moment they arrived.

Lady Hughes was delighted. She'd met several old friends and passed an enjoyable evening in conversation.

Even Jacob had seemed relieved when they left, though he'd been tense earlier.

But Emily was not pleased. While Jacob had reserved two of her sets and only one each with Harriet and Sophie, he'd failed to appear until that second set was nearly over. Not the mark of a gentleman. Even if he didn't care for her personally, he should have sent word that he'd been detained. That he hadn't, called her image of him into question.

Had she built him into a fantasy Prince Charming by assigning him traits that weren't there? While she'd known him most of her life, their meetings had been limited to his school breaks. And until that last summer, they had always included Richard, and usually Charles.

Her new fear was that she'd combined traits of all

three Beaux into her image of Jacob. And since he wasn't tripping over his feet to sweep her into marriage, she had better decide in the cold light of day whether he was truly whom she wanted.

Reserving two of her sets meant less than nothing. Charles had done the same—and had appeared for both. Each man had the same motivation—helping Richard. A full dance card when many girls had partners for only one or two sets would mark her as a success, raising her credit and drawing attention to her charms. She couldn't fault Richard's thinking.

But his meddling made it difficult for her. He had always forced his friends to include her in their childhood excursions. They had good-naturedly agreed, though neither had really wanted her along. Now he'd forced them to fill her card. It would not take society long to discount such coerced attentions, making her seem pathetic.

Did he really think her such an antidote that no man would look at her?

He might be right, she admitted. How often had gentlemen overlooked her as they vied for a word with the exotic Harriet or the vivacious Sophie? Caught between their courts and hidden by the Beaux' hovering, she might spend the entire Season invisible. It wouldn't matter if Jacob intended to wed her, but . . .

"I think that went well," said Harriet, following Emily into her room instead of heading up to her own.

Emily nearly threw her out—she needed to decide whether to abandon her dreams of Jacob and how to meet someone better if she did.

But Harriet would wish to discuss the evening—and who could blame her after the upheaval she'd experienced since dawn? And Emily had to explain the mistakes she'd made.

"The evening went fairly well," she agreed, "though you raised eyebrows more than once."

"I did not!"

"You did. London manners are much stricter than

manners in the colonies. You cannot refuse to dance with one gentleman, then accept another for the same set, no matter how much you prefer the second."

"But—"

"No exceptions. Lady Horseley saw you refuse Mr. Connoly, then accept Mr. Pierce. That was bad enough, but to do so while Mr. Connoly could hear you was unforgivable. She was appalled."

"Why? Mr. Connoly is still wet behind the ears. I don't enjoy the company of boys."

"It doesn't matter who your partner is, for you spend little time with him in a country dance anyway. You could have accepted Mr. Connoly, then joined the same set as Mr. Pierce if you wished to flirt with him. But manners forbid you to dance at all if you've turned down a partner."

"That is stupid!" Harriet threw herself onto the bed in a huff. "Ja—Lord Hawthorne will never expect me to court boredom."

"He will tell you that such rudeness is unacceptable. You must pay attention, Miss Nichols. Lord Hawthorne explained how your breeding compares to the other guests'. Mr. Connoly might be wet behind the ears, as you put it, but he is the heir to a barony, and as such, is well above your station. Your actions are gauche under any circumstances, but in this case, you looked vulgar."

"Vulgar?"

"Exactly. Society does not accept vulgarity. You must temper your exuberance. Ennui is the fashion. Never forget that. Flirt, but lightly. Restrain your laughter to a decorous titter. Never display displeasure in public."

"I saw ladies breaking all those rules."

"Not unwed ladies. And not anyone on the fringes of society. A duchess can do whatever she wants, and no one will protest. But your position is fragile. Without the support and approval of society's hostesses, you will receive no invitations. Lord Hawthorne's credit cannot overcome their fury if you flout them. The matrons always have the last word on society matters."

Harriet scowled, but finally nodded.

"Get some sleep," suggested Emily. "We will discuss the nuances of societal expectations in the morning. Also the topics of conversation that are acceptable for young girls. You must learn quickly, for the next day will be busy—Lady Sheridan's Venetian breakfast and Lady Horseley's rout."

Harriet finally left, but her departure did little to improve Emily's humor. Her own problems were too acute.

She had to wed this Season. Cherry Hill produced enough to cover Richard's quarterly allowance and support the family in the country. But its income would not stretch to a second Season.

Which brought her back to Jacob's intentions. If he was only helping Richard establish her, then she must look elsewhere.

Her heart screamed in protest.

"Behave," she snapped, rolling over to muffle her groans with a pillow.

Jacob might yet offer—Harriet's unexpected arrival had to have thrown his own plans into chaos. And she would certainly accept if he did. But it was irresponsible to assume anything. Unlike Sophie, who could afford to cultivate a gentleman for years, Emily had to settle now.

Which meant seriously looking at other candidates.

So far, they were an uninspiring lot. With the Beaux filling five sets, she'd spent time with only three others.

As Harriet had noted, Mr. Connoly was young, no more than eighteen, and had all the grace of a newborn colt. This had been his first ball, too, so he would improve with practice, but he would not be ready to wed for years. And at six years her junior, he would never consider her.

Sir Thomas Eaton was a better candidate—mid-twenties, nice-looking in a spindly sort of way, sober . . . Perhaps too sober. He hadn't smiled once during their entire set. Granted, ennui was the fashion, but he hadn't even cracked a smile when Lord Ross had sent staid matrons into the whoops with his tale of a contretemps at Grafton House between two women determined to claim the last length of blue silk. Their antics had ultimately ripped the fabric in two.

Then there was Mr. Larkin. Twenty-eight. Entertaining. Decent income. But she feared he was another reluctant victim of Richard's arm-twisting. They'd been schoolmates. Mr. Larkin's eyes had gleamed far brighter when fixed on Harriet than on her.

So tonight had done little beyond shatter her illusions and force her to confront reality. Tomorrow's court presentation wouldn't help, since only ladies would be present. Thus her next opportunity to see Jacob or anyone else would be at Lady Sheridan's Venetian breakfast.

She must be ready.

Two days later, Emily drew a deep breath as the Hughes carriage pulled up before Sheridan Manor an hour north of Mayfair. Warm brick glowed in the midday sunlight, but the sight did not warm Emily's heart. Nor did the magnificent yews flanking the drive, the brilliant blue sky, or the glimpse of water in the distance. An hour of Harriet's chatter could turn the hottest coals to ice.

Lady Sheridan had set up her Venetian breakfast beside the lake where the hills caught and concentrated the sunlight, creating a warmth that allowed her to stage comfortable alfresco events weeks before her neighbors.

The walk to the lake wound from the terrace through the formal garden, then past the ha-ha to a generous expanse of parkland, and finally into the valley sheltering the lake and adjacent pavilion.

"This path is awful," hissed Harriet, grabbing Richard's arm with both hands when her ankle turned. "Why would anyone choose to eat outdoors in the cold and damp?"

"It's a lovely day," insisted Emily from Richard's other arm, though the loveliest aspect was Richard's recovery from infatuation—two days of Harriet's chatter had canceled any interest, for which Emily thanked Fate. Harriet as a sister was too revolting an idea to consider. "As for the path, I warned you to wear half-boots. You've no one to blame but yourself that you insisted on slippers."

Harriet grumbled.

"Easy," snapped Richard. "Don't embarrass yourself by arriving in a lather. You don't see Emily growling like a mad dog."

Emily bit her tongue. Richard's comments increased Harriet's fury, but chastising him could only make matters worse. It would never do to arrive with all three of them at odds.

Two days with Harriet proved that she was incorrigible, the sort who would only learn from painful experience. She was so certain that every man would worship at her feet that she refused to believe London society could ever turn on her. Yesterday's remarks about prying old busybodies increased Emily's dread over this outing. Unless Harriet paid the proper obeisance to society's matrons, she would be cut.

Emily would bear the blame.

Jacob would never speak to her again.

Taking a deep breath, she focused on the gardens, which contained surprising vignettes around each corner. This one was an irregular bed rioting with primroses, buttercups, and tulips, some descended from bulbs that had been worth fortunes during the seventeenth-century tulip mania. A clipped box hedge formed a backdrop, order and disorder combining into an odd harmony.

This harmony enhanced a broader vista of grassy slopes and specimen trees from around the world. Below, a pavilion in the form of a Grecian temple perched next to a cobalt lake. Tables and rugs dotted its shore. Half a dozen boats awaited rowers. Several others were headed for a tiny island in the lake's center.

Charles and Sophie were among the fifty guests who had already arrived.

"Two beautiful flowers to grace the day," exclaimed Charles, nodding to Harriet before raising Emily's hand to his lips. "Enchanted, my dear."

Sophie rolled her eyes.

"Where is Ja—Lord Hawthorne?" demanded Harriet.

"Delayed. But he should arrive in another hour." Charles set Emily's hand on his arm. "Walk with me. As I recall, deer delight you. There is a herd with several fawns just over that hill."

"I would love to see them," Emily said, responding to the plea in Sophie's eyes—the dark-haired gentleman was approaching the tables. "Bring Harriet," she added to Richard. "English fallow deer will be a treat for her."

Charles scowled at the inclusion of Harriet, but Emily drew him ahead of Richard, chatting gaily so he wouldn't notice that Sophie wasn't following.

The deer were as graceful as always, the fawns frolicking with a playfulness that made Emily long to join them. But she was too old to run through the grass and must be content with this civilized stroll.

Judicious questions drew Charles farther along the lakeshore. Richard had to follow, forcing Harriet to keep walking. It was the perfect way to control the girl until Jacob arrived. And it gave Sophie a full hour to cultivate her gentleman.

She ignored the voice reminding her that it also kept her from meeting eligible gentlemen for that hour.

"Did you attend yesterday's Drawing Room?" Charles asked as they headed back to the pavilion for refreshments.

"Yes, though I remember little of it." She'd been too nervous to do more than pray she wouldn't trip.

"I'm not even sure who presided. The queen is too ill. Princess Augusta, perhaps? I didn't notice much until I'd backed out of the presentation room without incident."

He laughed. "Much like my first introduction to the king, though levees are not as formal as Drawing Rooms. But you can be sure that the next time you attend court, you will be more relaxed."

"I couldn't possibly be less so."

"Now that the worst is over, you can enjoy town. I presume you've received your vouchers."

"This morning. Mama is in alt. Harriet, on the other hand . . ."

"She can't expect Almack's." He lowered his voice, leaning closer so only she could hear. "She should rejoice to be here at all. You have your work cut out for you, my dear. That girl will be trouble if she doesn't settle down. Her tongue is sharp and doesn't know when to cease moving. It quite detracts from her looks."

"She may yet settle—the change from being a local diamond to being barely tolerated has to be difficult. A tantrum or two is hardly a surprise."

"You have more patience than most. And far more tolerance." His approval warmed her heart. Now if only Jacob felt the same way . . .

They rounded the pavilion to see Jacob and Sophie talking to Lady Sheridan.

Charles clucked his tongue. "Lady Sheridan really should not wear yellow," he murmured in her ear. "It makes her look like a lemon—and she's sour enough as it is."

"Charles!" But he was right. Yellow emphasized Lady Sheridan's roundness and her sallow skin. The green cap perched atop her gold hair made it worse.

Before Emily could say more, Harriet escaped and raced to Jacob's side. "My lord. I must speak with you."

"In a moment." Irritation clouding his eyes, he finished his conversation with Lady Sheridan before moving to one side. Harriet immediately laid a beseeching hand on his arm.

Emily shook her head at Harriet's impatience and joined Sophie. Jacob now had another grievance against her.

Jacob shook Harriet's hand from his sleeve and glared. "That was badly done, Miss Nichols. Interrupting a conversation displays atrocious manners."

"Forgive me. I wasn't thinking. I was too glad to see a friendly face after being locked away for two days."

"Hardly locked. I've received enough accounts to know you spent most of yesterday shopping."

"And enduring smirks from half the shop owners," she snapped.

He bit back a sharp retort. "I can't believe that, Miss Nichols. You must stop assuming that everyone is plotting against you."

"But they are," she insisted, sidling closer. "They won't allow me to do anything. In Bombay—"

"This is *not* Bombay." He stepped back and glared. "It does not matter what you did in India. This is London. Now let's concentrate on the activities Lady Sheridan has provided for your entertainment."

"I'd rather stay with you. It is ever so pleasant." She smiled up at him, again grabbing his arm.

"That is impossible, Miss Nichols. I have business to conduct."

"But—"

"No." He moved toward the lakeshore where several people chatted near the boats. Lord Ross grinned when he spotted Jacob. A little high for Harriet, but a good choice for now.

"Hawthorne," Ross called. "I am organizing races. Will you man a boat?"

"Perhaps later. But my ward would enjoy a ride if one of the boats has a vacant spot."

"Of course."

Jacob introduced her, then waited until Ross settled her in Crawford's boat before turning back to the pavilion. Several lords had retreated to the farthest table to discuss an upcoming debate. He joined them.

Two hours later, Emily was finally relaxed. She had not seen much of Jacob, who had spent the afternoon discussing politics with one group of men after another. But she had enjoyed time with several others. Mr. Gresham would never make an acceptable husband—Sophie was right about that—but he'd offered droll comments on the boat races they had watched together. Mr. Larkin had strolled with her once the races were over. And now Mr. Penfield had invited her to walk along the shore.

Sophie had exaggerated Mr. Penfield's character. While he was too sober for Emily's taste, he was far from a prosing bore. They were chatting lightly about the ducks swimming in and out of the reeds when a voice erupted from a nearby thicket.

Charles.

"I swear I'll throttle her if she doesn't settle this Season," he swore. "But every time I try to talk to her, she falls back on her *waiting for love* excuse. How can she believe such tripe? If she hasn't found love in four years, she never will."

"True," answered Jacob. "Love is merely a fancy word for lust and a trap for the unwary. It doesn't last, and when it dies, she will feel betrayed. She would be better off seeking an arrangement based on mutual interests."

"You know that, and I know that, but try convincing her. She is obsessed by those damned novels she reads."

"Tell her about Richardson and the Smythe-Gower chit. Starry-eyed, the both of them. Swearing eternal devotion. Spouting maudlin poetry night and day. Six months after their wedding, he resumed his rounds of the brothels, and she turned to flirting with every man she meets. I doubt they have spent five minutes together in the past year. Westlake did better by accepting an arranged marriage. The moment he begot an heir, he released his wife to seek her own pleasure while he sought his. They are better friends now than when they wed."

Penfield's progress took Emily out of hearing, but it was too late to salvage her heart. It had cracked painfully in two. Jacob didn't love her . . . had never loved her . . . did not even believe love existed.

Somehow she kept up her end of the conversation for the remainder of their walk. But she was so desperate to be alone that she dismissed Penfield quite abruptly when they returned to the pavilion.

A quick glance proved that Charles and Jacob were still gone. Harriet was in a boat with young Connoly, laughing so loudly she drew disapproving eyes from shore. Richard was glaring and would likely chastise her when she landed. Sophie had used Charles's absence to again speak with her dark-haired gentleman.

Yet escaping notice from her friends wasn't enough to assure the solitude she needed. Lady Sheridan was too competent a hostess to leave any guest alone for long. So when a chattering group of girls set out around the lake, Emily quietly joined them. As soon as they entered the woods, she dropped back and slipped off the path, heading for a sunbeam visible through the trees. It marked a tiny dell containing a convenient boulder where she could sit.

With heavy heart, she reviewed Jacob's hurtful words, hoping to find another interpretation. But there was none. Not only did he not believe in love, he had no intention of being faithful to a wife.

This explained why he never bedded the same courtesan twice. And it explained why he changed interests so often. He might not believe in love, but he feared it existed. So he made sure that he would never become attached to anyone or anything.

She released a shaky breath. Now she knew why he'd fled ten years ago and never returned to Hawthorne Park. She had misread him completely. He didn't want her love and would throw it in her face if she offered it. But he needed it even worse than she'd thought.

What had hurt him so deeply? Nothing she'd learned from either Richard or Lady Hawthorne could explain it. But his pain was real. She'd heard it threading his voice.

Movement in the nearest tree momentarily caught her eye, but birds held little interest for her today.

This changed everything. Jacob would not be sweeping her away to declare undying devotion. And if she pressed, he would likely flee. So she must concentrate on deepening their friendship. He admired the way Westlake had wed a friend.

They had truly become friends that summer. If she offered only that, maintaining the ennui that was customary in town, he might welcome her as his wife. Then she could teach him to love.

She was recalling his most recent interests—as related by Lady Hawthorne—when a voice interrupted.

"There you are!" Charles erased his frown as he entered the clearing. "Is something wrong? What are you doing out here alone?"

"Watching a robin feed her young."

"You shouldn't wander off," he chided.

"I know." She took his arm and headed back to the path. "But I'm unaccustomed to crowds and needed a few moments to recover."

"London can be hectic," he agreed, patting her hand. His eyes twinkled. "Not that you need to fret. Not only are you a diamond of the first water, but you possess kindness and sense as well."

"What fustian." She shook her head. "Not that I don't appreciate your efforts, Charles, but you must confine your exaggerations to the realm of possibility if you hope to be believed. Else you will be considered naught but an empty-headed flatterer."

"I? A flatterer? My dear Emily, you cannot have such a low opinion of yourself. Do you not know that sunlight turns your eyes to pure gold? The Graces are clumsy compared to you. I look upon your face and see a goddess, a—"

She laughed so hard, she had to grab his arm to keep from falling. "Too, too droll," she finally gasped. "You have lightened my day immeasurably. Now be a friend and tell me about the man rowing with Harriet." She'd changed boats while Emily was away.

"Borden?"

"If that's his name. Will he do as a suitor for her?"

"You want her settled soon."

"Of course." She met his eyes. "Wouldn't you?"

He nodded, then dismissed Borden, along with most other guests. Those who might do were an unprepossessing bunch that Harriet would reject without a second glance.

Emily sighed.

Chapter Five

*E*mily felt numb by the time she left for Lady Horseley's rout that evening. Rekindling her friendship with Jacob would be difficult. He spoke of nothing but Harriet when they were together, putting her in an impossible quandary. If she criticized Harriet or even alluded to her intransigence, he would think envy made her exaggerate, unless he concluded she couldn't handle the simple task he'd assigned her.

Yet she could hardly claim that all was well. Harriet's expression had been surprisingly satisfied since leaving Lady Sheridan's. The look was so at odds with her complaints that Emily feared she'd arranged an assignation. Such behavior would ruin her.

She'd rehearsed several warning speeches for Jacob that she hoped would demonstrate her concern without condemning Harriet out of hand, but she still didn't know which one to use. The uncertainty kept her tense as she entered Lady Horseley's drawing room.

He wasn't there. Was he not coming?

The question kept her on tenterhooks for the next hour as Richard introduced a dozen people she'd not yet met. Her heart leaped into her throat when Jacob finally appeared in the doorway.

But in the end, she had no chance to use any of her speeches. Jacob swept Harriet away without even pausing to greet Emily or Richard. The only glance aimed in her direction had been full of fury. What had she done now?

Only Charles's arrival a quarter hour later cut short her brooding. His droll wit soon had her laughing.

Jacob wanted to tear his hair out. Two cubs in the receiving line had been parodying Harriet in a most unflattering fashion. He'd dampened their humor, but it was clear that her ignorance was drawing notice. If she didn't settle soon, that notice would turn to censure.

What was worse was his reaction to Emily. His tongue had nearly hit the floor when he'd spotted her. That yellow gown had turned her eyes amber, but tonight's green added flecks that made him think of sun-drenched forest glades. Her gown was simplicity itself, but the cut emphasized her curves, the effect making him want to sweep her away to the country and devour her at his leisure. He'd never reacted to anything this strongly, and it terrified him.

He'd had to abandon the idea of hiring a chaperon for Harriet. Hughes House was too small. So he must continue dealing with Emily—which made his sudden lust an even bigger problem.

To regain control of himself—and to make sure Harriet behaved—he took his ward firmly in hand to complete the introductions he'd begun at Lady Penleigh's. Without approval from the hostesses, she would receive no invitations.

He also intended to warn her against alienating potential suitors. Her conduct at Lady Sheridan's made it unlikely that she would receive attention from any of the gentlemen she'd met there.

Yet she was no better tonight.

He soon realized that she disdained women, casting new light on Lieutenant Stevens's claim that Wentworth had kept Harriet confined. Jacob suspected that Harriet had refused invitations she considered boring, especially those afternoon teas beloved of the wives.

He backed her into a corner where they could speak without being overheard. It was too late to cancel her come-out, so he must make her understand that her interests would best be served by following the rules.

"Your manners are atrocious," he hissed, brushing her hand from his sleeve.

"What about theirs?" she hissed back. "They treat me as though I'd crawled out from under a rock."

"In their eyes, you did," he said in a milder tone. "*Not* because of your breeding," he added over her protest. "But because of your manners. You cannot snub people with impunity."

"That's not what Miss Hughes said," snapped Harriet. "She told me to ignore anyone who made me uncomfortable."

"You misunderstood. She was referring to rakes and lechers. Stay away from such men if you value your reputation. But you must be scrupulously polite to everyone else."

"She was not talking about men. I'd asked about the ladies who glare at me."

"Nonsense."

"You mean she lied?" Tears shimmered in her blue eyes, turning them to a transparent window to her soul. Or so a gullible fool might think. Her mother had used the same trick. He'd seen the woman practicing it in front of a mirror.

"Ladies don't lie, Miss Nichols. You were confused."

"No. She did it deliberately so I would ruin myself. She wants me to fail. How can you force me to live with such horrible people? They gloated because I couldn't go to court yesterday and laughed in my face when I didn't receive vouchers to Almack's. Miss Hughes threatened to turn me out on the street if I told you about it. You must take me away from there before they ruin me. I can't—"

"Stop this fustian at once," he snapped. "I've known the Hughes family for years. They would never harm a guest."

"You don't know that," she continued, pressing

against his arm. "Miss Hughes resents me. She hates sharing her Season."

Fury nearly choked him. "She has too much sense to play childish pranks. Pay attention, Miss Nichols. It is your own misbehavior that threatens your reputation. This is your last chance. If you annoy any more hostesses, you will receive no invitations." He again reviewed the rules, pointing out evidence that she was eroding her credit with each new infraction.

But as he listed her errors, her charges echoed through his mind. How well did he truly know Emily? He'd not seen her in ten years. Even Richard was rarely home to observe her for himself. Many likable young girls grew into selfish ladies who might well resent having a Harriet thrust into their homes—especially for a come-out that had been postponed so often. Might Emily sabotage Harriet's chances out of pique?

He thrust the question aside, unwilling to believe it. But he would have to watch her closely, just in case. Tomorrow would offer an excellent opportunity. Harriet had no invitations, so everyone was attending Astley's. Without the press of society around them, he could study how the girls got on together.

"I knew she hated me," Harriet swore when he finished his lecture with another injunction against arrogance. "That's the opposite of what Miss Hughes said. She is trying to turn me into a savage."

"Nonsense. You are hysterical."

"It's so different here." Her grip tightened as she moved closer. "It frightens me that I can ruin myself without realizing it. It's more frightening to realize that you are the only one I can trust."

He cursed, recognizing the power of her eyes even though he knew it was an act. If she turned that look on Richard or Charles, she might drive them to do her bidding. He must warn them.

In the meantime, he would make one more stab at penetrating her selfishness. "England is different only in your mind, Miss Nichols. Now pay attention. Routs are places to meet people and discuss the latest news. Your goal is to befriend as many hostesses as possible so you will have something to do this Season."

"But you—"

"—can do nothing further. I wrested a few invitations for you on the promise that you were presentable. But now that the hostesses have met you, only their opinions matter. We will continue around the room. Either treat everyone with deference, or I will send you home. I won't risk my own reputation by claiming you are civilized when their own eyes prove different."

Her eyes blazed briefly, then softened. "I will do my best, my lord. But you cannot leave my side. Without you to support me, I'm sure I will make more mistakes."

Manipulative wench. He wanted nothing to do with her. But escorting her was the only way to prevent a scandal that would reflect badly on Richard's family, so he grudgingly nodded. "Tonight only. After this, you are on your own. Linking your name with mine will destroy you."

Fuming, he led her back into the crowd, determined to find someone to take her off his hands. Too bad Bates avoided insipid entertainments like routs. He and Harriet were two of a kind, both wanting more than they deserved. Bates had women panting after him wherever he went.

Sir Bertram was absent, too. He'd looked for the man ever since Lady Beatrice had recommended him, but Sir Bertram seemed to have vanished.

Emily nearly groaned when Jacob and Harriet rejoined their group two hours later. How could he let Harriet cling so tightly? It made her look brazen and him look smitten. Finding her a suitable match would be harder than ever.

His words to Charles echoed ominously. Surely he didn't think Harriet would make an acceptable wife!

No matter what he thought of love, he owed the earldom an heir with impeccable breeding.

Shaking off her sudden fear, she turned back to Charles, who was entertaining her with descriptions of society's leaders.

"I see Lord Sedgewick Wiley is gracing us with his presence this evening," he said as an Exquisite paused in the doorway to survey the room. "After Brummell fled his creditors, Lord Sedgewick became the highest authority on fashion and manners. Note the perfectly tied cravat, the refined line of his coat, the discriminating choice of waistcoat, the elegant use of his glass."

Lord Sedgewick was so well turned out that other men seemed either overdressed or too plain. He leisurely quizzed Miss Lutterworth, taking in her blue crape gown with its vandyked bodice, full sleeves, and white crape rouleau above the flounce. More vandyking at the bottom drew eyes to her trim ankles and blue satin slippers. Simple, yet elegant. When Lord Sedgewick nodded approval, Miss Lutterworth seemed happier than when the princess had complimented her gown at yesterday's Drawing Room. Her modiste's credit would soar by morning.

"Watch him with young Bailey," murmured Charles, tickling her ear with his breath. "The lad's manners are rough. There was an incident yesterday that demands censure. I've no doubt Lord Sedgewick means to straighten him out."

A brief comment turned Bailey's face red. Another elicited a vigorous nod, followed by a deep bow. Bailey immediately left.

"Off to make amends, I'll warrant," said Charles.

"Surely such power is dangerous." Emily shook her head.

"In the wrong hands it could be, but Lord Sedgewick won't abuse it. He takes his position as society's conscience seriously, and he wants everyone to succeed. But you needn't fret about him. He will judge you a valuable addition to London. Your gown is ele-

gant without excess, a perfect foil for your beauty. I
especially like the way those knots of ribbon set off
the flounce. And the color adds green flecks to those
astonishing amber eyes. They remind me of the sun."

She blushed. Despite her afternoon objections, he
continued pouring the butter boat over her head. The
compliments sounded strange coming from a man she
recalled as a scrawny boy who'd broken his arm falling
from an apple tree at age twelve. But it fit his reputation as a flirt. If only Richard hadn't demanded he
help look after her. Charles must resent wasting his
talents on someone so negligible.

But he couldn't abandon her at the moment. Richard had disappeared. Jacob was busy with Harriet. Sophie was surrounded by her usual court, augmented
tonight by the dark-haired man. Emily still hadn't discovered his name. None of the Beaux had introduced
her, though she'd noted several mothers pushing their
daughters in his direction, so he must be a desirable
party.

"Who is that?" she asked Charles, nodding toward
the newcomer.

"Lord Ashington." His voice turned to a growl.
"What the devil is he doing bothering Sophie?"

"I can't see that he is." She stepped forward to
prevent him from charging. "What's wrong with him?"

"He's the worst rogue in town. Underhanded. Dishonorable. Why is he even here? He never attends
routs."

"He's talking. Just like we are. Relax, Charles." She
laid a hand on his chest. "He isn't hurting Sophie, but
if you attack, the scandal will reflect on both of you.
And there's no need. See? He's already moving off.
He only wanted a word with Mr. Pierce." Or he'd
noted Charles's glare and decided to play least in
sight.

"Apparently." Tension drained from his shoulders.
"Thank you for stopping me." He covered her hand
and smiled.

"One day you must tell me why it was necessary."

If there was a point to Charles's reaction, she must warn Sophie, though the girl obviously expected trouble. Why else was she so secretive? But if Charles was right to condemn Ashington, Sophie must listen to reason.

Yet Emily couldn't demand information in the middle of a rout. Too many people would notice if Charles lost his temper. It was almost as explosive as Jacob's.

Suppressing a sigh, she retrieved her hand and turned to greet Mr. Larkin.

"My dear Miss Hughes!" he exclaimed. "How delightful to see you this evening. I trust an afternoon outdoors did not weary you overmuch."

"Of course not. I am accustomed to the country, you might recall."

"Certainly. Certainly. My apologies for impugning your constitution. It is obvious that the Season agrees with you. Your eyes glow like twin suns, warming everything they touch."

"No need to exaggerate," she said, nearly rolling the eyes in question. It sounded even less sincere because Charles had said nearly the same thing.

"But he exaggerates so well," laughed Sophie, drawing them into her circle now that Ashington was gone. "My very first Season he convinced me his horse could jump a ten-foot wall." Her head shook.

"Now, I'm sure I never said *ten* feet," said Mr. Larkin.

"If it's the horse he rode to hunt that year, I doubt it could clear three." Jacob joined them, grinning.

Emily's heart leaped, despite the way Harriet plastered herself against his side. She deliberately focused on Mr. Larkin while she brought her breathing under control.

"That was quite a different beast. One I sold as soon as possible—to Delaney."

From the groans emanating from every male throat, Emily deduced that Delaney was not a respected horseman.

"The horse Lady Sophie recalls was Pegasus, a wondrous animal."

"But not the flyer his namesake was," said Jacob.

"Not quite," Mr. Larkin admitted, winking at Emily. "But can you blame a man for bragging on his favorite?"

"Of course not." She smiled. "No man could resist."

Sophie laughed.

Emily shifted so she no longer faced Jacob, then threw herself wholeheartedly into the banter.

When she next took stock, Jacob was gone, as was Charles. Richard had returned and was taking his turn at chaperoning the girls.

She accepted Mr. Larkin's invitation to drive in the park and promised a set at an upcoming ball to Lord Francis. By the time she left the rout, she had two more invitations.

But Jacob had said nothing, not even asking his usual questions about Harriet.

Harriet again followed Emily into her room when they arrived home.

"What a dull gathering," she groused, throwing herself across the bed. "Everyone says the same things, over and over and over. *Did you hear that Lord Seaton caught Devereaux in his wife's bed? . . . The Hunt girl has already received two offers! . . . I was shocked— shocked—by the costumes at Drury Lane! That theater is becoming positively vulgar!*" She produced a high-pitched parody of Lady Auden, whose girlish voice was recognizable everywhere, and who always injected an astonishing range of emotion into her recitation of the latest news.

"Gossip is the mainstay of society conversation," Emily reminded her. "Fashion. Theater. Scandal. Courtship. Be glad you know the details. It proves you are part of society. But don't mimic others in public. You haven't the credit to carry it off without insult. If you hope to find a husband, you cannot afford to seem rude."

"I'm already betrothed, so it doesn't matter." She flashed her secretive smile.

"What? Lord Hawthorne said nothing of a betrothal."

Harriet sat up, preening. "I should not have mentioned it, of course, for he wants me to take my time so I have no regrets later on—he is postponing the announcement until the end of the Season. And I must admit that flirtation is fun."

"Who?" But her pounding heart already knew.

"Jacob."

"But you just met him!"

She shrugged. "Our parents arranged the betrothal when we were children. They were the best of friends."

"I can't believe it." Her protest was automatic. "He would have told Richard. They have been closer than brothers since school."

"Maybe he thought a fever would kill me—fevers are common in India and strike the English harder than the natives. Or perhaps he wished to give me a choice—since no one in England knows about it, I could terminate it without hurting either of us. But I can't imagine anyone better. He is a very attractive man. And his title and fortune are a bonus Papa couldn't have foreseen when he arranged the match."

"True." And it was that single fact that convinced her. To a pair of army officers in far-off India, pairing their children would seem logical. Only the addition of an earldom turned it absurd. But the earldom had come later.

No wonder Jacob had insisted on pushing Harriet into society despite the breeding that made her inclusion questionable. His wife must have entrée. If he merely wished to settle her, he could have arranged a marriage to any of a dozen men near Hawthorne Park. A village shopkeeper, perhaps, or the blacksmith, who needed a wife to look after his three young children. Or one of the Hawthorne tenants. And there was a vicar two parishes beyond Cherry Hill who remained unwed. The . . .

She slammed the door on that sort of thinking.

This also explained why he let Harriet cling and why he'd ignored the London beauties who dangled after him each year. And he'd had to denounce love to Charles because he would never experience it. The examples he'd cited were the only ones he dared see— Emily had already spotted a dozen couples who made no effort to hide their love, many of them wed long enough to have produced several children. The pain threading his voice had not arisen from a long-past hurt but from having no control over his future. He could only sire an heir, then go his own way, clinging to the illusion that he was happy.

Her heart broke for him and the barren life he faced—Harriet cared for no one. But even more, it broke for herself.

As Harriet chattered excitedly about being a countess, Emily fought back tears. So much of Jacob's past now appeared in a different light. He'd fled their embrace out of guilt—as a gently bred female, she was off limits to any gentleman who couldn't court her. His one-night-only policy had avoided any attachment that might disprove the lies he used to justify accepting his future. Even his insistence on calling her *Tadpole* kept her firmly in the role of Richard's baby sister so he needn't look at her as a woman—which would likely terminate their friendship. He was the most honorable man she knew.

Her love flooded back, stronger than ever as she considered the quandary he must have faced for so long—bound to a stranger who might not live long enough to wed him, yet unable to betray her. Nor could he force her, which meant suffering yet another Season in silence so she could come to him freely— and dying a thousand deaths every time her antics raised frowns.

Harriet would choose him, of course—Emily hadn't missed the flash of avarice when the girl had mentioned his title and fortune. And there was nothing she could do about it. Even if Jacob knew Harriet was a fortune hunter, honor forbade him to jilt her.

So he was truly lost to her, condemned to a life he would never enjoy. As was she. Not only must she continue helping Harriet—teaching the girl proper manners was the only way to make Jacob's life easier—but she must find another husband for herself.

Tomorrow.

Tonight she had to escape Harriet before she surrendered to fury and slapped that gloating face.

"Men can be so silly at times," Harriet was saying. "It would be so much easier if we married immediately. He should not have asked you to share your Season."

Emily gritted her teeth. "That is something you should discuss with him. I believe your maid is waiting," she added as hers appeared in the doorway. "Tomorrow will be full of morning calls, so you need sleep."

She held herself together while Huggins readied her for bed. But the moment she was alone, tears poured out. She'd been unbelievably stupid and had only until morning to pull out her renowned sense and convince her heart to seek another. If she failed, she would remain forever a spinster, for her father could never afford a second Season. She did not want to play maiden aunt to whatever children Richard produced. She especially did not want to live next door to Harriet. So she must find a husband.

In desperation, she examined Harriet's tale, seeking some flaw or a hint of exaggeration. Was it possible the girl was lying?

Yet she'd detected no hint of dishonesty before. Arrogance, of course. And stubbornness. But not lies. Harriet's breeding might be less than her own, but she was a lady. Ladies didn't lie. If anything, the girl was too honest for her own good, refusing to use the social lies that covered boredom.

The betrothal must date to Harriet's infancy, for Jacob's family had returned soon afterward, and his parents had died only six months later. But such arrangements happened. And they were binding.

Chapter Six

$\mathcal{J}$acob watched as Emily settled into the box he'd taken overlooking the stage and ring at Astley's Amphitheater. He was looking forward to her pleasure.

Emily would never disparage a show some considered more suited to children and the lower orders. She loved horses and riding, so she would enjoy this exhibition. Many of the tricks were performed nowhere else, for the acrobats of Astley's were the best in the land. And Grimaldi's fame as a clown had spread well beyond London.

He hated to admit that Harriet had been at least partially right about Emily's coolness. Though he'd seen no overt antagonism, Emily remained as far from Harriet as possible, answering the girl's questions with a minimum of words. At the moment she was at the opposite corner of the box, laughing with Sophie.

It might be no more than a momentary tiff, of course. Harriet could be aggravating. He considered asking Richard, but doubted if he would know the truth—or would say anything against Emily if he did. So he must speak to Emily himself. Only then could he decide whether Harriet was exaggerating to stir up trouble or was a victim of spite.

He still couldn't believe Emily had a spiteful bone in her body.

When Charles drew Sophie away for a moment, Jacob slipped into the chair at Emily's side.

"Words cannot express how grateful I am that you

agreed to take Miss Nichols under your wing, Em. I hope her presence does not interfere too badly with your own plans."

"Of course not." She smiled warmly, though her eyes flashed a different message. Irritation? It was gone before he could tell, but his heart sank. Clearly the sun did not shine at Hughes House.

"I spoke to her last night about her manners and hope that she understands better now," he continued doggedly.

"I've no doubt her understanding is quite firm," she agreed, turning to watch several horses parade into the ring.

He waited for her to add the qualification promised by her tone. When she remained silent, he prompted her. "But what?"

She sighed. "Understanding the rules is not the same as following them. I remind myself that England is more rigid than a military outpost. Frustration often makes people lash out. I'm sure she will settle soon. It is in her best interests to do so."

He frowned, though she didn't see it. "You are right, of course. Is she disturbing your mother?"

"No." Her denial was firm. "They rarely speak. Mama remains upstairs much of the day, joining us only to make calls or attend events. I hope this evening is not too strenuous for her," she added, casting an assessing glance at Lady Hughes.

"She will be fine," he quickly assured her. "Laughter is wonderfully invigorating. Everyone enjoys Astley's."

"Hardly a surprise." She turned back to the ring as Miss Astley cantered into view, standing on her horse's back. A roar rose from the pit, where merchant children jostled for a better view. As Miss Astley set her hands on her mount's withers, vaulting from the ground on her left to the ground on her right before landing atop the horse again, the entire audience inhaled in an audible gasp.

"How does she do that?" demanded Emily.

"Much practice." Her flushed face and bright eyes

warmed his heart. Whatever complaint she had with Harriet was forgotten for the moment.

"Look!" she gasped, grabbing his arm as Miss Astley assumed a new pose—arms out to the side, one leg back, body forward like a ship's figurehead, her only support a single foot. Her diaphanous costume fluttered as the horse continued to canter.

"She is well-known for that trick," he said absently, wondering why Emily's grasp seemed so different from Harriet's. Probably because she was sharing pleasure rather than demanding attention.

His own attention suddenly shifted to a man skirting the ring. As he watched, the fellow hurried through the door leading to the Green Room. Sir Bertram, in the flesh. At last.

"I just spotted someone I need to see," he murmured in Emily's ear as he rose. "I'll be back in a moment." Without further ado, he hurried off to find the fellow.

Emily kept her eyes firmly on the ring as her other senses followed Jacob. She couldn't turn back to Sophie or Charles until she could control her face.

She had awakened that morning, hoping Harriet was ill-bred enough to have lied. But she was deluding herself by letting fantasies again take hold of her mind. Ten years of dreams was enough. It was time to face reality.

Jacob had focused all his attention on Harriet tonight, just as he'd done for days. Even his brief conversation just now had dealt solely with Harriet. He knew his wife must take her place in society. He trusted Emily to make it happen.

She could warn him that Harriet was worse in private than in public, but it would do no good. Complaining that Harriet snubbed Lady Hughes at every opportunity would sound like jealousy. Reporting that Harriet demanded a new shopping expedition nearly every day would look like envy of the bottomless coffers Harriet had at her disposal. And repeating even one of Harriet's snide remarks must sound like sour grapes from a woman with no matrimonial prospects about a woman who was settled.

All she could do was try her best to teach Harriet the skills she'd not needed in a Bombay military outpost. More than blood set aristocrats apart. They acted different, talked different, dressed different, and thought different from merchants or tenants or soldiers. Teaching all that was a daunting task, especially when every lesson would remind her in the most painful way that she had lost the man she loved.

No! She did not love him. She had exaggerated a childish infatuation into a fantasy of a perfect union. The infatuation would have died long since if she'd seen him. He was very different from the boy she remembered. Grimmer, more rigid, with less care for others. She needed a man who could laugh, who would share his concerns and listen to advice. With the Season well underway, her chances were diminishing daily.

Sophie reclaimed her seat as Harriet laughed uproariously. Charles quickly moved to whisper in the girl's ear—probably an injunction to temper her exuberance.

As Grimaldi tumbled onto the stage, Sophie leaned close, as if telling Emily about the fabled clown.

"Ashington is here," she whispered. "He just slipped into the corridor. Come with me."

"You can't chase after him," warned Emily. "Charles will have a fit."

"That's why you are coming. We will go to the lady's retiring room. Quickly, before anyone questions us."

Emily glanced at the others. Charles was still berating Harriet. Richard bent to Lady Hughes. Jacob had not yet returned from his errand. "All right, but if you do anything wrong . . ."

"Never. I only wish to bump into him in the hall."

And to Emily's surprise, that was exactly what happened.

"Lord Ashington! What a surprise. I didn't know you enjoyed Astley's."

"Lady Sophie." His brown eyes twinkled as he raised her hand to his lips. "How delightful to see you again. But who is your friend?"

"Miss Hughes, Richard's sister." She smiled. "Emily, this is Lord Ashington, heir to the Duke of Argyle."

Ashington murmured the correct greetings.

"So what brings you to Astley's?" asked Sophie.

"My nephews." He grimaced.

Emily laughed. "You look just like my brother when he was plagued by a demanding little sister."

"And mine," added Sophie.

"Not that I mind," Ashington was quick to note.

"Of course not," said Sophie soothingly. "But we all know family obligations often ignore personal preference."

"As you must know all too well," he nodded, leaving Harriet's name hanging unspoken in midair.

They continued talking for some time, giving Emily a chance to study his lordship. While he lacked the overt masculinity of the Beaux, beneath his urbane exterior was a man just as dependable—and just as steely. The brown eyes might seem warm and friendly, but she had no doubt he could be as hard as Richard when crossed. What she did not see was evidence of dissipation, dishonor, or disrepute. His quarrel with Charles must be private indeed.

"Are you enjoying the Season?" he asked, turning to Emily.

"Very much. London lives up to its reputation for splendor."

"And squalor." But he said it lightly.

"True, but what city doesn't have that? I do not expect perfection, though I do pursue it in my own life."

"Well said."

Sophie glanced over her shoulder as music swelled

from the ring. "We must hurry, Emily, or you will miss the pantomime. It is spectacular."

"Of course." She took her leave of Ashington, then watched as he and Sophie exchanged several silent messages.

"You arranged that," hissed Emily the moment they reached the retiring room.

Sophie blushed. "Not exactly, though I did mention that we would be here tonight, and he mentioned that, by coincidence, so would he."

"He seems quite nice."

"He is more than nice. I have every intention of wedding him."

"Why does Charles hate him so?"

Her face clouded. "I don't know."

"Can't you guess? He said something about dishonorable rogues."

"He says that about half the gentlemen in town." She checked her hair in the mirror. "They attended school together and remained friendly rivals until three years ago. I know no details, but from snippets of rumor, I suspect there was a duel. Whether they were principals or seconds or merely onlookers, I don't know, but they must have been on opposite sides. And the result must have been serious, for both left town for a time—as did Richard, Jacob, and several others. Since no one will discuss it, I've no way to discover the truth."

"Oh, lord."

"Exactly. I refuse to let a quarrel between two stubborn fools interfere in my happiness. Ashington is everything I want in a husband, and since he is now seeking a wife, I intend to have him."

"You likely will. There is a gleam in his eye when he looks at you."

Sophie exhaled in relief. "So you see it, too. I was afraid I was imagining it."

"No." She bit her lip, but had to continue. "You can't ignore Charles's objections, though. If you truly

want Lord Ashington, you must discover the truth of
their quarrel and convince Charles to call a truce. Do
you want to tear your family apart? Charles is stubborn enough to cut you if you ignore his advice."

"True. Perhaps Lady Beatrice can help. She knows
everything. In the meantime, please don't tell Charles."

Emily followed her back to their box, wishing she
hadn't participated in a meeting with all the overtones
of an assignation. But she had given her word.

The moment she resumed her seat, Charles slid into
the chair next to her.

"Where did you go?" he demanded sharply.

"To the retiring room."

"You should have told me you were leaving."

"Why? You were engrossed in a conversation. I
took Sophie along for propriety. Should I have announced my departure to the entire theater?"

"Of course not." His fury dwindled to irritation.
"But you could have waited long enough to let one
of us know you were leaving."

"Some things can't wait." She glared at him.

"Oh. Uh." He actually blushed. "Very well. I'm
sorry to scold, then. But I was concerned when I found
you gone."

"Then I forgive you." She turned to the ring, where
another horse cantered around the ring, its rider doing
a handstand on its back.

Jacob returned some time later, his face twisted in
frustration. Whatever had sent him rushing away had
not been concluded to his satisfaction.

He took the seat behind Lady Hughes. When Harriet beckoned him closer, he moved behind her, laying
a hand on her shoulder as he leaned forward to ex-
change confidences.

Emily didn't see the pantomime at all, despite staring at it with great determination.

The next afternoon, Jacob turned his horse through
the gates of Hyde Park, joining the press of carriages

and horsemen jostling for position on the narrow road. He generally avoided the fashionable hour, for he had long since wearied of matchmakers assaulting his bachelorhood. But today he'd had no choice.

Maybe he should find that insipid wife and surrender. He could then concentrate on Parliament and whatever affairs took his fancy, safe from pursuit.

But he couldn't bring himself to do it. Not yet.

Maybe never.

The thought shocked him, for he hadn't considered abrogating his responsibility to the title.

Yet why couldn't he? The next in line was a cousin who would carry on at least as well as he. The family obsession would remain a problem no matter who held the title, but leaving the succession to others would at least remove his mother's influence.

Lost in thought, he barely noticed Lady Marchgate sweep past.

Harriet's arrival had forced him to examine his childhood through adult eyes. It was just as sordid as he expected, but his analysis cast troubling doubts on his plans. If he wed only to produce an heir, then walked away, was he any different from Mrs. Nichols? The woman had acted solely to improve her social and financial position, ignoring honor, duty, and any other virtues that stood in her way.

Wedding with the intent of walking away was equally selfish. He expected to choose a wife he despised, then abandon her. Granted, he would leave her with a title and wealth instead of a gravestone, but the plan was just as cold. And what if she formed an attachment? Could he risk hurting another? Yet could he live with someone he despised?

He would be better off avoiding marriage altogether.

The decision should have buoyed him, but instead it triggered surprising melancholy. He had actually looked forward to rearing a son, helping him in all the ways his own father had never done. But it wasn't possible. He was too much a product of his breeding, his quick temper and sudden lusts confirming the worst of both parents. He would spare future generations at least part of that.

A shout jerked him from his reverie. He was blocking the road. Setting heels to his horse, he looked around, hoping to spot Sir Bertram. Last night's search had failed.

According to the baronet's best friend, Sir Bertram rarely missed a sunny fashionable hour—he was a dandy to the core and needed an audience to admire each day's sartorial creation.

Lady Beatrice rarely made mistakes, so suggesting Sir Bertram as a match for Harriet meant the man must be seeking a wife. To a dandy of his caliber, sporting an Exotic on his arm would improve his credit. Harriet fit the bill quite well, and she should jump at the chance to wed a full-fledged baronet.

That presumed Jacob could introduce the pair. So far, Sir Bertram remained elusive. It seemed that everyone had seen him but Jacob.

As usual, the park was jammed with open carriages of every description as the *ton* took advantage of the warm sunshine. Young ladies strolled across emerald lawns, their bobbing parasols forming a field of exotic flowers. Dandies strutted alongside, waving scented handkerchiefs languidly before their faces.

If Jacob hadn't been on horseback, he would have made no progress at all. But even his mobility didn't help when Lady Debenham gestured imperiously.

"You weren't at the Marchgate Ball last night," she accused him the instant he reached her side.

"My apologies, my lady." He doffed his hat. "The Beaux took our charges to Astley's."

She harrumphed. "That's another thing, Hawthorne. Where did that ward of yours come from?"

"Bombay." He sighed. Lady Debenham sought sensational scandal even when it didn't exist. If he didn't bury her in details, she might think he had something to hide. "Captain Nichols served in my father's regiment and was also a close family friend. I still grieve

over his death in action. Thus it was no surprise that
when Mrs. Nichols remarried, she suggested Hawthorne as her daughter's guardian in case anything
happened to her."

"That Hawthorne died nineteen years ago."

He shrugged. "Captain Nichols was my friend, too.
I'll do what I can for her. With her looks, I expect an
offer soon."

Lady Debenham frowned. "She has looks enough,
and you must be commended for making the most of
them. But it might have been better to polish her manners before bringing her out. Her breeding's too close
to the line to tolerate rudeness."

"Perhaps I rushed," he admitted, adding the smile
that generally charmed older ladies. "But she should
settle in another day or two."

"Maybe. Maybe not." She met his gaze. "Girl's got a
sly look I've seen before. Miss Parker comes to mind."

He nearly groaned. Miss Parker had come out two
years earlier to minimal fanfare. *Dull* was the best way
to describe her. She'd done everything right, deferring
to the matrons, listening politely to the other girls,
smiling sweetly at eligible gentlemen while avoiding
rakes like Devereaux—and the Beaux. Everything had
seemed perfect until the morning her parents awoke
to discover that she'd eloped with a here-and-therian
she'd met on one of her clandestine late-night excursions to a gaming hell.

Jacob shuddered. "You really think—" The idea
was too awful to put into words.

"I don't know." Her ignorance clearly annoyed her.
"But she has a look in her eye I don't trust. Settle
her before she ruins herself."

He thanked her, wondering how Lady Debenham
would have described Mrs. Nichols. Captain Nichols
should have requested that a London gossip pass judgment on his bride before she left for Bombay.

He would have to warn Richard and Charles to
watch Harriet more closely. And this made it even
more urgent to find Sir Bertram.

But the baronet was nowhere in sight.

Half an hour later, Jacob gave up and headed for the gates. Perhaps Sir Bertram was at his club. Or maybe he'd joined a party for Richmond. It was early for picnics, but groups sometimes drove out to eat at the Pig and Whistle.

He spared a passing landau only the briefest nod, then froze.

This stretch of road was momentarily empty, giving approaching drivers a chance to show off their skill. A high-perch phaeton raced along at a dangerous pace, Larkin at the ribbons. He nearly overturned as he swung around the knot of gentlemen admiring the newest diamond, then skidded precariously when his horses shied at a squirrel.

Emily clutched the low rail of the unstable seat. She looked lovely today in a dark green pelisse, her tawny curls framing her face. But even at twenty paces, he could see her white cheeks.

Fury licked his veins. What the devil was Richard thinking to let his sister drive out with a ham-fisted cawker as likely to overturn as to breathe? Insanity! Phaetons were notoriously unstable, especially the high-perch variety. Emily might be injured—or worse. Larkin had no more sense than a rock to risk her safety.

He was also a blatant flirt who should avoid impressionable girls. If Larkin was the best candidate Richard could find, Jacob would have to take charge of judging her suitors.

The phaeton flew past as he sat staring. Larkin sawed on the ribbons when a loose stone pushed the carriage off course—no wonder his horses tried to escape. Their mouths must be in shreds.

Instead of exiting the park, Jacob turned to catch Larkin, coming up on Emily's side, where the phaeton's high seat left them eye-to-eye. At least Larkin had the horses under control for the moment.

"Larkin. Miss Hughes." He nodded.

"Lord Hawthorne," she acknowledged coolly.

"Is Richard here today?"

"I doubt it." With the phaeton now stopped, she relaxed her death-grip on the side. "He mentioned going to Jackson's, then to his club. But that might have changed. I've not seen him since Astley's last evening."

Lady Cunningham paused on the other side to greet Larkin, letting Jacob lean close so only Emily could hear. "Didn't Richard warn you to stay out of phaetons, Miss Hughes? They are unstable and fast."

"The horses might be skittish—I'm not impressed with their training—but we can rarely move quickly in this crush."

"Don't pretend ignorance, Tadpole," he snapped. "You know I meant the disreputable sort of fast. Your reputation is too important. Don't risk it."

She recoiled, raising an urge to smooth the shock from her forehead. He suppressed it. He hadn't meant to scare her, but that might be a good idea. Larkin wasn't suitable.

Yet the urge to soothe remained. He actually tugged at his glove—stroking her brow without removing it might abrade her tender skin. It glowed even in the shade of her bonnet. Satin. Smooth. The perfect place to drop a row of gentle kiss—

He jerked back, appalled at the images forming in his head. Emily was no courtesan. She was Richard's sister, for God's sake.

His horse pranced, sensing his agitation. He took a moment to bring it under control.

Emily was staring as if she'd never seen him before. Larkin waved Lady Cunningham on, then laid a hand over Emily's before taking up the ribbons. The possessiveness of the gesture was clear, as was the lust heating Larkin's eyes.

Jacob snapped out a farewell that probably sounded like a threat, then left before he could choke the life from Larkin. Richard was insane to trust his sister to the idiot. Emily deserved better than a man who was only mildly intelligent and would expect his wife to accept his brood of by-blows.

He would watch until Emily returned home, then warn Larkin away. She was too sheltered to handle the man's flirtation and too naïve to know that some men could never become loving husbands.

Emily was glad the crush of other vehicles kept Mr. Larkin busy. She needed a moment to settle her senses. Jacob's appearance had cracked her armor, and his anger still rattled her nerves.

Not that she could blame him. London had more rules than she'd expected. Richard's lectures to Harriet had revealed several new ones. Now here was another.

She quickly reviewed his exhortations, wondering if she'd missed something. But she could recall nothing about phaetons. Avoiding gallops, yes. Avoiding Bond Street after two and St. James's Street anytime, yes. Avoiding intimate walks in dark gardens, yes. Avoiding phaetons, no. He must have forgotten.

She couldn't blame Jacob for being furious over her faux pas. Everyone knew she had charge of Harriet, so her behavior would reflect on his betrothed. Jacob would hate her if she besmirched Harriet's reputation. It was fragile enough already.

She must be more careful about accepting invitations without asking about the details. And she must share all her invitations with Richard instead of assuming that a ride in the park with one of his friends was all right.

Had Mr. Larkin deliberately jeopardized her reputation to repay Richard for forcing him to dance attendance on his sister? She didn't want to believe it, but why else would he court disapproval?

She concentrated on keeping her smile in place as the real ramifications of this confrontation burst through her head. Richard must think she was hopeless if he'd asked the Beaux to watch her as well as

Harriet. Jacob had the afternoon shift today. Charles would likely appear next.

Sophie's words suddenly sounded ominous. *They will smother you while assuring themselves that they are protecting you from harm.*

That did not bode well for the future. Unlike Sophie, she would have no second chance if she failed to wed this Season.

Yet she couldn't regret being the focus of Jacob's attention, even for such an unromantic reason. This would be the last time he would pay her any heed at all.

He looked magnificent on horseback, his legs rippling with muscle as they'd controlled the beast's restlessness. Anger darkened his eyes, but that made it easier to drown in them. His head had bent so close she could have cupped his cheek—

Thrusting the memory from her mind, she concentrated on Mr. Larkin's chatter. At least he was entertaining. This might be the best hour of her day.

Once she returned home, she would again face Harriet's megrims—the girl had thrown a fit because Emily was driving out without her; she refused to understand that society would not treat her like a countess until Jacob made their betrothal public. This evening Emily would have to watch Jacob monopolize Harriet and pretend that her heart didn't crack deeper with each intimate smile.

Chapter Seven

*J*acob ducked into the card room that night, hoping a few moments of peace would settle his temper. Nothing was going right today. Or almost nothing—he'd succeeded in steering Larkin away from Emily. But he'd still not found Sir Bertram. The man might have disappeared from the face of the earth.

At least Harriet was settled for the evening. The Cunningham ball included many men from the gentry—having ten daughters kept their dowries small, so the Cunninghams welcomed anyone respectable. By the time Jacob had arrived, every one of Harriet's sets was taken. So were Sophie's.

But Emily's card had been only partly full. He'd had to claim a second set to keep Connoly from annoying her. The cub was too green.

Now he cursed himself roundly. The first set had been a sprightly country dance that should have meant nothing. Yet that spurt of lust he'd felt in the park had returned, stronger than before. Annoyingly out of place for Richard's sister, especially considering his decision to die unwed, but he couldn't seem to shake it.

At least Emily neither noticed it nor shared it. She was still wary, flinching when he'd touched her unexpectedly. His fault, of course. He'd hurt her worse than he'd expected all those years ago. By striking out to cover his shock, he'd broken something precious. It was a mistake he ought to repair.

He'd been twenty, plenty old enough to control his

passions. With years of liaisons behind him, he'd been experienced enough to keep the situation under control. Instead, he'd stepped well beyond honor, then ruthlessly blamed her for enticing him.

It was too late for an apology, but he had to eliminate her fear. If he could reestablish the friendship they'd shared that summer, it would be easier to guide her toward a husband who would care for her as she deserved.

The latest Parliamentary debates would have to wait, he decided. Keeping unacceptable men away from Emily would require much of his attention. With his course set, he returned to the ballroom.

For two hours he hovered on the fringes of the crowd, discussing upcoming debates with other lords, deflecting an offer for his bays from a drunken Easley, and flirting lightly with Lady Jersey.

This was why he attended Parliament most evenings. Every year the social banter seemed more insipid. Who cared whether Shelford broke another of his own racing records? Why did it matter that Lady Willingham was leaving widowhood behind for Lord Hanson? Her liaisons wouldn't stop. Nor would his.

Emily was enjoying herself hugely, yet it became more obvious with each set that Richard was not paying attention to her.

"Sanders and Bradshaw danced with Emily," Jacob murmured as he and Richard filled plates at supper. Sanders was an increasingly jaded rake, and Bradshaw an inveterate gamester.

"Thank you. I'll deal with it." Richard shook his head. "Bringing out a sister is one headache after another. I had no idea what I was in for. How has Charles managed all this time?"

"Lady Inslip kept a sharp eye on Sophie that first year, and we had only one chick to watch instead of three. Too bad your mother isn't stronger."

"That was a nasty surprise. I'd always thought she exaggerated to keep Emily at her beck and call. Now I find out she's seriously ill."

"Sorry to hear that."

He nodded thanks for the sympathy. "By the way, I saw Harriet flirting with Featherstone. Probably nothing in it, but—"

"I'll warn her." Featherstone was another rake, older than Sanders and even less caring of propriety. Rumor credited him with three seductions of wellborn innocents. The Cunninghams would not have invited him, but that never stopped him from going where he pleased.

In addition to chastising Harriet, he must speak with sober-sided Sir Thomas Eaton and the frivolous Lord Ross. Each had danced attendance on Emily at Lady Penleigh's, remained close at Lady Horseley's rout, then claimed sets tonight. Another encounter any time soon would draw notice. Neither was worthy of her.

Harriet smiled as Mr. Phillips escorted her to the ballroom after supper. He was a dead bore, but at least he treated her well.

She couldn't say the same for Jacob. What was wrong with the man? She'd been the belle of every ball she'd ever attended. There wasn't an eligible man in India who hadn't been panting at her door, including Wentworth's second in command. Yet Jacob didn't look at her. She'd tried to save him two sets tonight, but Richard had filled them with dolts before Jacob even arrived.

She plied her fan to hide her fury. She would have to work harder to bring him to heel. He was hers, though he'd yet to admit it. His only comment all evening had been an admonition to stay away from Featherstone, the only man here who wasn't dull.

"Is anything wrong?" asked Mr. Phillips.

"A slight chill. I'm not yet accustomed to the English weather." Batting her lashes restored vapid infatuation to his face. Fool.

After a lifetime of enduring penury and her stepfather's derision, she was ready to embrace the life she deserved. Her mother had been a baron's daughter, and her father had connections to half a dozen great houses, making her worthy of the highest in the land. She'd managed her first goal—reaching London, the world's largest and most opulent city. The next step should be easy.

A score of officers had demanded her hand, but she'd refused. Never again would she live on an inadequate military income. She needed wealth—unlimited wealth—and the standing that would let her sneer at those self-righteous wives who had cut her so often.

In short, she needed Jacob. And she meant to have him.

The immediate problem was Miss Hughes. Jacob was watching her like a hawk. He wasn't courting her, but she knew men well enough to spot his interest. So she must keep the two apart, and that meant leaving Hughes House. As long as she remained there, Jacob would see Miss Hughes daily. But once he understood how miserable she was, he must move her to Hawthorne House.

So she put off Mr. Phillips and tracked down Jacob, catching him outside the card room.

"Lady Hughes refused to let Mr. Raintree drive me in the park," she complained, producing her most winsome smile. When she spotted Emily's eyes on them, she crowded closer, delighted when he grasped her shoulders to push her away. It would look quite intimate from afar. "You must drive me yourself so she understands that I can appear in all the usual venues. She is determined to keep me locked away so I don't overshadow her daughter."

"We've discussed this before, Miss Nichols." He glared as alarmingly as Wentworth—not that anyone else could see his face. "If she postponed a park drive, it can only be that you lack suitable clothing. In a few more days, all will be well."

"But—"

"Patience, child. If you rush your fences, you will

fall. The rules exist for a reason. Until you understand them, be careful. In the meantime, I will see that Raintree knows you did not reject him."

He left her fuming. Drat the man! She might have confirmed Emily's belief that Jacob was taken, but he was treating her like an infant. It was time to show him that his dear friends were not the paragons he thought them.

Jacob unclenched his fists as he escaped into the card room. The more he learned about Harriet, the worse she seemed. In less than a week she'd slipped from unwanted burden to impatient hoyden to vulgar harridan. Complaining about one's hostess was not done.

He had to find Sir Bertram before she irredeemably ruined her reputation.

The sound of the man's name pricked him to attention.

"No doubt about it," Pierce was drawling. "Got it from Lady Beatrice. Sir Bertram will wed the Chalmers chit in August. He left for her father's estate this morning. Doesn't care a fig for the chit, but she's a diamond, a perfect foil for him."

No! Jacob nearly screamed aloud. Now he had to find a new candidate for Harriet. Immediately.

He slipped out the far door, seeking the privacy of Lord Cunningham's library before someone spotted his fury and asked questions. But he hadn't gone two steps before running down Emily.

"Sorry, Tadpole," he said, gripping her arms until she regained her balance. Again the old name slipped out, but perhaps recalling that summer would lead to gaining her forgiveness. She seemed more relaxed than earlier.

"My fault. I wasn't watching where I was going." She shrugged.

"If you insist. What are you doing back here, anyway?"

"Retiring room. I caught my skirt on Major Harrison's sleeve—I cannot believe how many buttons his uniform has." She pointed to a rent in the lace.

"Old habit. Extra silver buttons are useful on campaign," he admitted, stifling irritation that Harrison had stood close enough to snag her gown. The Cunningham ball was always a crush. "A man can trade them to the locals for food when the supply lines break down. Are you enjoying your Season?"

"Of course." But the words were a shade too vehement, and her eyes again flashed wariness.

It was time to mend some fences. "I never thanked you for your advice and support that last year."

"I did nothing, Jacob."

"Hardly. You kept me from making a fool of myself. You directed me to men who could answer my questions. You built my confidence. Without you, I could never have wrested control of the Park from Stewart and the others."

"You would have managed, but I accept your thanks," she said modestly, then turned the subject. "Thank you for warning me about phaetons, Jacob. Richard forgot."

"Some men use flashy carriages to display their possessions," he said, leading her toward the library lest someone overhear his exaggerations and undermine his authority—phaetons were definitely unsafe, but there was nothing socially wrong with them. "You do not wish to be thought Larkin's possession."

"No."

"They are also dangerous, even in skilled hands. Larkin's aren't."

"It did seem rather unstable. Much like that up-and-down device you and Richard built that year," she added with a grin.

He rolled his eyes. "Don't remind me. You nearly broke an arm when it snapped."

"Ah, well. That must be fifteen years ago now." She paused, letting her smile fade. "Could you explain something that is puzzling me?"

"What?"

"Lord Ashington. Every time Charles sees him, he nearly attacks. Sophie claims they hate each other, but she doesn't know why."

"Not again," he muttered, gesturing her into a chair while he paced to the fireplace and back.

"It isn't a minor spat," she continued. "It's lasted three years. When I restrained Charles at Lady Horseley's rout, he called Ashington the greatest rogue in England, a dishonorable cad, and a few other names. So why is Ashington here tonight? Granted, he's a duke's heir, but the Cunninghams don't court rogues."

"Anyone can slip in if he doesn't care what society thinks—I saw Featherstone not long ago. He is a genuine rogue. But you're right. Ashington isn't."

"Then why does Charles hate him?"

Jacob ran his hands through his hair, wondering how to explain a feud rooted in a squabble over a widow's favors that had resulted in a farcical meeting at Chalk Farm. Neither man had wanted a duel, but each was too stubborn to back down from the drunken challenge. Both had fired wide, which should have ended the affair with pride intact. Unfortunately, one shot had ricocheted, striking Ashington's second. They'd all left town until the victim recovered, but the argument over blame had never been resolved.

There had been other clashes over the years—most recently over Gina LaRue, the French nightingale, who gave even better performances in bed than on the stage. But it had begun with the Widow Darnley. Personally, he thought the lady rated no more than a glance, but Charles had spent an entire month dancing attendance on her until Ashington swept her away. No one in history had been a less worthy subject for a duel.

"Well?" demanded Emily.

"Ashington is a decent enough fellow, though a bit wild at times," he said carefully. "But he and Charles butt heads often."

"Why?"

"Too many incidents to tell."

"Did Ashington steal his mistress?"

He jumped. How had she known that? "Perhaps," he conceded.

"Did they fight over it?"

Damn her for raising subjects no one discussed! "There are always rumors when two men are so obviously at odds. But I've not heard one word from anyone in a position to know the truth"—including himself, who never mentioned the incident aloud—"so I will not speculate. The confrontations I do know about include Ashington buying an estate Charles wanted and a suggestion that Ash caused trouble for Charles at the Foreign Office. Then there was the night Charles spilled wine down Ash's new coat, Charles buying a horse Ash wanted—"

Voices approached the library, reminding him that Emily was in a compromising position. To protect her, he opened the French window and led her into the garden. "What is your interest in the fellow?"

"None. But I was curious about Charles's reaction—more violent than one would expect of a gentleman, especially at a ball."

"Charles is generally insouciant," he agreed, turning away from the house. "But not when it comes to Ashington. Ignore the fellow. He is not seeking a wife, so you needn't consider him."

Emily paused as if searching for words, but finally abandoned the subject. "What are we doing out here?"

"I meant to ask your advice, but don't need an audience." Or some high-stickler screaming compromise. He'd been alone with Emily a hundred times before. This was no different than their strolls through the orchard.

"What is it?"

The graveled path pierced the shrubbery surrounding a small fountain, taking them out of sight of the terrace. "Miss Nichols, of course. She is far more rustic than I feared. And increasingly defiant.

Her arrogance rivals the most stiff-rumped duchess, making it a serious problem. Is she causing trouble for you?" He'd asked before, but hadn't believed her answer.

"Not trouble, *per se*," said Emily slowly. "Her taste is not as refined as you would like, but we have prevented her from buying gowns that would shame you. And her manners are slowly improving."

"I know that perfectly well." Her hesitancy annoyed him, for it sounded as though she feared his response if she failed to provide the right answer. The hell of it was that she ought to fear him. The moment they'd left the light, lust urged him to sweep her into his arms, kiss her senseless, then claim her for his own.

He couldn't allow it. Moving several careful inches away, so her gown didn't caress his thigh with every step, he continued. "Lady Debenham claims to see a sly look in Harriet's eyes. I've not seen it myself, but the lady is very astute, so you should keep a close eye on her. If she slips off alone, I will have to confine her. And tell me everything that seems odd, no matter how trivial."

Emily nodded. She would have done so anyway. The least she could do for him was keep his wife safe.

As they headed inside, she turned her thoughts to Sophie and Lord Ashington. Sophie would have her work cut out for her if she was set on Ashington. Jacob's verbal sidestepping hadn't fooled her, for she'd heard him utter similar half-truths before. Thus there had been a duel. Since everyone had left town, someone had been shot. Probably Charles. It wasn't an event he would forgive, let alone forget, and he made a formidable foe.

On the other hand, as long as he disguised his chaperon duties by playing the infatuated suitor, she could use his flirtation to soften his hatred for Ashington. If she could keep him occupied long enough for Sophie to establish a serious courtship, maybe he would accept Sophie's choice.

Watching Harriet. Helping Sophie. Overturning her

long infatuation for Jacob. The Season was moving ahead at breakneck speed, yet Emily had no time to address the most pressing matter of all—finding a husband.

Chapter Eight

"*I* don't know if I can survive another day with that girl," Emily confided to Sophie a fortnight later.

Harriet had decided that her knowledge of the world exceeded Emily's, so she ceased any pretense of listening. She was supremely confident of her power over men, using her exotic mannerisms and seductive accent to draw them near. She refused to understand that many of those she lured were dangerous.

Emily shuddered at the memory of Harriet laughing with Devereaux, the most dissipated rakehell in town, who took what he wanted, regardless of convention. Yet she dared not criticize. Harriet ignored her—or deliberately flouted her. Emily need only mention that something was improper to send Harriet hurtling off to try it. She was in full revolt, apparently believing that wedding an earl would overcome any censure— not that she cared what society thought; in that respect she was much like Devereaux.

Another insight Emily had gained too late was that Harriet despised all women, regarding them as unwanted competitors for men's attention. And she was selfish to the core. Jacob would have his hands full trying to control her. He could not pack her off to the country unless he stayed there, too. The minute his back was turned, Harriet would return to town.

But it was Harriet's private war on Emily that hurt the most. She resented any effort to curb her, reacting with criticisms that eroded Emily's confidence and made her doubt her fundamental worth. The attacks were all the more devastating because her misinterpretation of Jacob's kiss and ten years of blind infatuation were already calling her judgment into question. Too many of Harriet's jabs were true.

Sophie had been a godsend, listening to Emily's frustration, bolstering her confidence, and blanketing her in kindness.

"What did she do this time?" murmured Sophie now.

A quick glance around Lady Marchgate's drawing room assured Emily that they couldn't be overheard. Mrs. Trimble was breathlessly recounting the latest rumors about Lord Sedgewick's sudden marriage to a nobody five days earlier. Since Mrs. Trimble was a close friend of Lord Sedgewick's mother, Lady Glendale, her words held everyone spellbound. Lord Sedgewick hadn't been seen in days. Lady Glendale swore he was seeking an annulment.

Emily sighed. "You saw the Duchess of Woburn's gown last night."

Sophie stifled a giggle. "I don't know what the woman is thinking. Fifty if she's a day and built like a frigate, yet she decks herself in three flounces and enough ribbon to wrap a mummy."

"Horrible. But Harriet took one look and decided her single flounce was too plain. She insisted that Mama take her to the dressmaker's again. That is her tenth buying trip in two weeks. Mama is exhausted, and Jacob must be fuming."

"He can afford it." Sophie dismissed the cost. "If he has a complaint, it would be that she will never find a husband if she dresses like a mushroom."

Emily nearly revealed Jacob's betrothal, but bit back the words. It was not her place to reveal his secrets.

Sophie continued without pause. "But wearing your mother out is unconscionable, Emily. Talk to him about it."

"How?"

Sophie considered the problem. "You're right. You

can hardly carry tales, no matter how awful Harriet is. Nor can I. But Richard can. Talk to him. He should be as concerned as you."

Emily nodded, though she had already discounted using Richard as a messenger. Talking to him might pique his curiosity. Since her infatuation made her sound stilted whenever she mentioned Jacob's name, Richard would know her manner was far too quiet. Questions would soon uncover her naïveté. And if he told Jacob—

Heat rose in her face.

Fortunately, Sophie didn't notice. "Mr. Thompson returned yesterday," she said as Lady Debenham cut off Mrs. Trimble to announce that Miss Sharpton had accepted Sir Harvey Creevey.

Miss Everly slipped into an unbecoming pout, confirming that she'd had her eye on Sir Harvey for herself.

"Who is Mr. Thompson?" asked Emily.

"The Duke of Shumwell's grandson, through a daughter. He's of an age to need a wife, so I wondered if Harriet might like him."

"Duke's grandson. It's possible. Do you think he will be at the Jersey ball tonight?" Not that it mattered. A minor ducal grandson would never tempt Harriet away from a wealthy earl.

She ought to be glad that Jacob was clearly enamored with his ward. Most nights he whisked her away the moment he arrived, often without greeting her companions. Harriet regaled Emily with tales of kisses in gardens and anterooms and even behind a statue of Aphrodite in Lady Debenham's entrance hall. Emily had seen his hands on her more than once. So his marriage might offer him some enjoyment.

She wished she could believe he could be happy.

Emily reminded herself again that he was not the man of her fantasies. Whatever flirtation he'd dabbled in that summer was long over. If he had loved her, he would have claimed her when she turned eighteen.

And if he'd cared about his inheritance, he would have visited Hawthorne Park. She had naïvely ignored everything that might have exploded her dreams.

She let Sophie's chatter flow past while she reviewed the tale that proved Jacob was unworthy of her love.

He had coveted a piece of land that would become valuable once a nearby factory expanded. But Lord Raymond Perigord had already offered for it. Rather than make a higher offer, Jacob had accused Lord Raymond of fraud, forcing him to flee the country. By the time he'd returned with evidence of his innocence, Jacob had owned the land.

Emily clung to the image, repeating it over and over in an effort to throw off her lingering attachment. It would be easier if she had a viable alternative, but Harriet was right that she couldn't draw admiring eyes. Richard kept pushing his friends to consider her, but none remained at her side for long. Mr. Larkin had not spoken to her since their drive in the park. Others had skulked away after a single set. Only the Beaux paid her any heed, but they didn't count. Nor did the cubs who occasionally danced with her.

Damn the Beaux for hovering! she thought suddenly, clutching her teacup so firmly it nearly broke. Jacob's insistence on two sets at every ball was driving her to distraction. It didn't mean anything, for he continued treating her like Richard's baby sister. He talked of impartial things like Parliament, or his latest dispute with his tailor, or Harriet.

Always Harriet.

At first, she'd thought he was resuming their old friendship—why else would he treat her as a confidante? But as she watched the matchmakers stalk him, she realized that he saw his friend's harmless sister as a refuge. Or worse.

"He feels sorry for you," Harriet had said after the Wharburton masquerade a week earlier. Jacob had spent three sets with Emily that night, though they'd only danced two. "He knows your Season is a failure, but he must hide that until after we're wed so you don't tarnish my reputation."

It sounded so very plausible. And if she didn't find a suitor soon, he would likely find her someone desperate enough to accept a stranger. And she would be desperate enough to agree. She could not remain a spinster at Cherry Hill with Harriet lording it over Hawthorne Park next door.

She shuddered, for she had overheard Jacob and Richard discussing country suitors only yesterday.

"Are you going to accept Charles?" asked Sophie, shocking Emily out of her thoughts.

"What?"

"Charles. He's been mooning over you for weeks. Surely you've noticed. I hope you accept him. I want you for a sister."

"You can't be serious. He only dances with me because Richard asked him to."

"That was true in the beginning—just as both Richard and Jacob dance with me at every ball. But two sets every night is beyond duty. I've never seen him look at anyone the way he looks at you. Mama will be delighted. She's been concerned that he would end like Devereaux—forty-five and still swanning around like a cub."

Emily shook her head, trying to jar a coherent response from the chaos. Charles? Sophie had to be wrong. Two dances meant nothing. Jacob also demanded two. As did Richard on occasion. Her card wasn't exactly bursting with partners.

But the idea intrigued her. Might he really care? She'd never considered him as anything but Richard's friend. Even in childhood, her feelings had focused on Jacob.

Hope rose. At least she knew Charles. He would never mistreat her. Was this why Lady Inslip had begun taking her on morning calls?

She opened her mouth to demand details, but snapped it shut when Sophie stood.

"Come on. Mama is ready to leave."

"Where now?" murmured Emily.

"Lady Hartford, then Lady Beatrice." She rolled her eyes, careful to keep her face turned so only Emily could see her. "We will have to behave very properly there. I swear the woman can read minds."

Jacob slammed his library door and scowled. He was sick of Harriet's whining and begging. If she complained one more time that Lady Hughes was mistreating her or that Emily hated her, he would ship the girl back to India. Emily would never behave the way Harriet claimed. And how many times must he explain that he could not house her himself? Her hints had turned to demands, proving that her goal was to move out of Hughes House and into his.

It had been a serious blunder to inflict Harriet on Richard's family. He'd also erred in expecting anyone to tell him when Harriet misbehaved. Emily was a saint who would never utter a word against anyone. Richard might hint at trouble, but he was too easygoing to carry tales. Lady Hughes paid little attention to anything beyond her couch. Lord Hughes saw less.

So it was up to him to whip Harriet into line. Not only was she taking advantage of the Hugheses' goodness, she was obviously trying to stir up trouble.

"Miss Hughes refused to accompany me," Harriet had sworn when he'd run into her outside Madame Francine's shop. She'd clutched his arm. "I finally convinced Lady Hughes to come out, but she won't let me buy fashionable gowns. Look at this." She gestured to her walking dress. "I look a dowd! Lady Woburn is much better dressed."

"She is not a lady. She is a duchess and must be referenced as Her Grace of Woburn," he'd snapped. "That gown is perfectly suited to your age and station, so stop complaining. You have enough clothes. I won't pay for more."

She'd pouted and produced copious tears, but he'd remained adamant. He hated manipulative females.

Now he cursed as he poured wine. He'd been unconscionably stupid, bending over backward to hold her blameless for her mother's crimes. By doing so, he had ignored the instincts that suspected the daughter would be just as bad. He should never have introduced her to society.

Was that why Emily was avoiding him? Not avoiding, he admitted as a sunbeam fractured in his glass. She gave him two sets every night. But she'd withdrawn somehow, becoming aloof and masking her thoughts.

He missed the lighthearted girl of ten years ago. She had changed so much. Where was the fiery reformer whose eyes sparkled with laughter? Where was the sprite who had hung on his every word?

Only now that it was gone did he realize how often the memory of those meetings had steadied him over the years. In some ways she'd been a closer friend than Richard or Charles. He could tell her anything, secure that she would never ridicule him.

Unlike some of his schoolmates, Emily did not keep his misdeeds alive—which had let him put that scandalous kiss out of his mind. The good memories had calmed him in crises, influenced his stand on several issues before Parliament, and even affected where he invested his money. He supported several benevolent societies because of concerns she had shared that summer.

But that camaraderie was over. She no longer listened while he talked, no longer offered debate that might clarify his thinking, no longer welcomed him in her company. The last ten years had hardened her in ways he couldn't comprehend.

He wanted to ask Richard what had happened, but he couldn't. Such personal questions might hint at personal interest, raising hopes in the Hughes family that he could not fulfill. Besides, Richard might not know—he spent most of his time in town. Questions might send him home to demand answers, driving Emily further into melancholy.

And now that he thought about it, Emily's coolness

had started after reaching London. She'd been ani-
mated that first day, as full of life as ever. It was
Harriet's arrival that had changed her—but not because she disliked sharing her Season, as Harriet
charged. It had to be Harriet herself. And it was get-
ting worse. Emily seemed more strained every time
they met.

He surged to his feet, pacing as he reviewed Harriet's
complaints. Dismissing the substance, he concentrated
on her tone. Harriet was clearly a troublemaker. If she
was disrupting Hughes House, he must move her elsewhere. It was more important to give Emily some
peace. Only then could they recapture their friendship.

Harriet narrowed her eyes when Lady Jersey presented Charles to Emily as a suitable partner for the
waltz that evening. Jacob had made no effort to get
her approved. She should be dancing in his arms instead of promenading with yet another boring boy.

It was time to change tactics, she decided. Complaints did not faze him, but no guardian could ignore
actual danger. He would have to take her home with
him.

Emily smiled as Charles whirled her through a com-
plicated series of turns. Waltzing in public was an exhilarating experience, especially with a graceful dancer
like Charles.

Or like Jaco—

She stifled the voice. It didn't matter what Jacob
was or wasn't.

Sophie's claim that Charles cared had teased her all
day. Would he do? She'd known him almost as long as
she'd known Jacob. His lush auburn hair and brilliant
emerald eyes made him handsome enough to draw
covetous glances from every lady in the room—though
if gossip were true, he'd bedded nearly half of them.

She tripped.

"Sorry," he murmured.

"My fault," she countered.

Like all the Beaux, Charles was a rake. There was no reason to expect marriage to change that. Even setting up high-priced mistresses hadn't stopped him from seducing an endless procession of matrons—or so Richard had once claimed when he hadn't known she was listening. Sour grapes on Richard's part, perhaps, for he'd lost a conquest to his friend. But that made the evidence even stronger.

She had always assumed that Jacob would remain faithful once they wed, but honesty condemned that fantasy to the rubbish heap, too. Rakes rarely changed their habits, and since society didn't expect fidelity from any husband, Emily could hardly demand it. Wedding someone she didn't love gave her little bargaining power.

Another dream gone. While she might eventually come to love a husband, she was unlikely to do so before marriage. With the Season half over, gentlemen seeking wives were already culling candidates. Since the only one left in her court was Charles, love was out of the question. She could only hope that Sophie was right. He flirted with everyone, so she still couldn't believe he had intentions.

"Did you buy that horse you wanted at Tattersall's this afternoon?" she asked as they sidestepped to avoid a collision. He'd mentioned the horse last evening.

"Yes, and for a good price, too. You should see him. Not only will he draw all eyes in the park, but he has the stamina to hunt. Remember that gray I got my last year at Eton?"

"Beautiful animal."

He grinned. "This one's better, though I must change his name. *Bucket* would insult even a broken-down cob."

He continued waxing poetic over his new steed, but Emily no longer listened. A turn had brought Jacob's scowling face into view. His eyes speared hers like twin lances, radiating so much fury she nearly tripped.

What was wrong with the man? He acted as if she'd

disgraced everyone from family to crown. It couldn't be because of Harriet. The girl had done nothing gauche that Emily knew of. Nor could it be the waltz. Charles had done everything right before leading her out.

But she would find out all too soon. Jacob had the next set.

Charles's voice faded to a faint buzz for the remainder of the waltz. She only hoped her smiles and nods fit his questions.

Ten minutes later Jacob swept her away without giving her a chance to thank Charles. He was more furious than she'd ever seen him—more even than the day Richard had tossed him into the lake, ruining his favorite boots.

"I saw Harriet on Bond Street today," he snapped, his scowl drawing a disapproving glance from Lady Marchgate as they passed. "She has enough gowns. I won't pay for more."

"Of course." Keeping her answers brief kept her voice steady.

"I told her that." His softer voice lost none of its edge. "And I told her to stay with simple styles. One more flounce or spray of flowers will turn her into a laughingstock."

Emily's heart froze. He obviously blamed her for dressing Harriet like a mushroom. How could she explain that Harriet refused to listen to anyone? Even her maid's protests brought only threats to turn the woman off. She'd actually added another rouleau with her own hands to a gown already encumbered with three.

"She is rather headstrong," Emily tried. "Perhaps you will convince her that she is better suited to simpler lines. I'm afraid she ignores my admonitions."

"She has no sense," he complained. "How the devil can I penetrate that thick skull? Words roll off without effect. You must help me."

"You are her guardian," she said carefully. "You have more authority than I can ever wield."

"For all the good it does," he groused.

The music started, separating them.

Emily sighed in relief. She usually enjoyed listening to Jacob's problems, but not tonight. Why the devil had he criticized his betrothed? It simply wasn't done—unless he'd been about to blame her for Harriet's intransigence. He clearly hadn't believed her when she mentioned her own failure to penetrate Harriet's thick skull.

Stop thinking about him, she ordered herself as the pattern returned her to Jacob's side. *Concentrate on Charles. He treats you like a lady instead of a child or an oracle.*

Jacob touched her fingertips as they exchanged places, sending sparks up her arm. She turned gratefully to the next gentleman in line. By the time she returned to Jacob, she had herself under control. He was merely one of many men in this set, and of no more importance to her life.

She would encourage Charles. If Sophie was right, she could garner an offer soon, which would keep regrets from muddling her mind every day. An offer would let her plan for marriage and the children that would soon be hers. And it would put her infatuation for Jacob firmly behind her at last.

"For the last time, no!" Jacob hissed an hour later, pulling Harriet behind a statue in the hallway so they could escape detection by two dowagers climbing the stairs. "Cease dramatizing yourself. And if Richard says another word about you annoying Lady Hughes—"

"He lies. He wants to turn you against me." She grabbed his arm when he turned away in disgust. "It's true. I've seen the way he looks at me, like I'm a dish of sweetmeats and he is starving. Just so did Colonel Wentworth look at my mother before sending me to my room. Once he destroys your faith in me—"

His palm struck her cheek before he even realized it was moving. Her head snapped back.

"Leave me," he growled. "And take your filthy tongue with you. If you say another word, I will pack you off to the country so fast your head will spin."

White-faced, she stared, then fled.

Jacob leaned shakily against the wall, horror weakening his knees. He'd never struck a female in his life and couldn't understand how he'd done it this time. Even Harriet.

His father's violence had frightened him into vowing he'd never lash out in anger. He knew his temper was chancy, so he was careful to expend any fury in a round of boxing or a breakneck ride across the fields. But her words had beat against his ears, maligning his closest friend, hinting—

For an instant, she'd turned into Mrs. Nichols, begging, cajoling, pleading with her latest lover for help against a husband she swore beat her. Hah! A man whose life had been devoted to service, whose gentleness sometimes interfered with his duty to the regiment, who—

His hand pressed his eyes. Tremors attacked his legs, worse than the last time he'd endured a beating. He'd vowed to never become the tyrant Major Winters had been. But now he'd hit—

Dear God! He was turning into his father.

"What's wrong, Jacob?"

His eyes flew open to see Emily frowning at him. "Nothing." But the shaking grew until he could no longer hide it.

"You look terrible. Come in here before someone sees you."

He didn't protest when she led him into an anteroom. Couldn't. It required all his concentration to remain on his feet.

She shoved him into a chair. "Should I send for wine?"

"N-no." *Damn!* Now his teeth were chattering.

"What's wrong, Jacob?" She squatted so she could see his face. "Do you have an ague?"

"I—I hit her." He hardly noticed the words. His stomach was trying to heave up everything he'd eaten in the last week.

"Harriet? She can be exasperating at times."

"Yes—no—dear God! It's happening. M-murder. Just like them."

"Who?"

He couldn't answer. Saliva flooded his mouth. Lurching to his feet, he thrust open a window and vomited onto the rosebushes below.

Emily fought down the urge to pull his head to her breast in comfort. Whatever was wrong wasn't illness. He seemed in shock. What could Harriet have done that could shake him so badly? Had it banished his infatuation? Not that it would change anything. . . .

She led him to a couch and made him lie down. Tears leaked from his eyes, shaking her to the core. He covered them with an arm, but not before she'd seen his anguish.

"Talk to me, Jacob," she said softly. "What happened that distresses you so?"

For a long time he said nothing. She'd nearly given up hope before he finally spoke.

"The violence. I—I thought I could control it, but I was wrong . . ." Sobs punctuated his words. "Too strong . . . They both killed . . . Should never wed. Might pass it on."

"Who killed?"

"My parents. Cold-blooded killers. Both of them." Shudders wracked his body.

"What nonsense is this?" she demanded, pulling his arm from his eyes so he had to look at her.

"Truth. I saw them."

"What did you see?" She'd long ago sensed secrets in Jacob's heart. He never spoke of his childhood and rarely mentioned his parents. She knew that they had not gotten on and that their arguments had likely affected him. She knew his mother had accused his father of wanting her dead. But she'd never expected this.

"Major the honorable Edward Michael Winters," he spat. "With a name like that, you would expect a ruddy saint. Damn him to hell!"

"What happened, Jacob?" She kept her voice soft, hiding her shock at the hatred in his voice.

"He was a martinet who abused servants and ordered excessive punishments for his troops. He enjoyed floggings. Watching them. Administering them. His excitement . . ." His head shook as if scattering unwanted memories. "But his brutality didn't stop there. He killed anyone who stood in his way. The only survivor was my mother, though he tried many times to poison her."

"Why?"

"So he could marry his mistress."

The idea was so shocking that she nearly protested. No gentleman wed his mistress. But now that she'd pierced his wall, she dared say nothing that might stop him. "Are you sure he used poison?"

He nodded. "He first tried datura. It's an Indian poison that drives its victim mad—the sort of madness that leads to accidents like falling down stairs, leaping under horses, suicide . . ."

"But she didn't."

"No." He covered his eyes again. "Her maid was Hindi and recognized the poison. Without demonstrated madness to explain the accident he'd arranged, he had to change plans. He was furious."

This time when he paused, she remained silent.

"I heard him cursing the maid's vigilance—his man must have known his intent, for they were discussing it. He swore the next attack would work. Arsenic. Faster. More difficult to detect. Less risk of her surviving. I told Mother immediately."

"How old were you?"

"Ten."

Too young to bear such a burden.

"Before he could act, his brother died. He was summoned home to take up the Hawthorne title," he said wearily. "I thought that would be the end of it, but I was wrong. He couldn't tolerate a wife who knew of his crimes, so he planned a fresh start—a new wife to go with his new title and new estate."

"You can't—"

"I know everything." He glared at her. "I was a sneak in those days—poking, prying, listening at doors and under windows. My punishment was overhearing his cold-blooded plans. I'd heard others before, but paid little heed, for they had nothing to do with those I cared for. But make no mistake, Em. I know exactly what he was. He tried again aboard ship. Disease had killed half the crew. One more death would not have been questioned."

"Who stopped him?"

"Fate. Mother didn't want tea that night, so she gave it to her maid. The woman died. I spent the next two months standing guard, fetching her food myself so I could be sure it was safe."

"Dear God!" How had he managed? She nearly asked why he hadn't enlisted help from the ship's captain, but snapped her mouth shut. Who would believe a boy over a military officer and peer of the realm?

"That wasn't the end, of course." He sat up, draping his hands between his knees and staring at the floor. "Once we reached Hawthorne Park, he banished me to the schoolroom, then changed tactics yet again. Maybe he feared that the staff would report suspicious behavior. Or maybe he knew I would turn him in if her death raised any questions. Whatever his reasoning, he decided an accident would be easier to explain. We later found a dozen traps he'd set. The one she tripped was the folly. The moment she sat down, the roof collapsed atop her. That was the day she realized that I was a target, too. We usually sat there together, discussing my lessons."

"But you were his heir!"

"Son of the woman he hated, nemesis in his campaign to kill her. He hated me as much as her by then. When I said he wanted a fresh start, I meant it. He vowed to sweep away all reminders of the past. What he hadn't counted on was Mother's devotion. She'd been willing to leave her own life to Fate, but not mine. So she poisoned his wine and coldly watched as he died at her feet, then smashed the glass to remove any evidence. That should have been the end of it, but her conscience could not live with her act. I hardly saw her again, but my few glimpses were of a woman on the verge of insanity. We buried him two days after his death. That night, she slipped into madness and poisoned herself."

"No."

He glared. "The doctor tasted the dregs in her glass. There is no doubt—"

"No." She wanted to howl at the pain he'd suffered for so long. Needless pain. "Listen to me, Jacob. Your mother did not kill your father. If she died of poison, it was another of his traps. And if she seemed mad, he must have left datura where she would use it—a bout of madness after barely surviving an accident would seem normal to uneducated servants. But she would never have poisoned herself. She loved you too much to leave you parentless. And she would have had no reason to kill herself, because she was innocent of any crime."

Jacob closed his eyes in pain, then rose to pace restlessly around the room. "You can't know that, Em. You were still in the nursery."

"But I do know that. Did you see her poison the wine? Did you hear her planning it?"

"No. I was stuck in the schoolroom—new tutor. I hadn't yet found a way to escape him."

"Jacob, listen to me. Your mother was innocent. Absolutely innocent. Ask your aunt. She was there."

He froze, staring. "How do you know?"

"I heard her describe that day to my mother several years later—I think I was about eight. Since I wasn't supposed to be in the drawing room, I hid the moment I heard footsteps. Then I was stuck there for nearly an hour while they gossiped."

"Wha-what did she say?"

"Your mother went straight from the folly to your father, storming onto the terrace still covered with debris. Your aunt was in the sitting room with a clear view through the window. They spoke so loudly, she heard every word."

"The wine?"

"He'd been sipping it while he stood at the balustrade looking out over the garden—perhaps recalling his childhood; your aunt claimed it was his father's favorite pose."

"Then what?" His face paled until Emily feared he would faint.

"Your mother thanked God that he was no longer subject to a court-martial panel made up of his friends. This time she would swear out a complaint with a magistrate, then take you to safety until the House of Lords convicted him. They argued. He swore no one would believe a hysterical woman with a history of madness—he could produce a dozen men who would testify that she was an opium eater and habitual liar. She laughed, claiming that she had letters describing his poison plots, signed by the regimental surgeon and the Company representative in Bombay. She also had witnesses to two previous incidents at Hawthorne—a carpet that unaccountably slipped, nearly tossing her down the stairs; a burr that found its way under her saddle, sending her horse into a frenzy when she mounted. He threw the wine in her face, then hurled the glass to the stone floor, smashing it."

"Threw—" He leaned weakly against the wall.

"Threw. Whatever his faults, your mother never lifted a finger against him. She swept back into the house, calling for a footman. He was alive, but furious, when she left."

"So how did he die?"

"The butler had just taken delivery of the mail. It contained the letter your father had long awaited. He ripped it open, then screamed in anguish and collapsed. He was dead before he hit the terrace."

"The letter?"

"From a woman—his mistress, perhaps. I don't re-call the name, but your aunt sounded disdainful of her."

"Dear God," murmured Jacob, sinking wearily into a chair.

"She announced that she was tired of waiting for him to redeem his pledge, so she had taken a husband. Then she congratulated him again on his new position. That shock, added to your mother's threats and the realization that he could no longer hide his plans, killed him."

Jacob stared, trying to realign twenty years of cer-tainty. "So Mother didn't kill him to save me from harm."

"No." Emily's expression softened. "She loved you more than anything else in the world, Jacob. But even love does not drive an honorable person to dishonor. I've no doubt she would have defended you from di-rect attack, but she would never stoop to poison. Her solution was to summon a magistrate and press charges, regardless of the scandal. Since you found so many traps after his death, any magistrate would have treated her complaint seriously."

He wasn't sure he believed her—his father had al-ways bent people to his will—but this was no time to argue. Voices reminded him where they were. She had already been gone long enough to draw notice. "Thank you for the information," he said, formally bowing his head. "It eases my mind. You'd best return to the ballroom."

Something flashed in her eyes, but she left before he could identify it.

The moment he was alone, he rested his head in his hands. Could he really remove part of the stain from his blood? It sounded too good to be true.

Ask your aunt.

Immediately. The ball was nearly over anyway. Slip-ping out, he headed home to write a letter.

Chapter Nine

"What do you want now?" demanded Jacob the next night when Harriet dragged him onto the terrace outside the Debenham ballroom. He dug in his heels, refusing to move another inch.

Tears sparkled in her eyes. She was an even better actress than her bedamned mother.

"It's R-Richard," she choked, producing a sob. "He k-kissed me last night and t-tried to force his way into my r-room. I t-told you he was dangerous. You have to help me."

Jacob grabbed her shoulders to shake some sense into her, but reined in his temper before he struck her again. He should have expected this after yesterday's scene, but he'd thought his slap had finally knocked some sense into her head.

This newest lie proved how little she understood society. A lusty man might well seduce a maid—something Mrs. Nichols had known from her brief term as a servant—but he would never touch a girl he'd sworn to protect.

"Please?" Harriet reached up to clutch his arm, wrinkling his sleeve. "You can't leave me in that house another instant. I barely escaped his attack."

"Nonsense!" He backed away, brushing her aside. "Stop this idiocy at once. Every word proves what an ungrateful mushroom you are. If Richard did attack—which I don't for a moment believe—it's because your behavior marks you as fair game."

She gasped.

"It's time you faced facts," he continued relentlessly. "Captain Nichols might have connections to several great houses, but the nearest was three generations back, so you have no claim on society."

"You can't know that!"

"You forget that I knew him well for ten years. He was closer to me than my own father. Nor do you understand how well society's ladies know family trees. They also know family scandals. It would need little time and less effort to discover that your mother was the bastard daughter of a whore."

"How dare—"

"Facts, Miss Nichols. Her father might have been a baron as she claimed—or perhaps not; her mother serviced too many men to know which one actually fathered her. When raising a child interfered with the woman's business, she left your mother at the workhouse."

"No! She grew up in her father's house after her mother died in childbirth!"

"Lies. She had hundreds of them. Every time she described her past, she embellished it further to make herself sound better. But people noticed those changes, especially the women. And Captain Nichols knew the truth."

"B-but—"

"We let her get away with the first lie—the *orphan recently left to the parish* tale. It harmed no one. But the truth is a common enough story," he continued relentlessly. "She'd been in the workhouse for ten years when Captain Nichols's father died. He asked the parish to find him a wife, because he was the last of his line. The parish leaped at the chance to rid itself of an uncooperative charge who had been turned off within the week from every servant's post they found her. So they sent your mother to India. Captain Nichols didn't discover her background until it was too late." The parish had posted specifics but didn't wait for a response before sending the girl. Unfortunately the ship carrying the letter didn't arrive in Bombay until a week after Nichols's marriage. "In the end, the marriage was for naught. You aren't the son he wanted."

"Mother swor—"

"She lied. It was her worst habit. Don't deny it," he added when she tried to protest. "We lived next door, so I heard her lies and saw the truths behind them. Quit putting on airs, Miss Nichols. I gave you a chance to improve your station. Many younger sons and members of the gentry will accept a wife of lesser breeding if she meets his other needs. But to attract one, you must drop your arrogance and cease criticizing your betters. Every person at this ball has higher breeding than you. It's time you admitted it."

"I'm at least as well-bred as the Gunning sisters," she spat, eyes snapping. "They made excellent matches. One even wed two dukes."

"True," he admitted, shaking his head. "But they came to London in 1751, and the girls had impeccable manners. The men who wed them already had heirs, so the girls' breeding was less important. But times change, and attitudes change. I doubt they would have such success today."

"But—"

"No. They may have inspired countless matchmakers and hordes of impecunious or ill-bred maidens, but in sixty-seven years, no one has repeated their feat. Now be a good girl. Listen to Miss Hughes, and follow her instructions to the letter. Don't bother Lady Hughes—"

"You can't expect me to stay at Hughes House," she wailed, interrupting. "They hate me. You cannot imagine all the ways they slight me. Half my gowns are ill pressed because their maids won't let mine use the irons. My wash water is always cold. They criticize everything I do."

Exaggerations. Again. If her clothes were pressed last, it was because her maid had less precedence than the others. He made one last try to explain. "If Miss

Hughes criticizes, she is trying to help you. Your behavior has already barred you from many events."

"Help?" she squealed in outrage. "Does she think lying helps me?"

"Enough." His glare sent Harriet back a step. "When will you admit that this is not India? Maybe no one noticed your antics in Bombay—or maybe they were so desperate for English company that they didn't care. But here, a dozen people see every breath you take. Half of those are skilled enough to discern your thoughts from the faintest change in your expression. Every lie is obvious. Every arrogant word. Every selfish deed. If you want to manipulate people, go back to Bombay. It won't work here."

"I don't—"

"No more." He turned her toward the ballroom. "I might remove you from Hughes House, but only because you are hurting my friends."

Shoving her inside, he headed for the back of the garden, where he could find peace. It was obvious that thrusting Harriet into Hughes House had hurt Richard's family. Emily had skipped two prestigious balls because Harriet wasn't included. She'd also passed on an outing to Richmond, Lady Woodvale's soirée, and an evening at Almack's. By choosing lesser gatherings, she reduced her chances of making a good match and left herself vulnerable to cawkers like Larkin.

He'd never intended to harm Emily, but he'd done it. Instead of enjoying her come-out, she was stuck chaperoning a bad-tempered, spoiled child whose antics might redound upon her. Harriet turned any attempt to curb her excesses back against Emily.

Stripping the needles from a yew branch, he let them drift downward until his foot crushed them into the gravel path. He would like to do the same to Harriet.

Richard seemed strained lately, which meant he was biting back complaints. Emily had sunk into melancholy, rarely smiling. She never spoke unless he asked a direct question.

No more.

It had been a mistake to place Harriet at Hughes House. Lady Hughes lacked the stamina to cope with a headstrong miss. Richard helped some, but Emily had no help during the day. She was too kind, too sweet, too naïve to control Harriet. He needed someone harsher. Much as he hated acceding to Harriet's demands, he must move her elsewhere.

Returning to the ballroom, he nearly ran down Sophie and Ashington, who were twirling through a waltz.

Ashington?

Emily's question about the man suddenly made sense. What the devil was Sophie doing with him? What was he doing at a ball, for that matter? He usually avoided such gatherings, for he hated dodging matchmakers.

Damn Harriet to hell! She had demanded so much attention that he'd ceased watching Sophie altogether. Ward or not, it was time to let her sink. Her megrims were making him ignore his vows to his friends.

He set off in search of Lady Inslip. She could spot trouble a mile away and take immediate steps to prevent it. So could Sophie. Four years on the town had built the confidence that made her as formidable as her mother.

Granted, Harriet would spend many evenings at home while the Inslips attended entertainments that excluded her, but she needed a lesson in humility. He was willing to raise her a little, but she couldn't expect miracles.

Nor could he. She had already cut enough London gentlemen that she stood little chance of garnering an offer in town—another reason he didn't care if she stayed home. Her court had dwindled to cubs and a handful of would-be rakes with no interest in marriage. So he must intensify the search for someone desperate enough to accept a wife sight unseen and strong enough to control her once they were wed.

Detaching Lady Inslip from a group of matrons, he led her to an anteroom.

"I have a problem," he admitted when they were alone. "It was a mistake to bring Harriet out in London, but I have nowhere else to put her. Hawthorne Park will never do. She would drive my aunt to distraction in a week."

"Agreed," said Lady Inslip. "She has quite the most vulgar tongue I've heard in some time."

"Which makes my request even more difficult." He ran his fingers through his hair. "She will not find a husband in town, but it will take time to find someone who will accept her."

"Inslip can query his stewards."

"Thank you. But my immediate problem is where to keep Harriet until I find a suitable match. Lady Hughes cannot handle her."

"You want me to take her." It wasn't a question.

"I know it will be an imposition. She cannot attend half the events you do, and she is likely to annoy Lady Sophie."

"Sophie would never let a mushroom intimidate her. We will manage. Inslip's cousin arrived last week. She rarely accompanies us out, but is more than capable of controlling a headstrong miss. She will enjoy the challenge. And if Miss Nichols behaves, I will allow her to accept whatever invitations come her way."

Jacob sighed in relief. "Thank you, my lady. I will deliver her tomorrow morning."

A tremendous weight slipped from his shoulders as he returned to the ballroom.

"What are you doing?" Emily frowned as Jacob led her outside instead of joining the next set. Not that she was surprised. He never waltzed, so the music had likely startled him.

The real surprise had come when he'd claimed his usual two sets. After yesterday, she'd expected him to avoid her. Men did not enjoy baring their souls. She'd thought embarrassment would keep him away from her—had looked forward to it.

As they moved deeper into the garden, she decided she was glad he'd chosen not to dance. Touching him for an entire waltz would have been painful. He looked grim, though.

"I'm moving Harriet in the morning," he said without warning, dropping her arm as he half turned away.

"What?" Was this his response to last night's revelations? It was an excellent way to avoid her.

"Your mother looks on the brink of collapse, Em. She needs peace. Having to chaperon two of you is too much. I should have known better." He glanced over his shoulder.

Emily gritted her teeth. He was lying. She could see it in his eyes. Citing her mother was a way to dismiss her without condemning her outright for her failure to control his betrothed. Much as she'd wanted Harriet to disappear, she hadn't wanted it done this way.

He must have heard about Harriet's escape after being denied another shopping trip. Emily had thought that invoking Jacob's orders had settled the matter, but the moment she'd left for morning calls, Harriet had headed for Bond Street on foot. Alone. At a time of day when the street was crowded with gentlemen.

Richard had brought her back an hour later, ignoring the obscenities she threw at him. He must have informed Jacob.

Jacob blamed her. He knew that Lady Hughes had nothing to do with instructing Harriet or with enforcing the rules. It was Emily who dealt with her day in and day out. Now he'd decided that she was an inadequate mentor.

"Very well," she said as she turned to leave.

He grasped her arm. "Where are you going?"

"To tell Mother." She shook off his hand, furious that his touch raised sparks. When would her body accept that she didn't love him?

"Later. What's wrong with you, Em? I've never seen you this grim. Is it Harriet?"

"Of course not!" She fled further into the garden. How could she criticize Harriet now? Believing her incompetent, he would think she was lashing out in anger.

"Talk to me, Em," he urged softly. "I can't stand to see you unhappy. I owe you too much."

"You owe me nothing."

"Nonsense. You taught me patience ten years ago. You opened your doors to Harriet, despite that it meant sharing your Season. And I can't begin to describe what last night meant to me. I'm grateful."

I don't want gratitude! she wanted to scream. *I want love.*

But love wouldn't help. He was tied to another.

"It was nothing," she repeated, cloaking herself in calm. By concentrating on his betrothal, she could stay in control.

"It wasn't." He gripped her shoulders, forcing her to meet his eyes. "You have no idea how much you helped."

She pushed on his chest to loosen his grip. "Very well, Jacob. I'm glad you are satisfied. What time will you come for Harriet?"

He sighed, letting her break his hold. "Ten would be best. That way she can get settled before anyone calls."

Surely he didn't intend to take her home with him! "Where—" She couldn't get the question out.

"Inslip House. Lady Inslip's cousin will act as her companion."

She nodded, but Inslip House was nearly as bad. It meant she would still have to deal with Harriet every night. And now that Jacob openly distrusted her, Harriet would be insufferable. Inslip House also meant that he would soon announce his betrothal. Marrying out of Inslip House would give Harriet more stature than out of Hughes House.

"I'll see that she's ready." She couldn't keep the strain from her voice.

"What's wrong, Em?"

"Nothing." She headed for the terrace. "The set is nearly over. I must return."

"Nonsense." He stepped forward, blocking the path. "It has a quarter hour left. Tell me your problem, and I'll make it right."

She shivered. How could she explain that she'd stupidly built him into a fantasy lover who would guarantee her a perfect life? How could she confess the naïveté that had exaggerated one kiss into an undying love affair? How could she bare her soul to be trampled into the ground like the yew leaves someone had crushed into the path?

"You are chilled," he said, shrugging out of his coat and settling it over her shoulders. His warmth remained in the fabric, burning into her skin. His hands stayed on her arms as if unwilling to lose that fragile contact.

"Th-thank you," she managed, trying to step out of reach. But her feet refused to move. Her eyes rested on his well-formed mouth, desperately seeking some sign that she was wrong, that the last weeks had been a dream, that—

His hands tightened. His mouth swooped, clamping over hers, just as it had done in the orchard.

All thought fled as he pulled her against him, devouring her as if he were starving. His arms crushed her closer, his tongue plunging, deepening the kiss beyond her wildest dreams. Every star in the heavens exploded behind her eyes.

She curved her arms around his neck, pulling his head lower and knocking his jacket to the ground. The body she'd touched only in dreams imprinted on hers, tightening her breasts.

More! screamed her mind. *It isn't enough.*

As his scent wrapped around her, she squirmed closer, reveling in his heat, his touch, the wine that sharpened his taste. This was how she'd known it would be, this rightness, this certainty that they were two pieces of the same soul.

A laugh drifted across the garden. Loud. Vulgar. Harriet.

Jacob froze.

Emily bit off a cry. How could she compromise herself with a man committed to another?

Jacob jumped back, his lips forming an apology. But she heard nothing through the buzzing in her ears. Clamping a hand over her mouth, she fled.

Jacob stared as Emily disappeared around a hedge. A frown narrowed his gaze while he absently shrugged his coat into place. Why the devil had he kissed her?

You wanted to.

"That's no excuse," he muttered, slipping behind a tree to avoid an approaching couple. He'd been tempted by pretty girls before, but he never dallied with innocents. Even ten years ago, they hadn't fit his plans for the future. That was even more true today.

For thirty years he had carefully planned every action, aware that his temper could cause trouble if he released it. Allowing free rein to any emotion could trigger obsession, luring him down the same dark road that had destroyed so many others. He'd recognized the danger inherent in his father's detour onto that road, eavesdropping at every opportunity so he would know if the man's obsession threatened others. And he'd devised a strategy for every conceivable betrayal—like warning his mother in case his father turned murderous.

So how had he kissed Emily?

Twice.

She had no place in his plans.

He shuddered, swept again by the need to hold her, comfort her, protect her from harm. Her descent into melancholy hurt, and not just because he feared he was responsible. He would feel the same no matter what the cause. Emily deserved happiness.

You love her.

"Like a sister," he insisted, leaning weakly against the tree.

But his protestations could no longer hide the truth. He loved her. Had loved her even as he'd fled the orchard ten years ago. That love had made it easy to ignore the diamonds who tried to catch his eye each year, easy to postpone the day he would dust off his heartless plan to wed solely for an heir, easy—

He pushed away from the tree. He had to find her, tell her—

Tell her what? She'd fled in disgust, so upset that she'd been on the verge of illness. She'd known he was lying about his reasons for removing Harriet. *Your mother looks on the brink of collapse.*

"Damnation!" he snarled inelegantly. He knew Lady Hughes had nothing to do with Harriet. And Emily knew he knew.

In his need to hide his unacknowledged love, he'd hidden his true reasons—that Em was suffering from Harriet's presence. But his lies must have convinced her that he considered her incompetent. He'd seen that flash of pain.

It hurt, as did his fear that his love would hurt her if he pursued it. Obsession—and what was love if not a form of obsession?—made him dangerous. He might hurt her in a fit of fury. And if she ever came to love him, it would be worse. What dishonor might her love embrace if she thought he needed help?

"Stop this," he snapped, squeezing his temples.

Only yesterday she had sworn that his mother had *not* killed for his sake. He'd yet to hear from his aunt, but he trusted Emily's word. And it was far too late to walk away from her. Admitting his love had shattered a barrier around his heart.

At the very least, he must atone for again attacking her without warning. If she forgave him, he would tell her the rest of his family's sordid history. Once she knew what he was offering, he could court her.

Taking a deep breath, he set out to find her and apologize.

But she was gone.

* * *

Emily fought back tears as she fled toward the darkest corner of the garden. She could not return to the ballroom with puffy eyes.

How could she have been so stupid? She should never have let Jacob lead her outside. Knowing how hard it was to forget her infatuation, she shouldn't even dance with him.

She was still castigating herself when she rounded a rosebush and slammed into Charles.

"Are you all right, Em?" he asked, echoing Jacob as he clutched her arms to steady her.

"Of course." Her heart slowed, knowing she was safe.

"Hmm." He looked her up and down. "Amber eyes glowing. Satin skin pearling in the moonlight. Gorgeous gown—have I told you how much I like this one?"

"All three times you've seen it." She wanted to sigh, for she should have changed the trim by now to make it seem new.

"You remember." His teeth gleamed when he grinned. "So tell me why you are racing around a dark garden alone."

"Seeking a few moments of solitude."

"Again? What did Harriet do this time?"

She refused to respond.

"I understand the need to escape, my dear, but this is not a sun-washed clearing. It's a very bad place for an innocent alone—too many rakes lurking in the shrubbery."

"Like you?" Elation soared as she realized he was jollying her into a better humor. She did not yet love him, but this was a start.

He laughed. "Your point, Em, though I was not lurking with intent. You have set my feet on the path to reform."

"I must be judicious about wielding such power." She took his arm. "Imagine how staid London would be without rakes."

"Horrors!"

She giggled.

"My set, I believe," he added as the musicians began a new tune.

"Of course."

The country dance separated them almost immediately, giving her time to recover the rest of her poise. It also gave her time to consider the ramifications of Jacob's announcement.

Charles kept his own rooms, but he often called at Inslip House and would undoubtedly see Harriet there.

No matter how lofty the Marquess of Inslip might be, his cousin could never keep Harriet in line.

Harriet hated Emily and was doing everything possible to make her life miserable, including luring anyone who displayed interest into her own court.

At first, Emily had thought the migration was an inevitable result of Harriet's sensuality—who could see Emily when Harriet stood nearby in all her exotic glory? When she realized that Harriet was deliberately drawing men to her side, Emily had tried to believe that it was merely Harriet's need to be the focus of every eye. Only later had she admitted that Harriet worked her wiles especially hard on those men who showed interest in Emily.

Emily wanted to believe that Harriet would leave her alone now that she was moving, but the girl would probably strike out anyway. If Sophie thought Charles cared, everyone at Inslip House must think so, too, which meant that Charles would be Harriet's next target.

Needing time alone, she pleaded a headache when the set ended. Since her mother was weary, they left immediately.

But Emily's fears increased as the carriage took them home. Harriet's acid flowed freely tonight, and not only because they'd left early. Some new complaint was bothering the girl. Never before had she made her hatred so plain.

Charles was the best husband Emily could hope to attach, so she could not let Harriet drive him off, too.

Every day increased his attentiveness—now that she was looking, it was obvious; only her own blindness had missed it earlier. His fortune made her modest dowry acceptable. His Foreign Office job meant living in town, but he would meet Jacob mostly at his club.

Yet until he actually offered, Harriet posed a danger, so time was of the essence. She had to bring him up to scratch before Harriet poisoned his mind against her.

"Lord Hawthorne will pick you up at ten," she informed Harriet as they headed up the stairs. "You had best get some sleep."

"I knew he would agree," Harriet exclaimed. "He should have taken me to Hawthorne House in the first place."

Emily opened her mouth to correct the assumption, then gave up. Let Jacob deal with her. Harriet was no longer her responsibility.

Closing the door in Harriet's face, she concentrated on Charles. They would attend the opera tomorrow evening. Surely she could let him know that she would welcome his hand.

She didn't love him, but they had been friends for many years. Few couples had that much affection when they first wed.

It would work. His love would give them a framework. Her own feelings would match his in time.

Ignoring the voice that insisted no one could love her, she fell into a thankfully dreamless sleep.

Chapter Ten

As footmen loaded the last of Harriet's luggage into Jacob's town carriage, he joined her on the seat of his curricle. How had two modest trunks burgeoned into six in only three weeks? To say nothing of a dozen hatboxes. He had clearly not seen all her accounts.

Irritation sharpened his tongue. "Move over, Miss Nichols. I can't drive with you hanging on my arm." Her touch made his skin crawl. Being in the same room with her was bad enough. Sharing a carriage seat was intolerable.

"I am so glad you are taking me away," Harriet cooed without moving. "I don't know how you can consider those people friends. Not only did they mistreat me, but the things they said about you—"

"Move over!" He glared pointedly at her hand.

A tiny frown creased her forehead, but she moved two inches and dropped her hand into her lap. "They were ghastly last night," she continued. "Calling me the worst names, then celebrating my departure—except Richard, who scowled so fiercely I feared he would attack. He was furious to discover that you'd foiled his plans."

Turning down Brook Street, Jacob closed his ears to her lies, praying that Lady Inslip's cousin could control her until he could find her a husband—one with sufficient strength to handle her. Preferably one who lived far from London and nowhere near Gloucestershire. He never wanted to see her again.

He picked up speed, darted around a lumbering delivery wagon, then ducked down Davies Street.

"Where are you going?" she demanded, grabbing his arm. "Grosvenor Square is the other way."

"But Inslip House is this way."

"B-but I thought you would look after me." She produced tears to glisten in the morning sun.

"Tears don't affect me, Miss Nichols." He urged his team to a faster trot. "You cannot stay in a bachelor establishment, as I've explained before. It would brand you a harlot, and I would be chastised for bringing a light skirt into my home."

"But—"

"I've had enough of your megrims. And more than enough lies."

"I never lie!"

He snorted. "I knew your mother, Miss Nichols. She might have fooled some, but not me. You use the same mannerisms when lying, the same innocent voice when wheedling, the same—"

"I don't!"

"You do, and it's not attractive. Nor is your disdain. Do you think I'm stupid? Richard could not have glowered at you last night. He was with me. Now stop this. Your headstrong ways have damaged Lady Hughes's health, placed unpardonable burdens on my dearest friends, and annoyed society. I won't tolerate them another moment. Nor will Lady Inslip. You will follow her orders. Is that clear?"

"Of course, but—"

Again he interrupted. "You will not receive invitations to most of the events she attends. On those days, you will remain home with her cousin and behave yourself. If you anger anyone at Inslip House, I will send you to the country. Under guard, if necessary."

"You wouldn't!"

"I would. Society is very strict. It is willing to tolerate those of lesser breeding if they behave, but it owes them nothing and will turn on them in a trice if challenged. My gratitude to Captain Nichols does not stretch as far as you seem to think. If you can't or won't adhere to the rules, I will remove you permanently. You have embarrassed me and my friends for the last time."

"Embarrassed!"

"Exactly. Lord Inslip has agreed to house you as a personal favor to me, but he knows you have no chance of wedding one of his peers. Instead of throwing tantrums, you should be grateful to be here at all. But don't set your sights above younger sons, or you will fail."

"I will do my best, my lord," she said, lowering her eyes demurely.

"Thank you." Not that he believed her. He'd caught the flicker of her eye as she gauged his reaction to her apparent capitulation.

Damn the chit! She obviously hoped to attach him—an impossible task. If she continued on this course, he would have to disclose every detail of her mother's scandals, condemning her to the demimonde. Society would not only ostracize her, it would heap censure on him for thrusting her into its drawing rooms. He should not have repaid Captain Nichols's kindness by trying to do her a favor.

He turned into Berkeley Square, stopped in front of Inslip House, and escorted Harriet inside. Lady Inslip was waiting.

"Welcome, Miss Nichols." She smiled coolly. "I trust you will enjoy your stay. May I present my cousin, Miss Beaumont? Alice will chaperon you when our schedules differ."

"Of course," said Harriet faintly. "I'm pleased to meet you, Miss Beaumont." But her eyes pleaded with Jacob over the woman's head.

Jacob relaxed. Miss Beaumont reminded him of his nurse. A frown pinched her lips as she took in Harriet's frivolous morning gown. Her head shook as she met Harriet's gaze. She might not approve of her cousin's request, but she was determined to whip Harriet into shape.

Just like Coocoo.

He smiled at the memories, for he'd not thought of Coocoo in years—his infant tongue had stumbled over *Miss Cotherington,* and the name had stuck. There had been but one way to do anything—hers. And while she could be kind and loving to well-behaved boys, woe betide anyone who flouted her orders.

Once he'd learned to control his temper, they had got on quite well, remaining inseparable until her death on his sixth birthday condemned him to a series of lazy or incompetent tutors who had let him run wild. How much easier would his life have been if Coocoo had been there to keep him at home? He would not have witnessed Mrs. Nichols's many transgressions, would not have known of his father's mistress or heard him plot his mother's murder, would not—

He cut off the pointless speculation. Without those years, he would also be ill equipped to deal with Harriet. But his ward was now Miss Beaumont's problem, and she seemed capable of handling it.

"Come along," Miss Beaumont ordered, gesturing to Harriet. "We will look at your invitations, then discuss what you will wear."

Before Harriet knew what hit her, she was hustled out of sight.

Thanking Lady Inslip, Jacob headed for Jackson's Boxing Saloon. Tonight he would begin courting Emily. It shouldn't take much effort. Not only had she no serious suitors, but she'd responded to his kiss as hotly as he could desire.

As the first act of the opera drew to a close, Emily shifted her chair closer to Charles. The box was crowded with all the Beaux, their charges, Lady

Hughes, Lady Inslip, Miss Beaumont, Ashington, and an elderly gentleman who had arrived too late for introductions.

She had maneuvered Charles to the opposite corner from Sophie and Ashington—which also separated them from Jacob and Harriet. Charles had been furious to discover his enemy consorting with his sister. It had taken all Emily's skill and a glare from Lady Inslip to keep him quiet, but if he cared enough to tolerate an enemy for her sake, she could surely wrest a declaration from him.

Concentrating on that goal made it easier to ignore Harriet's whispered confidences with Jacob and forget the way he'd kissed her last night. It was another reason to press Charles. She could not risk Jacob using her to ease his frustration with Harriet's manners. Once she was safely betrothed, that danger would fade.

"Who is the lady in yellow?" Laying her hand on Charles's arm, she nodded toward a lord's box across the way. "I don't think I've met her—or anyone else in that box, for that matter."

"Lady Wrexham rarely visits London. Lord Wrexham is beside her. The couple behind them is Colonel and Mrs. Caldwell. They only returned to town yesterday and have yet to accept invitations. Caldwell is one of Wellington's aides and heir to the Earl of Deerchester, though he refuses to use his courtesy title."

"Mrs. Caldwell looks familiar." She frowned. "I believe she was coming out of Blackthorn House when I passed this morning."

"Quite likely. They are great friends. I must introduce you. You will like them immensely."

The final aria concluded in a flurry of notes.

"Thank you." She let her hand slip slightly, caressing his arm. "Lady Wrexham is so attentive to the stage, she must enjoy music, so why would she remain from town?"

"Because she is a devoted wife and mother." His eyes gleamed as he covered her hand. "Wrexham adores her and keeps her very busy."

"Doing what?" The question was unnecessary, for his tone told her exactly how Wrexham busied his wife.

"I will explain another time when we don't have an audience," he murmured into her ear.

That audience grew as three cubs crowded into the box to greet Harriet. Two more followed, looking for Sophie.

"It is a bit of a crush," she agreed, smiling as she plied her fan. "A stifling crush, I might add. Perhaps you know of a cooler spot where I might catch my breath. You know how crowds bother me."

His eyes brightened. "Of course, my dear." He led her away as yet more gentlemen descended.

"What a relief," she murmured, borrowing one of Harriet's tricks by snuggling closer. "All those voices quite drowned out your words. You were describing how Lord Wrexham occupies his wife."

"I was explaining that some topics are inappropriate in crowds."

"But we are quite alone." He'd led her away from the refreshment room where gentlemen could purchase lemonade for their ladies. Now he slipped into an alcove screened from the passage by a heavy curtain.

"Persistent, aren't you?" He grinned his lopsided rake's grin. "Very well. He touches her. Quite lightly. Like this." He ran a finger along her jaw and down her throat, not stopping until he hooked the bodice of her gown and tugged her a step closer.

"Mmm." His touch lacked the spark Jacob raised, but it was warm and not at all unpleasant. "I suppose she touches him back." Her hand cupped his cheek, her thumb rubbing his lips.

He turned to place a kiss on her palm. "Careful, little one," he murmured. "Such provocation is dangerous."

"But not with you, Charles. You would never hurt me." She let her hand slide down his chin. "How else might a man entertain his wife?" Her face heated at so forward a question, but perhaps he would attribute it to passion.

"You don't know what you're asking." His voice sounded strained. "This was a bad idea, Em. We'd best return."

"No." She boldly met his eyes. "I want some time with you, away from jostling crowds and prying eyes that prevent us from speaking plainly."

"You do?"

"Of course I do, so stop changing the subject. How else does a man occupy his wife?"

"Like this." Heat flared in his eyes. Before she realized his intent, his finger skimmed beneath her bodice, hooking around a nipple to stab such pleasure through her that she nearly shrieked.

"Oooh," she sighed, watching his eyes darken with satisfaction. "Do that again." She slid her hands into his hair.

"Emily, I—" He paused as if undecided what to say—which was not at all like him.

She smiled encouragement, arching against the finger still in her bodice.

"I shouldn't be touching you," he groaned, but his finger tightened. His other hand closed around a breast. "Richard will call me out."

"No, he won't. I want your touch."

"You do?" At her nod, he dragged her against him, crushing her close from shoulder to knee. Words poured out as he nuzzled her hair and dropped kisses down the side of her neck. "Dear God, Em. I wasn't sure—You seemed so—I love you. Madly. Passionately. Eternally. I want you. Need you. Forever. Marry me, my darling. Give me the right to show you more." He flexed, sliding his male flesh against her stomach, though she could hardly complain after her own forward behavior.

"I am honored, Charles," she said, smiling even as that dratted voice in her head screamed *no!* "I accept."

"You do? Thank God! It will have to be soon. I'm going crazy wanting you."

"Very soon," she agreed.

His eyes blazed, then went hazy as he dragged her onto her toes and kissed her. The moment she parted to his tongue, he thrust hotly inside, licking and stabbing as if at war. Very like Jacob had done last night.

Forget Jacob, she ordered herself, curling her hands around his neck. This was her future. So she sparred with him, reveling in every sign that he wanted her. He was an experienced rake who could teach her much about the sensual world he loved—and was already teaching her, she realized when his hand again moved to her breast, calling forth an interesting tingle.

Charles didn't release her until the bell sounded for the second act. "We can announce our betrothal at Mama's ball tomorrow evening," he panted as he smoothed her skirt and his own coat. "I will call on your father in the morning."

"I will tell him to expect you."

"In the meantime, say nothing, not even to Sophie." He grinned. "For once in my life, I intend to surprise her."

You won't. But she didn't say it. Instead, she argued with that stubborn voice all the way back to the box.

The second act might have included the sweetest music ever written or a chorus of mating cats. She was too busy waging war with herself to listen.

His kiss had raised less excitement than she'd expected—and she hadn't expected much. Oh, she'd enjoyed it well enough, for his response affirmed his love, and his offer meant she'd achieved the goal of every aristocratic young lady, marking her Season a success. If she'd never kissed Jacob, it would have seemed wonderful, the culmination of the most romantic of dreams. He was very skilled. But—

It would get better, she assured herself. Charles was a good man. She would come to love him in time. . . .

Soon. It had to be soon. A one-sided relationship

could not satisfy him for long, so she had to catch up. And she must never let thoughts of Jacob intrude on an intimate moment again.

By the second interval, she had herself firmly in hand. So when Jacob suggested that they promenade, she declined with a smile. This was no time to be alone with him. She did not yet trust her emotions. Thus she remained in the box and encouraged Charles to repeat the gossip he'd heard at his club that afternoon.

Jacob left before the third act. He'd never enjoyed the opera less. Emily was in a strange mood, and Harriet clung like a limpet. It had been a mistake to include her in the party, though excluding her would have drawn speculation from every gossip in town.

But it was Emily who worried him. He was very much afraid that last night's kiss had shattered her trust. She'd fled his embrace, left the ball before its end, and now refused to walk with him along a corridor thick with people.

She must fear him.

And why not? He'd treated her shabbily. Attacking her ten years ago. Forcing her to share her crowning moment with another. Attacking her again. He'd saddled himself with a huge handicap.

Harriet wasn't helping. Her blatant flirtation made him look interested, discouraging other gentlemen from courting her and likely raising questions with Emily, too.

All in all, this was the worst Season in memory.

He considered showing up at Hughes House tomorrow to take Emily driving in the park, but she might already have plans. And he was supposed to meet Wrexham to discuss an upcoming vote in Parliament. After dragging the man to town, he could hardly ignore him.

So his best course was to arrive early at the Inslip ball, claim two waltzes so he and Emily could talk, then begin that talk by telling her he planned a courtship. He would not press for an immediate answer, but she needed to know his intentions.

Emily arrived early for the Inslip ball. Charles immediately whisked her into the garden, where they could celebrate his news. "You won't believe it, but Mother managed to reserve St. George's of Hanover Square for June the seventh."

"That's in three weeks!" Her mouth dropped open. "She is amazing." St. George's was the most desirable venue for society weddings, thus was never available on such short notice during the Season. Shivers raced down her spine. Events were spinning out of control, giving her no chance to think.

"Three long weeks, though. I would wed you tomorrow if it wouldn't look too havey-cavey." He pulled her close as they passed beyond the terrace lights, out of sight of the guests already streaming into the ballroom. She was still trying to catch her breath when he changed the subject.

"I wish my brothers were here so I could show you off. George will attend the wedding, of course, but I doubt Andrew will even make that." George was Inslip's heir. Andrew captained an East India Company merchantman, but wasn't due in port until midsummer.

"I would have expected George to be here for the Season," she said. "I know his wife is with child, but it is early days yet."

"True. And she's never let her condition interfere in social affairs in the past. But this time, the midwife ordered her to rest."

"Complications?"

He nodded.

"I hope it isn't serious."

"George said something about twins, though it is far too early to tell. But he's not taking any chances."

"Did you tell Sophie about our betrothal?" she asked. Discussing children made marriage seem too real.

"I haven't seen her, but Papa claims she already knows. I swear she can read minds."

"Gossip rarely surprises her," Emily agreed, grinning for the first time all evening. "She even stole a march on Lady Debenham yesterday. I thought the woman would expire on the spot."

"Why?" His green eyes glowed in the fading light.

"Sophie mentioned Miss Towhay's less than stellar behavior at Richmond Park last Tuesday, hoping Lady Debenham could add details Sophie didn't know. But Lady Debenham hadn't heard a word of it."

"You cannot mean it!" Charles roared with laughter. "So Sophie beat the old bat. I always suspected she would prove as formidable as Lady Beatrice one day."

"I—" A swell of voices from the ballroom cut her off.

Charles glanced at the house. "It is nearly time, my love," he announced, drawing her against him. "I can't believe you are mine."

"Forever," she murmured, meeting his eyes.

"And I am yours, only yours, forever." He raised her hand to his lips, then dropped a light kiss on her nose and a longer one on her mouth. Much longer.

"Come, love," he murmured when he finally pulled away. "They are waiting in the library. It's time to shout our news to the world." Grabbing her hand, he headed toward a French window.

Emily forced another smile, but her knees shook. Her doubts were back with a vengeance. Again Charles's touch had stirred nothing. His kiss felt flat. His excitement made her want to flee. Yet in another minute, she would enter the ballroom on his arm and announce that they would wed.

This is a mistake! screamed her conscience. *Run!*

But it was too late. She had given her word. He had bought her a ring. He and her father had spent two hours discussing settlements. A wedding date was set. They would look at houses tomorrow.

Richard smiled as she entered the library, then

squeezed her shoulder and shook Charles's hand. Lady Hughes fussed as she straightened Emily's gown. Lord Hughes beamed in relief.

"Don't be nervous, love," Charles whispered as his parents arrived. "I'll be with you."

"I know." Duty called. Smiling, she headed for the door.

The ballroom was large by private standards, holding nearly two hundred people. And such was Inslip's credit that it was already packed. Every eye turned when a fanfare announced their entrance.

Sophie grinned, then whispered something to Lord Ashington. Lady Beatrice was already nodding, as was Lady Jersey.

Jacob was nearly hidden by a pillar, speaking to Harriet. He seemed unaware that anything unusual was happening—unless he already knew the details; Charles must have told him by now.

Emily returned her attention to Charles as Lord Inslip finished his speech with, "We are delighted to announce the betrothal of Lord Charles Beaumont to Miss Emily Hughes."

The musicians struck up a waltz. Before she could think, Charles swept her into his arms and into the dance. Their parents joined them, then gestured to the guests to do likewise.

Knowing what people expected, Emily broadened her smile and locked her gaze with Charles's.

Jacob paid no attention to the fanfare. He was too busy glaring at Harriet. She had cornered him the moment he arrived, moaning about Miss Beaumont and swearing the woman wanted her dead.

Jacob sympathized. He wanted Harriet dead, too.

He finally told her to quit acting like a spoiled child. Miss Beaumont's job was to force Harriet into obedience. Unless she cooperated, she would spend the rest of the Season in her room.

Harriet was still gaping when Lord Inslip's voice shattered the sudden silence.

"—betrothal of Lord Charles Beaumont to Miss Emily Hughes."

Voices rose from all sides as Jacob's dreams collapsed. Justice had rejected him again.

He'd not known that Charles was considering marriage. If he had, he never would have trusted him near Emily. The thought of him leading her to bed made him ill.

He stared as Charles and Emily took to the floor. Em gazed adoringly into Charles's eyes, sinking another dagger into Jacob's heart that released another burst of fury.

Charles always discussed his plans with the other Beaux, so his secretiveness had to have been deliberate. It wouldn't be the first time he'd sabotaged Jacob's plans, but indulging in such tactics with Emily was intolerable.

Incensed, Jacob slapped Harriet's hand aside and plunged into the crowd. Every glimpse of Emily in Charles's arms hurt, but he had to move closer and verify that his ears had actually heard aright.

Emily let the dizzying whirl of the waltz put color in her cheeks.

"That wasn't so bad, was it?" asked Charles, a euphoric grin stretching his face. "Catch everyone by surprise, then give them time to recover before we let them approach us."

"I think you did that more to save yourself than to protect me," she dared, smiling back. "You know the gossips will descend *en masse,* demanding details—lots of details. Shall I tell them how you landed at my feet after falling from the dairy roof?"

"I thought it was you who landed at my feet."

"Never."

"Certainly you did. I distinctly recall the encounter. You fell from the apple tree."

"No. That was you. Two years earlier. You were hopelessly graceless as a boy."

"Very well." He chuckled. "But I doubt they need *that* many facts."

"Don't underestimate Lady Beatrice. It is news when a lord takes a wife. The marriage of a noted rake is also news. Since you are both, we can't escape. She will demand every detail of every meeting from your first visit to Cherry Hill."

"Let them suffer. We are entitled to our secrets." He flashed another smile, pulling her closer than was customary. For tonight, society would forgive them.

She kept her eyes on his as they circled the room. He seemed so happy. So confident. So proud. She must keep him that way forever. So noble a goal must surely make up for her deception.

"Relax, darling," he murmured, caressing her back as he twirled her down the ballroom. "The gossips won't bite. We'll allow one set for people to fawn over us, then dance again."

"Good." She started to say more, but Jacob's face flashed past, every detail clear though she'd barely glimpsed it. Her heart leaped into her throat, preventing speech. She swallowed, trying to force it down. Already the dance was drawing to a close. She must be ready . . .

Jacob might have been drowning. Shock muffled sound, slowed movement, and relentlessly drew him into a blackness no light could penetrate. Voices echoed hollowly, scraping his nerves raw.

How could he have erred so badly? Only a fool ignored his own needs. He should have known that he could never tolerate Emily wed to another. Why else had he condemned everyone who had displayed interest in her? Controlling his temper to protect her would have been easier than controlling his need to claim her despite that she belonged to another. Denying the truth had plunged him into the same predicament his father's cousin had faced.

His heart cracked, draining enough blood that he

swayed. By the time he controlled himself, the waltz was over, with Charles only a yard away. Duty called. Hiding pain and fury, he stepped forward.

"Congratulations." He clapped Charles firmly on the shoulder with as much bonhomie as he could muster.

It wasn't much. His hands were numb. Touching Charles felt like touching fog. Brushing the feeling aside, he continued, "Who would have thought you would be the first to settle? You've depths even the Beaux didn't recognize."

Emily struggled to compose herself before Jacob finished bantering with Charles and turned his delight on her. Her jaw was already cramping from her forced smile. Spots danced before her eyes.

You will never manage! snapped a new voice suspiciously like Harriet's. *You're hopeless! Look at you! Your knees are shaking. You can barely speak. How will you face him again and again and again without breaking? You know—*

She slammed a door on the intruder, but panic clawed up her spine.

"Emily! I can't believe you didn't tell me!"

She pulled herself together to accept Sophie's exuberant hug.

"Just what I wanted," Sophie exclaimed. "A sister!"

"I thought you already had one." Emily grinned. "Or did George wed a monkey?"

"You know what I mean. I rarely see Elizabeth, so we've never been close. But you are my dearest friend. And now you will be my sister. I'm so excited, I may swoon."

"You would never do anything so gauche," chided Emily. "Your mother would die of embarrassment."

"I know." She rapidly fanned her face, then leaned closer. "Guess what!"

"You are also betrothed."

"Not yet, but I'm closer. Ashington is driving me

in the park tomorrow. He never escorts ladies during the fashionable hour."

"Wonderful!" Emily suddenly remembered that Charles stood next to her, so she lowered her voice to a whisper. "What about Charles? He quivered every time he glanced your way last night."

"I'm counting on you to control him. He and Papa had words two days ago—I complained after Charles threatened to lock me up if I spoke to Ashington again. But I doubt a parental injunction will hold him for long."

"I'll do what I can." She would have said more, but people were crowding around, with Jacob in the lead.

"May I have the next set, Miss Hughes?" he asked, holding out his arm.

How could she refuse? Her infatuation aside, she needed more time before facing the gossips. They were far too adept at reading faces. Charles was already waving her away. If she balked, both men might wonder why.

"Of course." Effort kept her voice light.

It was another waltz.

Every curse she'd ever heard paraded through her head. But she could do nothing but wrestle her face into submission and pray.

His first touch demolished her excuses for accepting this dance. She needed this last contact.

His hand burned into her back, imparting all the heat and sizzle Charles's touch lacked. Electricity shot from his other hand to hers, despite their gloves. It was the first time they'd waltzed—and the last. She was in heaven. Or was it hell? Agony. Ecstasy. Was there no end to the emotions rampaging through her heart?

Somehow, she kept her face calm and managed an inane remark about the crowd.

Jacob hadn't realized that the second set would also be a waltz. The moment he took her in his arms, his eyes stung. Touching her was more painful than he could have imagined, recalling their kiss of two days ago.

Two days! How could she kiss him boneless, then accept another man only hours later?

Fool! he castigated himself as they circled the ballroom. Yes, he'd kissed her. Yes, he'd crushed her close. But he'd also pulled away, withholding any hint that he truly cared. She must have thought he was a cad.

It took determination to keep from ravaging her mouth to prove that conclusion wrong. She was all he wanted, now and forever. But he was too late. Obsession had driven others to dishonor, but not him. Since honor was all he had left, he must cling to it. He would not become the subject of gossip.

Custom kept his gaze on her face, but he blinded his sight so he needn't see her glow. Heat built wherever she touched, playing havoc with his control and increasing his grief with each new note.

He ought to talk lightly, discussing *on-dits* and exchanging comments on the weather like every other couple. But his throat was too tight. Even if he could prod his brain to work, his tongue could never spit out words. All he could do was hold her the prescribed twelve inches away and die a slow and exceedingly painful death.

They made a complete circuit of the room before he managed, "Congratulations, Em. I wish you the best. Charles is a good man."

Emily's struggle to stay calm muffled her ears, making his voice sound odd, almost strained.

"Thank you," she managed coolly. She nearly congratulated him on his own betrothal, but remembered that he had yet to announce it. Agitation might drive her to say something gauche if she again spoke, so she kept her mouth closed, indulging instead in sensation.

The set stretched interminably, yet was over in the blink of an eye. And when it was, she did as she had vowed, locking Jacob away so she could concentrate on her future with Charles. That was all that mattered now.

Jacob heaved a sigh of relief when the set finally ended. His control hung by a thread. Bidding Emily farewell, he escaped the ballroom, forgetting that he'd agreed to watch Harriet after supper.

"Sorry to leave so quickly," he told Lady Inslip, who had returned to the receiving line. "I had to put in an appearance in support of Charles, but I received an urgent summons from the Oakhaven steward."

"Of course," she said. "I hope it's nothing serious."

"We will see." Unable to utter another word, he fled.

Leaving town had not occurred to him until the words tumbled from his lips, but it was the best solution. He had to avoid Charles until he suppressed the need to throttle him. And pride demanded he remain away until he could meet Emily as a friend. Which might take forever.

Returning to Hawthorne Park had never sounded better.

Chapter Eleven

After supper, Harriet led Miss Beaumont to the Inslip House morning room and solicitously helped her lie on the couch.

"I'm sure your head will be fine shortly," she murmured, tucking a cushion in place. Not that she cared, but Miss Beaumont's sudden headache gave her a chance to escape the interfering busybody. She needed time alone so she could think.

She hadn't had a moment to herself since arriving at Inslip House. Miss Beaumont played shadow every waking moment. Even last night's outing to the opera had allowed her no chance to speak with Jacob alone. After years of lax supervision, constant surveillance was intolerable. And tonight had been the final straw.

Lady Inslip's invitation to this ball had been so condescending that Harriet had nearly refused. Only her need to attach Jacob had stayed her tongue. But Lady Inslip had made it clear that Harriet lacked even the cachet of an invited guest at Inslip House. She would be Miss Beaumont's charge, with no connection to the family.

Fury burned hotter every time she recalled those words. It had to be Emily's fault. Emily and Sophie often whispered together, excluding her from their confidences. Emily feared competition from so blazing a diamond, so she and Sophie conspired to keep Harriet out of society. Sophie had convinced Lady Inslip to cut her.

Harriet scowled. They needed a stern lesson, and wedding Jacob would give her the power to teach it. They would pay, then pay again until every slight was avenged several times over.

Especially Emily's. Despite accepting Charles, she kept Jacob dancing attendance on her. He'd waltzed with her tonight, then left, forgetting the set Harriet had given him. So Emily must be punished.

And Jacob owed her an apology. She looked forward to accepting it. His guilt offered a new opportunity to bind him. Men were most vulnerable when begging forgiveness. She'd mastered enough of the seductive arts to bind him if given half a chance. He—

Miss Beaumont's fingers plucked at her arm. "If you could fetch me a glass of ratafia, dear. A small one will cure my head in a trice."

"You don't want your tonic?"

"No. Ratafia works better. I should have taken some earlier. Violins always bother me."

"Of course."

She hid her glee as she slipped out the door. This was her chance to make Emily suffer.

Miss Beaumont's cupboard held several bottles. Harriet poured a glass of ratafia, then added a generous dollop of laudanum. The ratafia's sweetness would cover any bitterness.

Half an hour later, laudanum and a boring monologue about India put Miss Beaumont to sleep. Harriet turned her mind to planning.

All her life, she'd been an unwanted burden shoved ruthlessly into the background. Even her mother had heeded her only when it didn't interfere with her own plans. Everything Harriet had ever achieved had come through her own efforts. Jacob would learn the same truth others had discovered too late. She allowed nothing to stand between her and her destiny.

So far, every step had succeeded. She had refused each offer in India in such a way that no one considered renewing his proposal no matter what inducements Wentworth tried. She had reached England and chosen the best husband for her purposes—better even than the previous Hawthorne, whom she'd planned to attach. It was his title and fortune she needed.

Society was stricter than she'd expected, but she could use that. A lifetime with the military had taught her much about strategy.

It was time to change her approach, though. Unlike most men, Jacob seemed immune to her charms. So instead of flirtation, she would try guile. Tonight's insult proved that he would never offer for her on his own.

The memory again heated her blood. By the time she'd discovered him gone, it had been too late to give the set to someone else. Several girls had gloated over her predicament. Others took the opportunity to snub her more blatantly than usual.

She fought her temper into submission lest it cloud her thinking.

Society's rules dictated her next step. Only a week ago, Lady Horseley had discovered Lord Sedgwick Wiley alone with a disheveled Miss Patterson. Despite their very different stations and the credit that should have allowed Lord Sedgewick to avoid a distasteful marriage, they had wed immediately.

So Harriet must get caught in Jacob's arms. He could not refuse her hand. Gentlemen prized honor above all else.

As for Emily, the best retribution would be to turn Lord Charles's head the way she'd turned Jacob's—an easy chore. His reputation revealed proclivities she could exploit.

With a nod of satisfaction, she checked her hair, made sure Miss Beaumont was sleeping soundly, then returned to the ballroom. Charles had promised his mother he would remain until the bitter end, so she could pick the best time to approach him.

Charles downed another glass of wine, wishing he could leave. He'd already danced three sets with

Emily, most recently the supper dance. Even a newly betrothed couple could not claim more, and there was no one else he wanted to partner. But not dancing left him open to an exhausting torrent of congratulations, risqué suggestions, and questions.

He marveled at how fast his life was changing. He'd offered for Emily with none of the consideration he usually accorded decisions. Now their respective families were rushing ahead with wedding plans, suggestions on houses, hints that he would soon be a father. . . .

He quelled his rising panic.

Sophie's laugh raised new fury. She was again talking to Ashington. His fingers longed to squeeze the life from the cad. But his father had forbidden any confrontation under his mother's roof.

Turning his back so he needn't see them, he accepted a new glass of wine from a passing footman, parried another lewd comment by a fellow rake, and tried to figure out why kissing Emily froze his soul. He loved her. He'd known her most of his life and had long considered her a friend. Nothing about marriage could make him nervous.

Last night's disappointment had been understandable. He'd rushed his offer because Jacob's precipitate removal of Harriet had raised speculation about Emily, something he could not counter until she was his—no one would dare criticize a Beaumont. But their hurry had made it impossible to fully enjoy their kiss.

He bit back a sigh. Love changed so many things. One of them was the excitement he always found in flirting with danger. Stealing a kiss from an innocent was dangerous. Doing so in a public place was worse. But this time, discovery would have changed nothing. They were already betrothed and planning an early marriage. At most they would have drawn an indulgent smile and a quip about young love. There would have been no irate fathers pounding on desks, no insulted husbands to demand satisfaction. . . .

He shivered at the reminder of last year's narrow escape.

Tonight's kiss should have been better. He'd deliberately led her outside to show her what the future held. He'd accomplished his goal, but his own reaction had been even more insipid than before. What the devil was wrong with him?

He meant to settle down after marriage, but that was a decision he'd made many years ago and actually anticipated. His family had a long history of fidelity. Even his uncle, whose notoriety had once bordered on contemptible, remained faithful to his wife. And it wasn't as if he was giving up anything valuable. A life of endless conquests had long since grown stale.

It was the suddenness of his betrothal that was confusing him, he decided as he moved through the dwindling crowd—it was late enough that many of the guests were gone. He'd not had time to contemplate the idea, so his body had not yet switched focus. For years he'd allowed lascivious thoughts only about courtesans or matrons interested in dalliance. Since Emily wasn't a courtesan, his libido did not yet consider her delectable. But that would change.

Satisfied, he relaxed, and promptly tripped over his foot. His head whirled. He'd drunk more than he'd thought.

"Are you all right, my lord?" asked Harriet, grabbing his arm to steady him.

He was grateful. It would not have done to fall in his mother's ballroom, especially on the night he announced his betrothal. People might question his devotion.

"Quite fine." But he swayed, leaning more heavily than he'd intended. He had to grab her shoulder to keep her from toppling.

"You need to sit down for a moment. This room is so warm it quite reminds me of India. You can't be accustomed to it."

"No. Too hot tonight." His words echoed oddly. She was right. He needed to sit until his head cleared and his stomach stopped churning. He usually kept closer track of his intake, but an evening of constant interruptions and congratulatory toasts had distracted him. He'd best leave before he cast up his accounts like a cub who couldn't hold his wine.

"This way, my lord." Her hand closed over his wrist. "Let's find someplace quiet. You are looking rather green."

"Shounds like a good idea," he slurred, letting her lead him away.

When he again stumbled over his feet, she shook her head. "Lady Inslip will not be pleased to find you in your cups." She smiled as if sharing a joke with him.

That smile did something odd to his insides, but at least she wasn't chiding him. His mother *would* be furious. He still recalled her scold when he'd stumbled into her drawing room after a long night of drinking. Even at eighteen, he'd been expected to conduct himself in accordance with his position—or her view of his position. Public drunkenness wasn't on her list. Or his. How had he lost control so thoroughly? He must have consumed three bottles to be this foxed.

"Right again," he managed, turning for the stairs. "My old room will do." The butler would keep his presence quiet. No point in telling his parents that he'd spent the night. They would want to know why. He could hardly admit that he'd drunk too deeply while contemplating his lack of response to Emily's kisses.

"Lean on my shoulder, Charles. I doubt you'll make it otherwise." Again her eyes laughed up at him, sending his spirits soaring. Her tone turned his condition into a joke. He hadn't been on a lark since moving into his own rooms had made surreptitious returns unnecessary—though it had been perfume as often as wine he'd been hiding. His mother demanded discretion in all things.

"You're good shport, Harriet—I can call you Harriet, can't I? Good shport." His knees wobbled. Only draping his arm over her shoulder kept him upright.

His next stumble skidded his hand down to cover her breast.

"Mmmm," she murmured, her nipple puckering into his palm. "Feeling naughty, I see. Well, come along." Her arm circled his waist to hold him steady.

He staggered, pulling her closer lest he fall. Her giggles kept embarrassment at bay and made it easy to forget that he was supposed to escort Emily home.

It took an age to negotiate the stairs. He couldn't walk straight even with Harriet's help, zigzagging so badly he bounced off both sides. When he turned toward his room, he couldn't straighten his feet fast enough to control his direction, finally crashing into the wall with Harriet pinned beneath him.

"Lord Charles, you are three sheets to the wind and then some," she laughed, pushing him away—or was she pulling him closer? His senses swam, unaware of anything beyond the breasts pressed against his chest, tipped by hard, excited nipples that stabbed deep, awakening rakish instincts and calling his shaft to attention.

He tried to recall what he was doing—and with whom—but her scent filled his nose, heavily exotic, excitingly erotic, scrambling what was left of his wits. His hand cupped her cheek—

"Drunk as a lord," she giggled, somehow caressing him from head to foot as she turned him toward his room. "Come to bed, Charles. You need to move out of sight before someone sees you."

Sweat popped out on his brow as he doggedly staggered down the hall, her arm again steering his course. Or was it her hip? How could she touch so many places at once?

By the time he reached his room, he was too dizzy to think of anything but the black-haired witch rubbing against his side, moaning with desire. His hand was again kneading her swollen breast. She was as aroused as he, her heart pounding wildly, her breath coming in excited pants.

"Ready for bed, my lord?" she murmured seductively, kicking his door closed. Her tongue circled her lips, focusing all his attention on their rosy fullness. Her hands stripped off his coat and waistcoat as she arched against his throbbing shaft.

Heat seared every nerve. His last shred of control vanished. Grinding his groin against her, he dipped his head and plundered. . . .

Jacob handed his horse to a sleepy groom and staggered through Oakhaven's front door. Exhaustion increased his pain.

Emily.

Lost.

But the hard ride had lessened his fury. How could he expect Charles to see what he himself had admitted only yesterday? Charles, who always knew his own mind, had recognized Emily's perfection and set out to win her. Jacob, the fool, had refused.

So pistols at dawn was out.

He cursed.

Yet if he was to avoid that dawn meeting, he must relinquish his friendship with Charles. Facing Emily would unleash obsession, driving him to dishonor. Honor was all he had left.

The future loomed, bleak as a Devonshire moor.

Grief welled.

Grateful that his valet would not arrive until morning, he threw himself across his bed and let the tears fall.

Emily was surprised when Richard escorted her home instead of Charles. She was more surprised when he accompanied her into the drawing room. He rarely came home after balls, preferring to go to his club or somewhere less reputable.

"You look radiant tonight, Em," he said, pouring wine.

"Thank you." She doubted it, especially after a long evening as the center of attention, but she tried to look radiant enough to satisfy him.

"I'm glad. I've been concerned these past weeks. You had lost your joie de vivre."

"Not really," she lied. "I found London subduing—something you've likely forgotten after living here for so many years. It seemed prudent to temper any unladylike exuberance until I was sure how it would be received."

"I suppose," he said skeptically. "But are you sure it wasn't Harriet? Several people claim she criticizes you."

She should have expected Harriet to repeat her snide little cuts to others. But at least she had no further reason to do so. Let Miss Beaumont try to control her megrims. "She's gone," she said quietly, crossing to the fireplace to stare at the banked coals.

"But people don't forget."

She shook her head. "There is no need to fret, Richard. If you must worry about something, concentrate on Mother. She is not as well as she claims."

Her ploy worked. Richard immediately demanded details of Lady Hughes's health, allowing Emily to relax her guard.

How much longer would she need such a guard? she wondered as she described Lady Hughes's latest swoon. Her future was assured. She and Charles would look at houses tomorrow. Once they found one, she would be caught up in duties—staff, refurbishment, learning how to properly entertain his diplomatic and political friends. . . .

Richard's questions soon wearied her, so she excused herself.

He stared after her, his face twisted into concern that had nothing to do with their mother.

Charles rolled over and groaned. His head pounded, and his mouth tasted like an ash bin, but that was nothing compared to the bad taste of the memories parading through his mind. What the devil had he done?

Words weren't harsh enough. Nor was execution.

Only hours after announcing his betrothal, he'd taken another woman to his bed.

Many in society wouldn't consider that a problem, for marriages were often arranged and involved nothing beyond financial and dynastic contracts. But his was a love match with a friend's sister. And instead of bedding a courtesan, he'd bedded another friend's ward, a guest in his mother's house. Worse, he'd violated his family's honor. He couldn't imagine his relatives even wanting another woman.

Which cast his love in doubt. Drunkenness was no excuse. How could he lust after Harriet instead of Emily?

He groaned, for even that question paled beside his real problem. How could he explain this disaster to Jacob? Not only had he defiled the man's ward, he'd discovered that Harriet was no innocent.

His stomach roiled, sending him to the close stool to retch his guts out. An eternity passed before he flopped, moaning, on the floor.

What the devil was he going to do? Harriet wasn't merely experienced. He'd had courtesans who weren't as skilled. And he hadn't forced her. Every moment remained etched on his mind, from the instant she'd halted his fall in the ballroom until she'd screamed in ecstasy as he pumped his seed into her just before dawn. She'd been as enthusiastic as he, teasing, caressing, stoking his passion until he'd been too crazed with lust to think.

She'd gloried in the encounter, riding him with abandon, using her hands, her mouth, and her body to bring him to completion three times in as many hours. Only the empty bedchambers flanking his room had kept their tryst secret.

Holding his head, he gingerly sat up.

No matter how he hated baring his crimes, Jacob needed the truth.

Guilt swamped him. He must go to a friend who was already behaving oddly and admit that he had bedded a girl they both thought was innocent. Could

Jacob keep his perfidy quiet, or would he tell Richard? The Beaux had always punished their own transgressions.

God, he couldn't bear for Richard to learn about this one. If Richard called him out for insulting his sister, he would have no recourse but to stand there and take the ball.

But even that image paled beside the bad news about Harriet. He had to inform Jacob that he'd introduced a wanton into society who could likely teach Harriette Wilson a thing or two.

His body heated as it recalled her attentions. Where the devil had she learned such things?

Jacob would be furious.

Then there was the question of Harriet. She could not stay at Inslip House. If her experience became known, it would tarnish his entire family. Sophie would lose most of her court. And while he would never mourn Ashington's departure, he could not hurt his sister.

Charles dragged himself wearily to his feet and looked around for his clothes. The coat and waistcoat were tangled together by the door. His cravat dangled from the washstand. His shirt—

He collected the pieces, his stomach turning over as he recalled how she'd ripped it from his body.

Swallowing hard, he found an old shirt he'd left in the wardrobe. Light stabbed painfully into his eyes. Each new detail made his behavior seem worse. This was not a confrontation he wanted. Especially now.

Jacob had seemed odd in recent days, and not just because Harriet drove him to distraction. The look in his eyes last night—

That's why Jacob's congratulations had sounded strained, he realized. The eyes had held fury, as if he wanted to challenge Charles to a sparring match but couldn't because they were in a ballroom. It couldn't be over Harriet—that had come later.

Charles must have done something to annoy him—

Jacob had long exploded over trifling incidents. But what could it have been?

Not the horse he'd recently bought, but maybe—

No, that couldn't be it. And pique that Charles hadn't revealed his betrothal before announcing it to the world would not drive even Jacob to fury.

He set it aside. There was no dealing with Jacob's little obsessions. He would have to deflect any anger, then risk a worse blowup over Harriet.

Sighing, he headed for the door.

Richard was the one who usually jollied Jacob out of his megrims. But not this time. He would have to face Jacob on his own.

Chapter Twelve

"*I*'m so furious, I could run Jacob through!" The usually insouciant Sophie paced Emily's drawing room a week later, showing more agitation than Emily had ever seen in her.

"What's wrong?" Emily asked calmly. For her, the emergency that had called Jacob to Oakhaven was a godsend. By the time he returned, she would no longer flinch whenever his name was mentioned.

"Harriet, of course." Sophie abruptly sat, downing half a cup of tea before continuing. "How you survived three weeks with her, I'll never know. That girl is worse than the most encroaching mushroom. I've never met anyone so willfully obnoxious or so determined to ignore anything she doesn't like."

"What did she do now?" She wasn't really interested, but talking about Harriet kept her mind off Charles. Every day he grew more morose until she hardly recognized him—which boded ill for the future. She had counted on his love and humor to see them through the early days of marriage, giving her time to learn how to please him. Now she feared he regretted their betrothal.

"What hasn't she done?" demanded Sophie crossly. "Her latest was flying into hysterics because she cannot attend the Hartleigh ball tonight—it hadn't been an issue until she heard Mama mention that the Regent would be there. She actually accused Mama of locking her away and vowed that Jacob will be furious when he returns."

"If he returns. The problem at Oakhaven must be serious to keep him this long."

"Very. I asked Charles about it, but he's heard nothing."

"Nor has Richard." She left it at that. Harriet received daily letters, but revealing that would raise the question of why Jacob would write to her.

The only good thing about Emily's week was that she'd only seen Harriet twice, but last night's tête-à-tête more than countered four days of peace.

Emily still didn't know why the girl was so spiteful. Though she and Charles had shared Lord Wrexham's theater box instead of the Inslips', Harriet had sought her out during the intermission to gloat over her letters and recite the most intimate parts for Emily's unwilling ears. Then she'd repeated what Charles had told Mr. Larkin in the park that morning—that he'd contracted a marriage of convenience out of pity for Richard's family; Lady Hughes's health and Lord Hughes's financial setbacks meant they couldn't afford another Season. If Emily didn't wed, they would have to find her a post as a companion, for they couldn't afford to keep her at home.

Emily didn't want to believe it. But no matter how hard she tried to forget the spiteful words, she could not ignore that Charles had been as condemning of love as Jacob that day at Lady Sheridan's. He hadn't kissed her since the Inslip ball, and at Almack's he'd claimed but a single set. If he'd lied about loving her, such coolness made sense. As did his neglect—he skipped half the balls.

She'd seen so little of him in recent days that she hardly credited Sophie's next words.

"I'm so grateful that you are keeping Charles occupied, Emily. It's given Lord Ashington the chance to court me properly. Charles hasn't glowered once since Mama's ball."

"Is that going well?" she asked, wondering where

the devil Charles had been if he'd avoided both her and Sophie.

"Very. I'm hoping for an offer quite soon. With you controlling Charles, I can accept without fearing an attack."

"I can never influence him."

"Don't be so modest. The man dotes on you. Why, he cried off dinner with Lord and Lady Marchgate last night so he could escort you to the theater."

Emily's heart warmed. She hadn't realized the sacrifice Charles had made for her. Dinner with a lord was the most prized invitation of all, for dinner parties were restricted to a select few. "So will Harriet stay home tonight?" she asked, returning to the original topic.

"No. She and Cousin Alice will attend the Smythe ball—a distant connection of Lord Tardale," she added when Emily raised her brows.

"Miss Beaumont had better keep a close eye on her drinks, then. I hate to think of the mischief Harriet might cause if she puts her to sleep again."

"Exactly, but you needn't worry. I've never seen Cousin Alice so angry. She hasn't let Harriet out of her sight since. And she makes sure a maid sleeps in Harriet's room so she can't slip away."

"Good. If society discovers that she escaped her chaperon, she will be ruined."

Sophie nodded agreement. "She doesn't care a fig what other people think. But we know her better now, so her tricks no longer work. Nor do her megrims."

"Is she making new demands?"

"Shopping."

"That's hardly new."

"This time she wants a court gown—Mama and Papa dined at Carlton House Monday night."

Emily groaned. "Not again. I've explained at least a dozen times that her breeding does not give her entrée to court. Even if she could find a lady willing to present her, the queen's secretary would never allow her name on the list. But she won't listen. It's not a matter of stupidity. She simply refuses to hear anything that contradicts her desires."

"Jacob made a grave mistake by bringing her out in town," said Sophie, accepting another cup of tea. "I'm amazed that he didn't wait until he'd met her before deciding to do so. It's not like him."

"No, it's not." Emily nibbled a lemon biscuit while she sought a new topic of conversation. She couldn't disclose why he'd had no choice. His wife had to know society.

But thinking of him tied to a nobody like Harriet stabbed her to the soul. The girl might have ties to several houses, but she was still too low for an earl. He deserved so much better. If—

She shook away her thoughts. "How did Harriet hear about the Hartleigh ball? I thought Miss Beaumont was watching her."

"For the most part. But she was speaking with Mama when Harriet awoke—about Harriet, I'm afraid. The discussion did nothing to sweeten her temper."

"What now?"

"They think her unsuited to town. Mama wants Jacob to move her to the country as soon as he returns."

"Why not write to him?" The question was out before she remembered that discussing Jacob was not in her best interests.

"She can't admit failure." Sophie shook her head. "Writing is too definitive. She would rather drop a gentle hint and let him work out the details for himself. I know," she added when Emily shook her head. "It sounds cowardly, but what else can she do? She promised to look after the girl. Complaining makes her seem incompetent, as though she can't even control one wayward miss."

"She can't. No one can, including Jacob. She should never have left India."

"But she did." Sophie resumed her pacing. "And I'm worried that she will start rumors about Mama and me. Whenever she feels slighted, she finds a scapegoat and attacks."

"What do you mean?"

"Surely you know that she blames you for her lack of invitations."

"Of course. But your family is safe from such criticism."

Harriet's remarks usually focused on Emily's inadequacies. Unfortunately, Emily couldn't even dismiss them as exaggerated, for it was true that she lacked the poise and social instincts so obvious in Sophie. Her inadequacies left her feeling uncertain and might harm Charles. What if she—

Without warning, Jacob's eyes floated before her, wide with shock. She'd forgotten that momentary reaction to their betrothal. He'd immediately smoothed his face, but she'd seen that flash of horror. He'd feared that Charles was tying himself to someone unworthy.

Stop this, she admonished herself. Wallowing in self-pity was useless. Charles loved her. She must see that he never regretted their marriage.

"Should I ask Richard about Harriet?" she asked Sophie at last. "He might have some ideas on how to control her. Or he might talk to Jacob about removing her from town." The best solution was for Jacob to cloister his soon-to-be wife in the country until she turned into a respectable lady—if ever.

But Sophie was shaking her head. "Mama promised to take care of Harriet. If Richard interferes, it would seem like a cut. We will have to make the best of it for now."

"Very well." But if Jacob didn't return soon, they would all suffer. It was past time for him to announce his betrothal so he could care for Harriet himself.

*　　*　　*

Jacob dismounted in Grosvenor Square, handed the reins to his groom, then climbed wearily to his door.

A week in the country had done little to settle his mind. But at least he could maintain his usual façade with others—which was more than he could have managed a week ago.

He had come to some painful decisions. Those angry vows of last week must stand. Facing Emily was impossible, for it would crack his composure, pushing him into dishonor that he would never live down. At least relinquishing his friendship with Charles would be easy, for imagining the man making love to Emily invoked a hatred nearly as powerful as his love. Thus the Beaux must disband.

He would remain cordial with Richard, of course. Richard was a neighbor and would one day own Cherry Hill. They must deal with each other, no matter what. And continuing that friendship would not bring him face-to-face with Emily. She would rarely visit Gloucestershire.

The most bitter loss would be his Parliamentary work. He could not remain in town knowing Charles and Emily were nearby. As soon as he fulfilled the obligations he'd already accepted, he would remove to Hawthorne Park and stay there.

His calm disintegrated the moment he reached his study. Four letters sat on his desk, including one from Charles. Sucking in a deep breath, he cracked the seal. It demanded a meeting—had Emily mentioned his attack in Lady Debenham's garden?

Emily's hand on the next one reinforced that fear. Would she add recriminations or warn him of Charles's temper? Or was she, too, demanding a meeting?

He needed two glasses of brandy before he dared open her note. The urge to stroke the paper she'd touched and trace the letters she'd formed cracked his composure, destroying every bit of peace he'd gained from his absence.

Her tone added new pain—polite, succinct, and completely without warmth, driving a stake through his heart. He stared at the page.

My lord,

Our long acquaintance emboldens me to warn you that Miss Nichols's tantrums have increased in your absence, distressing Lady Inslip and infuriating Lady Sophie. Neither of them can complain without straining your friendship, but a prudent guardian would take her sharply to task for her behavior. You should also know that to escape supervision, Miss Nichols drugged Miss Beaumont on at least one occasion.

Miss Hughes

Fury engulfed him, though this explained Charles's demand for a meeting. Charles would be incensed if his family was harmed. And they would be if Harriet caused a scandal while under their roof.

Thankful that Emily had warned him so he needn't face Charles, he consigned the latter's note to the fire and studied the two missives from Richard.

The first merely expressed hope that the emergency at Oakhaven had been resolved. The second suggested cards, then mentioned that he'd found several candidates to wed Harriet. There was no hint that the girl was causing trouble.

Jacob was glad that Emily had not disclosed Harriet's doings to her brother. It would be too much to have everyone annoyed at him.

He would meet Richard immediately and find out where Harriet would be that evening. It was time to read her the riot act.

Two hours later, Jacob joined Richard in the reading room at White's. It was empty. Few men were out this early, though the card room contained a table of whist players left over from last night.

"Who did you find for Harriet?" he asked when the footman had finished serving wine.

"A butcher. A blacksmith. A vicar. A—"

"Vicar?" Jacob laughed humorlessly. "She would precipitate the downfall of the church if she wed a vicar."

"She is a handful," agreed Richard carefully.

"Don't tiptoe around the truth," snapped Jacob. "She is headstrong, spoiled, and selfish to the core. I want her far, far away."

"She won't be pleased at leaving town," Richard said bluntly. "But if that's what you want, the best candidate is Mr. Barnes, one of Clifford's tenants. Barnes recently lost his wife in childbirth. His oldest is barely ten, so he badly needs a wife to care for his six children."

"Clifford's seat is in Yorkshire."

Richard nodded.

"Can Barnes control her until she settles in?"

"He spent fifteen years in the army, rising to the rank of sergeant before injuries forced him home. His last three years of service were in India."

"Barnes." He frowned. "I don't know the name."

"You wouldn't. He retired twelve years ago. Since he was born on the Clifford estate, he returned there and wed the daughter of another tenant. She had no brothers, so Barnes took over that tenancy after her father died. He is crusty enough that few women are willing to take him on."

"It sounds perfect." Barnes might even recall Harriet from India. "I'll speak to Clifford tonight. Harriet's dowry is five hundred, but I'll raise it to two thousand if Barnes keeps her busy in Yorkshire."

A sergeant. Exactly what Harriet needed to bring her to heel. The moment Barnes accepted the offer, he would pack Harriet off to the country, special license in hand, and be rid of her. Distressing Lady Inslip was the last straw.

"Is everything under control at Oakhaven?" asked Richard, breaking into Jacob's thoughts.

"It is now," he said, which explained nothing, but he refused to lie about a nonexistent crisis. Nor could he admit his reason for fleeing town. "Where will Harriet be this evening?" he asked to change the subject. "Charles is complaining about her behavior."

"Charles?" Richard sounded surprised. "Unless Lady Inslip told him—which doesn't sound at all like her—he wouldn't know anything. He hasn't been to Inslip House since last week's ball, and I doubt he's seen Harriet since then, either." He frowned. "We've none of us seen much of him, actually. There must be trouble at the Foreign Office. I'll ask Emily."

Charles was probably keeping Emily to himself, Jacob groused silently, cursing his blunder. Of course Charles knew nothing about Harriet. He was probably initiating Emily into—

He slammed the door on the thought.

"She might be at the Hartleigh ball tonight," continued Richard, not noticing Jacob's abstraction. "That's where everyone else will be."

"Good. So what happened while I was gone?" His valet would have the latest gossip by the time he returned to the house, but talking would keep Richard from asking questions he didn't want to answer.

"Glendale House is in an uproar."

"Still reeling from Lord Sedgewick's marriage?"

"In part. Glendale suffered an apoplectic fit and is not expected to live. Lady Glendale is no longer speaking to either of her sons. The falling out seems permanent. Ellisham left for France three days ago, leaving Lord Sedgewick to run the Glendale affairs. Rumors are flying that Lady Glendale will soon depart for Scotland and is not expected back."

"Good Lord!" Jacob stared. "What happened?"

"You know how top-lofty Lady Glendale is."

"Of course. She can't think much of Lady Sedgewick, though I've always liked the girl."

"As have I. But Lady Glendale tried to drive Lady

Sedgewick from town while Lord Sedgewick was away on business. She hoped he would seek an annulment. Not only did she fail, but both sons turned on her. Details are scarce, but that makes speculation irresistible."

Jacob shook his head, though a scandal of this magnitude would draw attention from Harriet's last days in town.

"Wellington accepted a cabinet post as Master of Ordnance," continued Richard. "Colonel Caldwell is looking for you, probably to discuss some new debate in Parliament."

Jacob made a mental note to avoid Caldwell so he needn't explain why he was retiring to the country, then directed their talk to ongoing courtships, surprised to learn that Sophie seemed seriously interested in Ashington.

Maybe *that* was what Charles wanted to discuss.

Emily stood with Charles at the Hartleigh ball that evening, but she might as well have accompanied a stranger. He spoke little and rarely met her eyes. Every day he grew more remote.

But her spirits soared when she spotted Sophie. Her friend was approaching so fast, her feet barely touched the floor. Waves of excitement rolled from her, heating the already overheated room—the Regent hated drafts, so every door and window was shut tight.

"Guess what!" Sophie whispered as she tugged Emily a step away from Charles's side. Not that whispering was necessary. So many people were talking that a shout could have gone unnoticed.

Emily smiled. "Harriet accepted an adventurer and will leave for China in the morning."

Sophie laughed. "Very droll," she managed at last. "I admit my news isn't quite that good, but Lord Ashington demanded two waltzes tonight, including the supper dance. And he's driving me to Richmond tomorrow with only one other couple in attendance."

"Wonderful!" Emily squeezed her hand. Such assiduous attention was as good as a declaration. The gossips would be buzzing—which meant Emily must keep Charles in line. Given his glumness, it seemed an impossible task.

Charles finally noticed Sophie's presence and turned a quizzical eye on them, so Sophie changed the subject. "Mr. Larkin kept Miss Cunningham on the terrace for the entire first set," she reported brightly, her eyes fixed on Ashington as he chatted with Lord Hartleigh across the room. "I think he's serious."

So did Emily, but she merely said, "They seem suited. She is very sweet, which is just what he is seeking."

"I expect an announcement quite soon. Lady Beatrice estimates two weeks, but I think one is more likely. He . . ." Her voice trailed off as Charles's attention shifted elsewhere. "I—uh—I need to speak to Lady Hartleigh," she murmured, drifting away, her eyes still on Ashington, who now spoke to their hostess.

Emily shook her head.

"What was that about?" Charles asked.

"Jacob is back." The words escaped without thought as she caught sight of him in the ballroom doorway, sending her treacherous heart into a gallop.

"Oh." His voice could freeze fire.

Shocked, she turned her full attention on Charles. What now? Had he detected her infatuation? That might explain the change in his demeanor. Or was it something else? His eyes held . . . fear? They slid away before she could be sure.

Not until she met Jacob's gaze did she realize that her own had shifted back to the door to drink in his broad shoulders and brilliant blue eyes.

Tearing herself away, she smiled at Charles, hoping she looked less strained than she felt. "This is your set, my dear."

"So it is." He swung her into the waltz.

When the first turn let Emily see the entrance,

Jacob was gone. Had he been there at all, or had her imagination conjured his image?

Jacob swore as he slipped from Hartleigh House. Emily had caught him staring like an adoring puppy— or like some lovesick swain spouting excruciating odes to her amber eyes.

He shuddered.

He ought to have stayed long enough to find Harriet, but the sight of Charles at Emily's side had ignited his rage yet again. Would the day ever arrive when he could face his erstwhile friend with equanimity?

So he left before he did something he would regret. His best course was to go home and stay there until he regained his composure.

At least he'd found Clifford. Barnes would receive an offer for Harriet in two days. Within the week, she might be settled.

Richard stared at the empty doorway, wondering what the devil was wrong with Jacob. He'd taken one look at Charles, turned white as a sheet, then fled.

Emergency, hell! Jacob had fought with Charles, then left town to keep the incident from the gossips— the Beaux always kept their troubles private. No wonder Charles had looked so grim lately. What the devil had sundered their friendship this time?

Somehow he must find out. He could not have his two closest friends at odds with each other. Once again, it was up to him to mend the hole in the Beaux' armor.

Why did Jacob and Charles have such hot tempers?

"Why is Sophie dancing with Ashington again? That's twice tonight!" hissed Charles during the supper dance. It was the first time in a week he'd taken two sets.

"Behave!" she hissed back. "You can't cause a

scene. The Regent is here. What would he say if one of his diplomats started a brawl?"

"He would agree that such provocation cannot be borne."

"Will you listen to yourself? A duke's heir is dancing quite properly with a marquess's daughter while surrounded by three hundred of his peers. No one can consider that a provocation. What would your mother say?"

"That seeing Sophie's reputation in shreds would be worse."

"It won't be."

"How can you know? Flirting with excitement is understandable. But why choose him? The man is the worst sort of rake."

"No."

He stared, shocked into looking deep into her eyes.

"You are the only man who has said a word against Ashington in all my weeks in town," she said calmly. "Everyone else considers him an exemplary gentleman and a good catch."

"But—"

"Please, Charles. I know you hate him. I've heard enough rumors to suspect why. But please set aside your quarrel for a moment and think. Sophie is not flirting with excitement. She loves him."

He tripped on her foot and nearly fell. "You can't be serious."

"I am. She's had her eye on him for the past two Seasons, but he wasn't looking for a wife. Or perhaps he was avoiding your animosity. Now he is ready to take what he wants, regardless of your opposition."

"Never. He's toying with her to irritate me."

"I don't believe that for a moment."

"He'll never change."

"Love changes many things, Charles. It changed your father and brother by all accounts. You claim it changed you. So why would it not change him as well?" She met his gaze, trying to force him to accept the truth. "I've spoken with him several times. His eyes blaze with love whenever he mentions Sophie. His face lights up with every glance. Talk to him yourself if you're not sure. But don't let your own grievance destroy Sophie's chance for happiness. She's waited too long for this. If she doesn't wed Ashington, she will wed no one. Do you want society to brush her aside as a confirmed spinster?" She was taking a huge chance, but Sophie needed more than a loving marriage. She needed Charles to accept her choice.

"Very well. I'll talk to him—without malice." He scowled. "But why the devil would she fix on someone like him?"

"Because he's exactly like her favorite brother."

Charles stared as if he'd never seen her before, then exploded in laughter, relaxing into the man who'd proposed to her. "By God, you're right." He spun her through a tight sequence of turns, pulling her close as he'd done after announcing their betrothal. "I suppose that's why we fight so often. Let's hope he's mellowed since we last locked horns." He pulled her closer on the next turn. "Thank you, sweetheart. You've kept me from making a fool of myself."

Emily smiled up at him, relieved that everything was all right. For Sophie's sake, he would give Ashington a fair hearing.

Chapter Thirteen

"*I* don't know how we can manage a proper wedding breakfast," moaned Lady Hughes a week later, waving her vinaigrette beneath her nose. "We haven't enough space. Mrs. Hodges can never manage that much food. We can't—"

"Stop fretting," snapped Emily crossly. "I'm not wedding a royal duke, for heaven's sake. The marriage of a third son to the daughter of a minor viscount is hardly the social event of the Season. The guest list is small, and Gunter's can help with the food."

Or so she hoped. While she'd discussed arrangements with Lady Inslip, she had no idea how many friends Charles might invite. They hadn't discussed their marriage since they'd chosen a house several days earlier. He'd been so aloof that she hadn't drummed up the courage to ask him. Or the enthusiasm, she admitted.

But they needed to talk about final arrangements. The wedding was only a week away.

His lightheartedness at the Hartleigh ball hadn't lasted beyond escorting her home that evening, confirming Harriet's claims that his offer had nothing to do with love. Emily accepted that, but she had no idea how to tell him that she would make no unwanted demands on him. He also seemed at a loss for words, despite his usually glib tongue. After his vow of eternal love, he could find no painless way to tell her that he'd exaggerated and expected no more than a marriage of convenience.

Or so she hoped. It wasn't the marriage she'd dreamed of, but dreams had little to do with reality. She and Charles had been friends for years and could surely regain that once they were clear on what their marriage would and would not encompass.

Knowing that he cared enough to consider her feelings should have made it easy to broach the subject. But it didn't, because something else was bothering him. Something serious. He jumped at the least sound, avoided half of the entertainments he should have attended, and rarely spoke—and then only when asked a question. It almost seemed as if he expected an attack.

In the past, the other Beaux would have taken him in hand, but none of the Beaux were behaving as usual. Richard was surprisingly grim for a man known for lighthearted insouciance. Charles was avoiding him. At first, she'd thought she was imagining things, but he'd actually fled Lady Hartford's rout last night when Richard arrived, leaving her to find her own way home.

As for Jacob, he might as well have stayed at Oakhaven, for he attended nothing, not even events that included Harriet. Emily might have thought her glimpse of him had been imagination if Richard hadn't mentioned meeting him at White's.

She reminded herself that she was glad Jacob wasn't hovering over her. She could not have endured the extra strain now that Charles—

"Lord Charles might be a third son, but his father is a marquess," said Lady Hughes, interrupting. "He is a rising figure in government and might well be prime minister one day. I won't have Lady Jersey think you unsuited to such circles—which means we cannot scrimp on the wedding breakfast."

"You also don't want her to think you are putting on airs. We should strive for elegance, not ostentation.

Do you wish to court comparisons to the Regent's extravagances?"

"Of course not. But—"

"Leave everything to me, Mama. I won't disappoint you."

Emily stifled a sigh. Lady Hughes was noticeably weaker than when they had arrived in London. Her swoons occurred more often, and swelling made walking difficult. Her color was worse as well, her face so yellow it drew comments.

It made Emily feel guilty for all the times she'd suspected her mother of exaggerating her illness to keep Emily at home. What difference would it have made had she reached London sooner? Her dreams would still have been exposed as fantasy. Jacob would still have been tied to another. She might have avoided meeting Harriet, but Charles would still have offered out of pity. It—

"Lady Sophie has arrived," announced the butler from the doorway.

"I will join her downstairs." Emily patted her mother's hand. "Stop fretting, Mama. We will finish this when I return."

Without waiting for a response, she picked up her pelisse and headed out for yet another shopping expedition. Matrons wore different clothing than innocents in their first Season.

"I barely escaped without Harriet," Sophie complained as they climbed into the Inslip carriage.

"Again? I thought Miss Beaumont had her under control."

With a clatter of wheels, the carriage rocked into motion.

"She does, but that doesn't prevent Harriet from wanting more clothes. You would think she'd been deprived for her entire life."

It was on the tip of Emily's tongue to say, *she was*. But she didn't want to talk about Harriet. A fortnight of rarely seeing her had been pure bliss. It was wonderful that her new status took her places Harriet wasn't invited.

"I told her to talk to Jacob if she needed more clothes," continued Sophie. "And speaking of Jacob, what happened between him and Charles?"

"I know of nothing. Why?"

"Jacob actually ducked into Michelle's Millinery yesterday when he spotted Charles approaching."

"That's odd," admitted Emily. Jacob's refusal to take a mistress meant he never had to clothe one, so he had no business in a hat shop. But his actions fit her other observations. Charles avoided Richard. Jacob avoided Charles. Something was terribly wrong with the Beaux.

"Has Charles said anything?" asked Sophie.

"Not a word. Nor has Richard, and if something were wrong, he would surely know. He spent the afternoon with Jacob just yesterday."

"But not last evening."

"Not that I know of. Jacob wasn't at the Hartford rout while we were there. They might have met later, but I wouldn't know about that. Richard is still abed."

"There is definitely a problem," swore Sophie. "I talked to my maid last night—she steps out with Charles's footman."

"So he said." He'd decided that Sophie had learned of his intentions because the footman listened at keyholes.

Sophie nodded. "She claims that Charles goes out only to the Foreign Office or to escort you. He sees no one else and accepts calls only from the builder working on your house."

"That's odd," she repeated. The house should be a minor matter, since all they were doing was refurbishing three rooms.

"Very odd. He even turned Richard away twice."

"Uh-oh." But this explained Charles's tension. Expecting a confrontation, he had fallen into his old habit of grousing at everyone when he was at odds with his friends.

Since Charles had been morose for a fortnight, the quarrel must have occurred before the Inslip ball. Jacob had also been strained that night. He had attended to hide their falling out from society's prying eyes, but had left at the first opportunity.

Idiots! All three of them.

Heaven only knew what silliness was causing trouble this time—she knew of other instances. Richard had broken from the group one year to cover embarrassment that he lacked funds to attend the Newbury Races. A few years later, he'd rescued the Beaux from a more serious rift when Jacob and Charles had bid against each other for something—she'd never learned exactly what. Charles won, but Jacob accused him of cheating. Competition gave way to fury. Harsh words ended in accusations that might have led to a duel if Richard hadn't suggested that the two pay for the item jointly, then donate it to the British Museum. Friendship was more important than ownership.

This quarrel would be equally silly, though it seemed Charles was the latest culprit—why else would he refuse to see Richard? And she feared that Harriet might be involved. Harriet did not understand the Beaux and was too selfish to share Jacob with anyone.

"I have to figure this out," declared Sophie. "Charles has been miserable lately. Their friendship is too important to let it die."

"I'll talk to him." Now that she knew his melancholy arose from an argument with Jacob instead of dissatisfaction with her, the words would be easy.

"Thank you, Emily. The question will be better coming from you."

Emily nodded as they entered Bond Street, then changed the subject to fashion. She should have known that Charles was brooding about something besides her—would have known if she hadn't let Harriet's snide remarks erode her confidence.

Perhaps the future was not as dark as she'd feared.

*   *   *

Jacob stared blindly at the report in his hand. Lords would soon open the debate on building new churches—so many people had left the country to find work that several hundred new parishes were needed. Parliament's problem was deciding how many, for the trend would likely continue long into the future.

A future without Emily. And without Charles.

It was harder to avoid them than he'd expected. He could skip social gatherings and stay in his study instead of visiting White's, but Mayfair was small enough that merely stepping outside could bring him face-to-face with acquaintances—he'd barely avoided Charles on Piccadilly yesterday. Yet staying home wasn't a permanent answer. Avoiding the clubs kept him from his other friends.

Then there was Richard. Their meetings were strained, for Jacob had to retain strict control lest he reveal too much. If Richard started asking questions, he would have to cut that connection, too. Richard might be lighthearted, but he had the tenacity of a mongoose. Once he went after something, he never quit.

So far, Jacob had steered their conversations onto innocuous subjects, but Richard suspected something was wrong and might well bring Charles to one of their meetings to help ferret out the problem. Walking out on them would solve nothing. So he might lose Richard's friendship, too.

He forced his eyes back to his notes, but Emily's face hovered over the page, eyes alight as they'd been at the Hartleigh ball. Every time he recalled how happy Charles made her, his own pain deepened.

Maybe he should abandon London immediately instead of waiting until Parliament adjourned. His voice would matter little in the upcoming debate, for Canterbury had all the votes he needed.

Setting aside his notes, he fetched the brandy.

He would do it—the moment he settled Harriet, which could be any day now. If only Barnes accepted her . . .

Brandy was a mistake. It relaxed him, freeing memories he'd tried to forget—Emily racing across a meadow, determined to reach the stream before the boys did . . . Emily knocking his hat off with a green apple, revealing her presence in the tree above him . . . Emily's eyes aglow as she waltzed around Lady Inslip's ballroom after her betrothal announcement . . .

"Stop this maudlin pining," he snapped, even as his hand poured another glass. "You lost. Unless you want to court dishonor, you must put her behind you."

Richard left Emily with Lady Inslip, then departed the ball. He was only there because Charles had sent word at the last minute that he could not escort Emily after all.

Richard wanted to know why. He'd had enough evasions. Emily's wedding was only a week away. If there was trouble between the two, he would step in and stop it. It was time for the truth.

Two hours later, he found Charles in a gaming hell on Jermyn Street. It was not a place he'd ever expected Charles to frequent, but neither of his friends was behaving normally of late.

Nor was Emily.

He'd returned home the night before to hear heart-rending sobs emanating from her room. It had taken tremendous effort to stay outside rather than rush in and demand answers.

But her tears were the last straw. She had changed since arriving in town, and not for the better. Her explanation was patent nonsense.

She had eagerly anticipated this Season, fairly dancing with excitement when she arrived in town, her laughter filling the house, her enthusiasm infectious.

Six weeks later, she never smiled. Her shoulders seemed to slump even when she was standing erect. Instead of bringing sunshine to any room she entered, she brought gloom.

At first he'd thought Harriet was to blame. Though

the girl was exotic, with enough sensuality to incite lust in a corpse, an hour of acquaintance had revealed a sharp tongue and selfish nature, killing his interest. But he had no doubt that she'd turned her vitriol on Emily. The girl was a schemer. So he'd applauded moving Harriet elsewhere, hoping the change would restore Emily's spirits.

But it hadn't. Nor had her betrothal. If anything, she was worse, as evidenced by last night's tears. He feared she did not want to wed Charles. So why the devil had she accepted him?

He'd paced his room for hours, but it wasn't until dawn that he'd found a possible explanation.

Em had always insisted on joining the boys for what she called adventuring. Whenever he was home on breaks, she pestered him for tales of school. When Brummell had coined the sobriquet *The Three Beaux,* the name had sparked her imagination, igniting an almost obsessive need to be part of the group.

Accepting Charles would accomplish that—but it was a poor excuse for marriage.

He also wondered if the ridiculous rift between Charles and Jacob had something to do with Em. Her attention had always sharpened when he mentioned Jacob. But if competition between the two had tied her to the wrong man . . .

He couldn't imagine anyone fighting over his sister, especially those two. Yet he could not deny that something was seriously amiss. It was time to learn what it was.

"How about a hand of piquet?" he asked Charles now. His friend was leaning over the hazard table watching Ardmore's throw.

Charles jumped, spilling wine as he trod on Ardmore's foot.

Ardmore yelped.

"What?" asked Charles, ignoring glares from several players.

"Cards. Join me for a hand."

Denial hovered on Charles's lips, but he could not refuse without drawing comment. He finally shrugged. "Why not? The dice aren't falling my way tonight."

Charles had never been one to bare his soul, a tendency worsened by his work at the Foreign Office. So Richard kept the conversation light while they played out the first hand. Ignoring that Charles neither mentioned Emily nor asked why he was here, Richard discussed Glendale's death two days earlier, laughed over Connoly's embarrassing fall from his horse, and pondered the effect a wet spring would have on the crops. He also kept Charles's glass full, occasionally emptying his own into it when Charles wasn't looking.

Two bottles of brandy later, Charles was misplaying cards on every hand. He'd unbuttoned his waistcoat to counter the heat and was sprawled precariously half out of his chair.

"Have you seen Jacob lately?" Richard asked as he shuffled the deck. "He hasn't been around much in recent days."

"No." Charles shuddered. "Well, once. Ducked out of sight."

"Who did?"

"Him. Can't blame him." He reached for his glass, but misjudged the distance, knocking it to the floor.

"Why would he run?" demanded Richard, handing him his own glass.

Charles drained it. A drop rolled down his chin when he hiccuped.

"Why?" repeated Richard, hoping he hadn't pushed Charles into unconsciousness.

"Hates me. Can't blame him."

"What happened?"

Charles opened his mouth, closed it, then shrank into himself. Every trace of color drained from his face. His hand shook, setting off larger tremors that knocked him from his chair.

Shocked, Richard pulled him up and dragged him outside. "We need to talk. Now!" he added when

Charles balked. His coach waited across the street. Bundling Charles inside, he slammed the door.

"No more running," he snapped. "What the devil is going on? You're a wreck. Jacob is so tense he will shatter at a touch. I can't believe you are acting like this."

"Harri—" He stopped, gagging.

Richard fished out the chamber pot he kept under the seat for just such occasions. He waited until Charles had cast up the second bottle of brandy, then returned to his questions.

"What about Harriet?"

"I—I seduced her at Mother's ball." He was shaking again.

"The night you announced your betrothal to my sister?" His fist slammed into Charles's jaw. No wonder Emily cried herself to sleep.

"I don't know what came over me," swore Charles, making no attempt to defend himself. Tears streamed down his face. "I can't stand her."

"What happened?" Charles was so haggard, Richard stifled his fury.

"I drank too much," he mumbled. "She helped me upstairs. The next thing I knew, I was ravishing her."

"So that's why Jacob is so upset."

"Maybe—I don't know. I wrote, asking him to call, but he never answered. I haven't talked to him in two weeks. But he must know, because he's avoiding me. Every time he sees me, he runs away. Why would he unless he fears he might kill me if he gets close?"

It made sense. Jacob had a ferocious temper. Whenever it started to slip, he hibernated until he had it under control. "Harriet probably told him. She must have told Emily, too. She's been upset."

"My God!" Charles turned green and lunged for the chamber pot. By the time he surfaced, he looked at death's door. "I never meant to hurt Em. You have to believe that."

Richard nodded.

"Harriet should never have been allowed in town."

"Agreed. But she is not your problem."

"Still is," slurred Charles. "I wasn't her first."

"Good God!" He stared. "Does Jacob know?"

"Have to tell, but couldn't put in letter . . ."

Of course he couldn't, admitted Richard as shudders wracked Charles's body. What a coil! It was a wonder Charles could function at all. He might flirt with great skill and hide behind a façade of gaiety, but inside was a deep core of honor that must be shrieking.

Damn Harriet. And to think he'd welcomed her into his home.

"Stop blaming yourself," he said at last. "It isn't your fault."

"Weren't you listening? I bedded—"

"Yes, but you would never have done it without help. Not even in your cups. Think! Harriet is utterly selfish. You proved she's also experienced. So why did she help you upstairs?"

Charles's eyes widened.

"Exactly. She deliberately seduced you, probably to hurt Em."

Charles groaned.

"But I have to know how susceptible you were. Do you love Emily?"

"I thought I did."

"Thought?"

"I must. I have to. I'll treat her well, I promise. But—" He rubbed his hands over his face. "Kissing her is like kissing my sister."

"Good God."

"I don't know what to do. Everything was fine until that night. Wonderful. Then—" He groaned, hiccuping several times before he continued. "I have to revive that spark. I have to. It isn't fair." Words gushed forth like a spring flood, detailing his growing fear that he would never be able to recapture the love he'd felt only a fortnight earlier. Every day was worse as self-loathing assaulted his senses, eroding his confidence and adding to his fears.

What a mess, thought Richard as he hauled Charles up to his rooms. He could not let Emily wed a man who couldn't love her, yet breaking the betrothal would ruin her in the eyes of the world. She didn't have the credit to jilt a marquess's son with impunity.

Then there was Harriet.

He shook his head as he turned toward Hawthorne House. Harriet would have grabbed the first opportunity to tell Emily about Charles's advances—which would explain her tears. What she hoped to accomplish by her cruelty, he didn't know. But he must stop her. It was time she left town.

Jacob was home. The butler tried to turn him away, but Richard refused.

"This is an emergency," he vowed, brushing past the servant. "I haven't time to cater to his megrims. Is he in the study?"

Giving the man no chance to reply, he hurried up the stairs.

Jacob was staring into the fire, an empty bottle on the floor, a nearly full one at his elbow. He raised bleary eyes, then shrugged and looked away.

Richard sighed. At least Jacob was already well into his cups, which would make his job easier. Jacob was too good at keeping secrets. That he was drinking alone indicated serious trouble.

Half an hour and three glasses of brandy later, Jacob had turned maudlin. "Ladies make no shensh," he slurred, filling his glass. "You think you understand them, then they do something you don't expect."

"Like Emily?" Richard dared.

"Szactly. She always liked me, szo why'd she accept Charles?"

"She liked all of us."

"Not like that. Special spark. Taste never did go away. . . ."

"Did you ever tell her?" he asked, reining in a demand to know why Jacob knew how Emily tasted. He topped off Jacob's glass. "She never mentioned it, and I didn't notice any particular regard."

"Never meant to wed. Too dangerous, though she said—" He scowled. "Maybe right, but what good is it? Doesn't want me."

Richard couldn't believe he'd pulled a near-admission of love from Jacob's lips. But he must move fast if he hoped to get more. Already he could see the shutters closing across Jacob's secrets. "Do you mean that you intended to court Emily but were so slow about it that she turned elsewhere?"

Jacob paused for nearly a minute. "Meant to start that night, but Charles betrayed me. Must have known. Bastard knows everything. Hates to lose, so jumped in to grab her. Trying to annoy me."

Richard stared. What an idiot! Jacob could be dense at times, but this was beyond anything he'd done before. "Charles pressed his attentions from the moment Emily arrived in London. Every gossip in town commented on it. How could you not notice?"

Jacob shrugged.

"So what will you do now?"

"Get rid of Harriet, then go home. Never should have brought the bitch to town. Just like her mother. Selfish to the core."

"If you want to go home, why come back at all? You were just at Oakhaven."

"Not Oakhaven." He slumped in his chair. "Hawthorne. Haven't seen it in years. Couldn't face Emily. Too young. Too damned young . . ." His head fell forward.

"Fool!" snapped Richard. But Jacob had passed out.

Richard remained for several minutes while his mind worked out the clues Jacob had let fall. The man was crazy in love with Emily, but he'd been so distracted by Harriet's arrival that he hadn't realized it— Jacob was the most stubborn man he knew. If he'd decided never to wed, he would refuse to consider anything that might change his mind. Thus he'd stayed aloof, even refusing to visit Hawthorne after Emily came of age. Emily thought he wasn't interested, so she'd accepted the offer from Charles. But they would be miserable together.

He headed home, turning an idea over in his head. There was no way to prove that Emily preferred Jacob. She would deny it if asked, for she was not one to abandon commitments. The only way she might break her betrothal was if Jacob declared his love in no uncertain terms. Jacob would never do it. Honor would stop him.

So they had to be tricked.

Chapter Fourteen

*J*acob strode into the Thompson ball the next night a changed man. He couldn't believe last evening's maudlin prattling, but that was over. The headache he'd awakened with had forced him to take a close look at what he was doing to himself. It had to stop.

He'd been stupid from the beginning. Why had he thought that Emily would accept friendship without wanting more? She'd been in town to find a husband, for heaven's sake! Since he'd shown no sign of offering for her, she'd turned elsewhere.

He could hardly blame Charles for stepping in to claim her. If he'd had an ounce of brains, he would have seen that their match was inevitable.

In truth, he couldn't even blame Harriet for this fiasco. Yes, she'd arrived at an inconvenient time. Yes, she'd reawakened memories he would have preferred to forget. Yes, he would cheerfully strangle her. But it wasn't Harriet's fault that he had refused to recognize his own feelings until it was too late.

Tonight he would begin a new life. Emily was lost. But he was a gentleman born, a belted earl with more than a thousand dependents on three estates, a man charged with the responsibility to guide England's policies at home and abroad. His honor would not allow him to renege on any of those duties.

He would take that break at Hawthorne Park—it was past time to personally inspect his seat. But he would not use the visit to cower and hide. So before he left town, he must make peace with Charles.

But first he had a more pleasant errand. He'd finally heard from Barnes. The man recalled Harriet as a quiet girl with sad eyes, who rarely mingled with other children. Since he'd respected Wentworth and admired Mrs. Wentworth, he would gladly take her to wife.

Tonight Jacob would break the news about her forthcoming nuptials. She would leave for Yorkshire in the morning.

The rented ballroom was crowded. He didn't know the Thompsons—Mr. Thompson owned coal mines in several counties; Mrs. Thompson was a baronet's daughter, which gave them access to society's fringe— so Jacob hadn't received an invitation to this ball. But no one on the fringe would dare turn away an earl. His presence would raise Thompson's credit several notches.

He pushed through the crowd, parrying greetings. In the end, it was Harriet who found him.

"Jacob! You're back!" If an outstretched hand hadn't stopped her, she would have flung herself against him. "I've been looking for you for days, but that awful Miss Beaumont wouldn't let me summon you. We have to talk." Grabbing his arm, she tugged him toward the balcony.

"We will." He changed direction, leading her to one of the anterooms off the main hall. But he'd barely crossed the threshold when a snick whirled him around. Harriet leaned against the closed door. Before he could protest, she ripped her bodice, then threw her arms around his neck and rubbed against him.

"Stop this!" he snapped, peeling her off. A shove forced her into a chair. "What the devil is wrong with you?"

"I've compromised you. Now you must marry me."

He shook his head. "You are mad."

"No. That's what happened to Miss Lutterworth.

When her father caught up with her, he had to approve the marriage, for she was hopelessly compromised." Her smile sent chills down his spine.

"You are a worse slut than your mother." He ignored her gasp. "And far more stupid. If you had paid any attention to our lectures, you would know how ridiculous you sound."

"Even Lord Sedgewick had to wed a nobody when he compromised her."

"There was no coercion involved, Miss Nichols. He'd been in love with her for weeks. It was obvious to anyone with eyes. Had they not wanted to marry, they could easily have escaped nuptials."

"But—"

"As for Miss Lutterworth, her father thought Mr. Lastmark young for marriage—he is barely twenty. The only way they could follow their hearts was to stage that silly elopement. They knew her father would catch up long before they reached Gretna Green. Having made their point, they will have the wedding they wanted. None of that applies to you, though."

"Are you saying you don't want me?" She batted her eyes.

"Exactly."

"But you'll take me anyway. A man in your position has to wed, and since the one you wanted chose another—"

His snarl stopped her cold. Damn her to hell! Somehow, she'd arranged Emily's betrothal. Had she set up a compromise scene so Emily had no choice? It would be just like her to remove someone she considered a rival. He had to talk to Charles. But first, he must rid himself of this parasite permanently.

"No, Miss Nichols. I don't have to wed. But even if I did, I would never choose you. I don't care if you ruin your reputation, so I feel no need to protect it."

"B-but all those lectures—"

"—told you what you needed to know to be accepted in town. We gave you a chance to improve yourself and the tools you would need. If you are too stupid to use that chance wisely, it is not my affair."

"But—" She started to rise, falling back when he glared.

He shook his head. "A lord does not reach into a cesspit for his wife. In your greed, you chose to spurn those who might have taken you. Now you have nothing."

"I'll ruin you if you don't wed me," she snarled.

He laughed. "The closed door? Forget it, Harriet. My credit is so far above yours, no one would ever accept your word over mine, even if I lied through my teeth. But in this case, the truth will protect me better than any chaperon. No one will think twice about me seeking privacy to beat some sense into my sister."

She blanched. "Sister?"

"My bastard sister. Your slut of a mother seduced my father. He was the only man she was entertaining that month, so there is no question about who fathered you."

"It was Captain Nichols!"

He snorted. "She married Nichols, and a good man he was, too. Far too good for the likes of her, though he learned that too late."

"No-o-o."

He ignored her protest. "My bedroom window overlooked hers, so I saw what sort of woman she was—you must know she never bothered closing her curtains. She lured others to her bed from the day she arrived. Do you want names? I can provide them. Every damned one. Eleven of them before she sank her claws into my father. Captain Nichols was immediately sent to quell a disturbance in the interior."

"I know." She glared defiantly. "Mama told me how tragic it was that he died six months before I was born, so he never even saw me."

"But she didn't mention that he'd been gone a full six months before his death." He let her do the sums, her face whitening as she realized the truth.

Nichols had never learned that his wife had conceived. She had hidden her condition from the regiment until after his death. But Jacob had heard her celebrating with his father when she confirmed her pregnancy. Their laughter had been larded with curses at Nichols's luck and with speculation on how much longer he could survive that suicide assignment.

That was the day he'd learned to hate the man who had sired him. Obsession had stripped away every vestige of honor. He'd murdered his best friend as truly as if he'd held the knife that slit his throat.

"You have to be wrong," Harriet pleaded. "Mama swore—"

"You were born twelve months after Captain Nichols left Bombay," he confirmed. "Your mother lied whenever it suited her. Didn't you wonder why the good captain was sent on that mission? Everyone knew the leader of the expedition would not return alive. There was no need to send anyone at all, for the decision had already been made to postpone a confrontation with that particular raja. But your mother begged my father to rid her of an inconvenient husband—who was one of the best officers in the regiment—thus Nichols was told to bring the raja to heel. In the meantime, the pair set about poisoning my mother so they could be together."

"No—"

"Yes. Your mother didn't love him, of course. She merely wanted the most powerful man available—just like you. If not for her maid, my mother would have died in India. He tried again, of course, but by the time he succeeded, your mother had found another protector in the person of Wentworth."

Harriet cringed into the seat, staring as if she'd never seen him before. "It can't be true."

"It's time you grew up, Harriet. The world does not exist for your benefit. Face facts. You are the bastard daughter of a whore, who was the bastard daughter of another whore. She dazzled Wentworth into marriage before he learned the truth—by then the entire regiment knew that you couldn't be Nichols's; they could count easily enough. But I doubt she changed her ways after marriage. She always tried to attach anyone who could raise her consequence."

He waited until her shoulders sagged, indicating that she'd finally accepted the truth. "We won't discuss this again. Out of deference to your blood, I gave you a chance to better yourself. You used it to anger my friends and alienate anyone who might have offered for you. I will not ask them to put up with your megrims another day. A carriage will collect you in the morning."

"To go where?" For the first time, her voice sounded forlorn.

"I can't house you without revealing your breeding, which would lower your credit even more. Bastard daughters have no entrée into society. Nor can I send you to Hawthorne Park. My aunt remains there. She is well aware of the damage your mother caused our family and would never allow you to set foot in the house."

"Surely you could demand—"

"No! I will not ask her to sacrifice her pride." He moved to the fireplace to put distance between them. "Since you have failed to attract a suitable husband, I accepted an offer from Mr. Barnes of Yorkshire. My secretary will accompany you and arrange that your dowry be handed over upon conclusion of the marriage."

"You can't!"

"Certainly, I can. I am your guardian. You are not yet of age."

"I'll run away!"

He shrugged. "If that is what you choose, I cannot stop you. But for once in your life, think before you act. Running away will sever any responsibility I have for you. You would face a choice between starvation and prostitution. There would be no gloss of elegance from setting up as a courtesan, for no gentleman would protect you after you deceived society by passing yourself off as a lady. Of course, the choice would likely not be yours. A procurer for one of the brothels would pick you up before you'd been on the streets a day. Once in a house, you would have no say in your future. The penalty for noncooperation is usually death."

"You exaggerate."

Jacob sighed. "Willful to a fault. No, I don't exaggerate. That is what you face if you run—assuming you survive the first night. Chances are equally good that you would be dead before morning. So I suggest that you pack your things and plan on living in Yorkshire. Don't flee along the way. Your chances of survival in the country are equally grim. There is no way you could find decent employment without a reference. If you turned to thievery, you would be transported. Otherwise, you would be tossed in the nearest workhouse. Marriage to Mr. Barnes is far better."

"M-Mama threatened me with the w-workhouse whenever I d-displeased her." Her remaining bravado collapsed in a spate of shuddering, stripping her of the exotic veneer she used to captivate men. She looked like a frightened child.

He hardened his heart against sympathy. He should have mentioned the workhouse earlier, but he hadn't thought Mrs. Nichols would have described one.

It was over. Harriet's future might lack balls and picnics, but it would be respectable. Given her background, it was satisfactory.

He opened the door, checked to see that the hall was empty, then led her down the back stairs to his carriage. A note to Miss Beaumont explained her sudden absence.

By the time Jacob left Inslip House, he was seething. Forcing Harriet to accept the truth had unleashed the rest of his memories.

He had long blamed Mrs. Nichols for seducing his father, but in truth, his father had not needed seduction. He had been obsessed with her from the moment they'd met—when Major Winters had stood up at his best friend's wedding. Only his dedication to duty, honed by twenty years in the army, had stayed his hand in the beginning. But with Nichols living next door, it had been impossible to avoid her. It hadn't taken him long to succumb. The result was Harriet.

Which returned his thoughts to his own obsession. He'd spent the day devising ways to convince Emily to break her betrothal to Charles. Yet that was the same dishonorable path his father had trod—sweep away all obstacles so he could take what *he* wanted.

He couldn't do it. He could not press her to an act most would consider dishonorable. Nor could he ignore the likelihood that she loved Charles. In many ways Charles was a better man than he. Harriet might have pushed the two together, but Charles was canny enough to avoid such traps if he didn't want to be caught.

Ignoring the pain searing his heart, he held his head erect and entered Lady Jersey's ballroom. He must speak to Charles—to inform him of Harriet's imminent departure if nothing else—then reinforce the congratulations he had offered Emily at their last meeting. But he must *never* reveal his love.

Emily jumped when Jacob suddenly appeared at her side. If not for Sophie, still hanging joyously onto her hand, she might have fallen.

"My lord." She nodded in greeting. "Welcome back to town. I trust you settled your emergency."

"Yes, thank you. You look well. Betrothal agrees with you." He turned away without waiting for a response, giving Emily a chance to control her face. If she looked well, it was due to Sophie's news.

Jacob noticed Sophie's excitement. "What happened, Soph? The sun is shining from your eyes."

Sophie squeezed Emily's hand to keep from shouting her joy to the world. "You have to keep this secret," she warned.

Jacob nodded.

"Lord Ashington will speak with Papa tomorrow."

"About you, I presume," he drawled, grinning. "Congratulations. I feared you would never settle."

"I'm so excited, I'm bound to give it away."

"You won't," said Emily.

"Especially if we discuss something else," added Jacob, holding out both arms. "Let's get something to drink while you tell me all the latest gossip. Come along, ladies."

Richard watched Jacob lead the girls into the refreshment room, then turned to Charles. "Tomorrow afternoon," he ordered, picking up their conversation. "Delay will worsen the scandal. Drive Emily to Richmond. I'll handle the rest."

"What about Harriet?"

"She will be gone—be surprised when Jacob tells you about it. He must have spoken to her or he wouldn't be here."

Charles raised his brows.

"Later. Concentrate on Emily. You claim you want her happy. This is the only way you can manage it."

Chapter Fifteen

*E*mily watched Kew Gardens slide past as Charles
tooled his curricle along the road. She'd been
delighted by last night's invitation to spend an afternoon at Richmond Park. Excitement had sparkled in
his eyes, hinting at a surprise.

Yet today he seemed nervous and unusually quiet,
his few comments sounding stilted. She knew he was
an excellent whip, so he didn't have the excuse of
needing to concentrate on the horses.

"Is that the famous pagoda?" she asked, pointing
to a slender tower visible beyond the trees.

"Yes." He didn't even turn his head to look.

"It seems so fragile! Why does it not blow over? It
must be taller than St. Paul's."

"It is shorter than it looks."

"But—" She counted. "There are ten floors, plus
that spire."

"Perspective, Em. Each level is progressively
shorter, making the building seem taller than it is."
He sounded exasperated.

She gave up on conversation. He had certainly displayed a different side of his character in the last fortnight. Away from society's gaze, he became moody
and unpredictable, mired in thoughts far more serious
than most gentlemen entertained. Whatever quarrel
was occupying his mind left no room for her.

It boded ill for the future. Could she tolerate a lifetime of silence? Or a lifetime of never knowing which

face to expect? In five days, this man would be her
husband. How could they manage if he would not
even speak to her?

The questions rolled around her head, pausing long
enough to stab her temples on each lap. The throbbing
set up a sympathetic roiling in her stomach, made
worse by each jolt of wheels across ruts.

Swallowing hard, she forced the doubts aside.
Seeing Jacob last night had reminded her that this was
her only course. He had treated her no differently
from Sophie, laughing over the latest gossip, congratu-
lating Sophie on her prospects, and demanding details
of the house Charles had purchased. He was so obviously content with his life that Emily had nearly burst
into tears. How could he accept being tied to a girl
who wanted only his money and position?

Her bravado collapsed as Charles turned through
Richmond's gates.

What if Harriet was right? What if Charles had proposed as a favor to her brother? Richard had expressed fear that she would never find a suitable
match—not to her, of course, but overhearing his
words to their mother had hurt. And Richard knew
their financial position even better than she did, so he
might have stepped in to make sure she was settled.
Charles might have agreed out of friendship without
really considering the matter until it was too late.

Yet what could she do? If would be a terrible blow
to her family if she called off her betrothal.

The very fact that she'd put the thought into words
startled her, for she hadn't consciously considered it.
Yet she did not see how she could spend her life with
a man who didn't want her.

Many women do.

She clenched her teeth, but it was true. Aristocratic
marriages were seldom made for personal reasons.
Lords enjoyed many privileges, but the price of privi-
lege was duty. She had a duty to her family to wed
well. Her duty to Charles was to provide an heir and

run his household. It was a system that had worked well for centuries.

Despite her childish dreams, love had no place in society, though most couples formed congenial relationships in time. She should count her blessings. Charles was an admirable man and an excellent catch for the insignificant daughter of an impoverished viscount. He would accord her respect at home and in public. Whatever he did in private was none of her business, so she must stop fearing that wedding a lady who did not love him would blight his life.

If she hoped for a comfortable future, she must put the last of her childhood dreams behind her. Immediately. The humiliation of spinsterhood and the pain of living next door to Harriet justified accepting any offer, even one from a man far worse than Charles.

"We are here," he announced as his groom rushed to hold the horses.

He lifted her down, then led her to where servants were laying out lunch. Three other couples had already arrived.

Smiling up at him, she commented lightly on the herd of fallow deer watching their progress. It was a beautiful day.

Her temples pounded harder.

Two hours later, Emily accompanied Charles on a stroll along the riverbank. Food had settled her stomach and diminished her headache.

Much of the park lay well back from the Thames, its highest point a hill from which both St. Paul's and Windsor were visible on clear days. Like today. She had hoped to take in the view, but any walk with Charles was good. He'd not sought to be alone with her since his mother's ball.

"You seem excited today." He smiled as they rounded a clump of trees and turned along a worn path. Swans glided downstream, oblivious to their presence.

"Not exactly." She lifted her face to catch the breeze, wishing she could remove her bonnet and feel the wind in her hair. "But fresh air is wonderful. I am weary of coal dust and smoke. Richmond is a lovely park."

"True. But it does have dangers. Stay on the path," he cautioned as it curved. "The river erodes the bank at this point so one never quite knows where it is safe to walk."

"Do you come here often?"

"Half a dozen times a year. As you said, it is nice to escape town, especially in August. London becomes quite stifling then."

Richard had mentioned the summer heat when he first moved to town. In recent years, he'd passed those weeks at house parties or home at Cherry Hill. But Charles had a job.

They walked in silence for several minutes.

"Oh, look." She pointed to a clump of yellow flowers at the base of a rock between the path and the river. "Buttercups. Is it safe to pick some?"

"As long as you're careful. In fact, you might want to rest here a moment. I just remembered that Larkin is leaving early. I need to speak with him. Would you stay here until I return? I won't be long."

"Take your time. It's quite peaceful."

"Thank you. Just don't walk nearer the bank than the rock. I don't wish to haul you out of the river."

"It wouldn't be the first time."

He laughed, then kissed her lightly on the cheek and headed back, taking a shortcut through a stand of trees.

She frowned, for his kiss had been no more exciting than the ones Richard used to give her when he left for a new school term.

Stop this!

She stared at the shifting light patterns on the water, forcing her mind back to duty. Tomorrow she would hire upper servants for her new house and talk to

Gunter's about food for her wedding breakfast. Or perhaps her new cook could lend a hand.

The delicate scent of buttercups tickled her nose. Birds trilled from the trees. The balmy sunlight and glistening water relaxed her, letting her mind wander—organizing her own home . . . another court presentation once she was wed . . . an unwelcome reminder that Harriet would attend the Cavendish rout with them tonight . . . a wish that Sophie and Ashington had accompanied them to Richmond, though that might have annoyed Charles. His acceptance was still too new to trust.

The ever-changing patterns of light mesmerized her, reviving memories of the best moments of her life—waltzing until she floated among the stars . . . laughter that lingered hours after parting . . . deep drugging kisses that involved so much more than a meeting of lips . . . drowning in eyes that glinted sapphire blue no matter how much she tried to make them green. . . .

Her fist crushed the flowers.

What was she to do?

Jacob trudged along the path, wondering for the thousandth time why Richard had insisted that they drive to Richmond today—using Jacob's curricle, no less. Granted, London grew wearisome at times, but he'd just spent a week in the country. Now that Harriet was gone—his footman had watched her climb meekly into the carriage at dawn—he wanted to concentrate on Parliament. Immersing himself in work was the best way to put this disastrous Season behind him.

Playing the carefree friend with Emily last night had been so hard that he'd decided to skip the rest of the social Season. With Emily taken and Sophie on the verge of a betrothal, his obligations to the Beaux were over. By next year, his role as a confirmed bachelor would be so established that he would no longer be tempted.

"I'm worried about Emily," said Richard without warning.

"Why?"

"She isn't herself lately." He waved a hand as if uncertain how to express his thoughts. "I've never seen her this quiet. It's as if she's hiding a mortal wound. I'm afraid that Charles coerced her into this betrothal. She will never renege on a promise directly, but I fear she might throw herself in the river rather than wed him."

"Absurd. She would never distress your family." But his heart clenched. The oddest people turned to suicide. His mother—

But Em had sworn that his mother was innocent, and she'd been right. His aunt had confirmed it, adding details that left no room for doubt. And in debunking his fears, Emily had made it clear that she considered suicide the height of dishonor. He tried to explain, but Richard cut him off.

"Under normal circumstances, I would agree. But even the most levelheaded person can break if the stakes are high enough. Look what happened to Rothmore after he lost everything to Hardesty."

"Rothmore was drunk and stupid. He'd been hounded since birth by a disapproving father and a harridan of a mother, who reminded him constantly that he would one day be responsible for eleven females, then intimated he would make a muck of it. When he lost everything, he couldn't face her with the truth." And if Rothmore's father had entailed his estate like any sensible man, the family would have been protected, as his had been after his great-grandfather's stupidity.

"But that's exactly my point with Em," insisted Richard. "Mother has been telling her for years that she would have but one chance to wed. Failure will keep her at Cherry Hill, condemned to spinsterhood. Why wouldn't she believe it? She knows Mother can never survive another trip to town. This one has weakened her considerably."

"Sorry to hear that."

"Thank you. That doesn't matter at the moment, though. It's Emily I am concerned about. Harriet deflected several suitors, stripping her court of everyone but Charles."

Guilt slammed through Jacob's chest, muffling Richard's words. He'd driven off several men himself, including the very eligible Larkin. Such acts should have told him from the beginning that he was in love with her. His blindness had forced her into Charles's arms.

Richard was still speaking. "I can hardly share my suspicions with Charles, but I am truly worried, Jacob. You must help me jolly her out of her megrims before she does something stupid."

Jacob nearly groaned. The last thing he needed was to seek out Emily to lighten her spirits.

He'd barely survived last night's ball, for he'd been aware of every breath she took, even when he was looking at Sophie. But Richard was right. Emily was not her usual self. He'd assumed she was merely tired, or possibly hurt by some jibe of Harriet's, but now . . .

"I'll do what I can, but it would be better if she put off marriage until she finds someone she cares for."

"A nice idea, but she would never consider it. You know she takes honor as seriously as any man."

Jacob's heart sank as he stifled an offer to take care of her. He had no evidence that she would accept him.

Richard continued. "But thank you for helping me. She is with a group just over the next hill. It should be a pleasant outing, but her eyes looked odd when she mentioned it. I've never heard her speak of rivers in quite that way. I can't risk losing her, so we can watch from that grove of oaks and make sure she is safe."

So that's what this was about. Richard was crazy if he thought spying on his sister was a good idea. But before he could protest, Richard grabbed his arm.

"My God," he hissed sharply. "She's going to jump."

Eyes closed, Emily was rising from a rock perched a dozen feet above the water. Currents had undercut the bank to a dangerous degree. She stepped closer, then closer yet . . .

"Get her away from the cliff," hissed Richard. "I'll fetch help."

Before Jacob could respond, he was gone.

Emily stretched her arms up and forward, as if to dive into the river. Another step would hurl her over the edge.

Jacob's disbelief vanished. She was truly contemplating suicide.

Afraid to shout lest he startle her, he sprinted forward, circling so he could approach between her and the water. If she flinched, he must be in position to catch her.

He hadn't gone three steps before the ground collapsed, plunging him into the river. Water closed over his head.

Lungs bursting, he forced his way to the surface and gasped for air. But he couldn't stay afloat. The river was shockingly deep at this point. Currents sucked at his leaden clothing. His boots could have anchored a warship.

A shout pulled Emily from her reverie. She'd been too lost in dreams of Jacob's arms to realize that she had stood, reliving their most recent embrace.

A splash drew her eyes upstream. Someone had fallen in. Charles?

She was whirling to run for help when a head broke the surface.

Jacob.

"My God." He couldn't swim. They'd laughed about their mutual lack of ability after he'd pulled her from the lake—

Do something!

The current would sweep him past in seconds, but the bank was too high to reach him. Cursing, she rushed down the hill to where the bank was lower.

He again broke the surface. His arms flailed wildly, but his soaked clothes would drag him down, as she knew all too well. She would never forget how her gown had nearly drowned her that day.

He was too far away to catch, and moving farther

out every moment. The current swept away from the bank.

"Kick!" she shouted. "This way!"

He must have heard her, for he turned toward her voice. But the current was too strong. He would never make it.

A branch lay under a willow tree farther downstream. Where she found the strength to lift it she didn't know, but somehow she flung one end into the river.

"Grab this."

"Too heavy," he gasped. "Pull you in, too."

"Grab it! If you don't, I'll have to jump in after you. You know I can't swim!"

He splashed harder, catching the end and nearly pulling her over. He was heavier than he looked.

Emily braced her heels on an exposed root and leaned back against the trunk. "You have to pull your way along the branch, Jacob. I haven't the strength to drag you."

He managed, though the effort was nearly too much for him. When he tried to stand, he fell.

She waded out to hold his head above water and help him to safety. They collapsed on the bank.

Jacob didn't move.

"Jacob!"

Her hands frantically searched for injuries. She found no obvious broken bones and no blood. But he remained inert.

"Jacob! Wake up!"

His chest rose and fell, so he was breathing. Tearing off her bonnet, she set an ear against it, reassured when she heard his heart.

"Damn you, Jacob! Wake up!"

She brushed the hair from his forehead.

His eyes flickered open.

"Are you all right?" Her fingers found a scrape along one temple.

"Out of breath." He struggled to sit, then frowned.

"You should be whipped for taking such a chance, Em. You might have drowned."

"If you were dead, it wouldn't matter." Tears flooded her cheeks as relief shattered her barriers. "Did you expect me to sit here and wave as your body floated past?"

Jacob was so shocked at her admission that he barely registered her sarcasm. She cared!

His resolutions dissolved as he pulled her into his arms.

"Em!" Rolling her beneath him, he plundered her mouth. Her taste exploded on his tongue, recalling the orchard, Lady Debenham's garden, and every erotic dream that had plagued his sleep in the weeks since. All the love and passion he'd been suppressing roared out, doubling and redoubling as she melted beneath him. Her lips molded his. Her hands pulled him closer and closer yet, flooding his senses. Heaven could be no better than Emily's arms.

Suddenly she gasped, shoving him away. "What are you doing?" she demanded, shock blazing in her eyes. "Harriet will be furious."

"Wha—Harriet has nothing to do with us."

"Don't lie to me. She told me about your betrothal weeks ago."

"What?" He sat up, horrified to see that she was serious. "That scheming little witch!"

"Don't deny it. I know you wanted to announce it later, but she told me the whole story."

"What story?"

She scowled. "How your parents arranged your betrothal before you left India, but you wanted her to have a Season before you made it public in case she changed her mind. She—"

"Enough." Jacob held her head so she had to look at him. Fury burned so hot, he nearly strangled on it. So that's how Harriet had forced Emily onto Charles. "Every word is a lie, Em. Yes, Harriet is betrothed. To a sergeant she knew in India. I accepted his offer yesterday. She left for Yorkshire this morning."

"She's gone?"

"Gone. As for her tale, my family left India six months before she was born. Captain Nichols was already dead. His wife was my father's mistress. I didn't know of Harriet's existence until two months ago."

"You can't mean . . ." Her eyes widened.

He nodded. "She is my father's bastard. My half sister. A half sister I wish to hell had never been born. Her mother caused endless trouble twenty years ago, and Harriet is causing worse today."

"But why would she claim—" Again she stopped.

"Greed. Like her mother, she covets money and power. I should never have introduced her to society, but I'd made the arrangements before I knew anything about her beyond her birth date."

"Which told you her parentage." Her hand lifted to cover his.

He nodded. "It wasn't her fault her mother was a slut. I thought I owed her something in deference to our shared blood."

"She didn't know, did she?"

He shook his head.

"So everything was lies?" asked Emily. "I can't believe it."

"Everything. She's no lady, Em. I doubt she would recognize truth if it slapped her face."

"What happened, Jacob?" She struggled to her feet.

He shook water from his hair, then led her away from the river into a sunlit dell that captured enough warmth to keep them from catching a chill. With luck, its seclusion would prevent anyone from seeing them—his clothes had soaked the front of her gown, making it obvious what they'd been doing. "I told you my father was a murderer."

She nodded.

"It was Captain Nichols that he killed." He shook his head. "Not in person, you understand. But Mrs. Nichols mesmerized him, obsessing him until he could think of nothing but possessing her. Under her spell, he sent his best friend into a fight he couldn't win and tried to poison my mother."

"None of which was your fault," she said, hearing traces of guilt in his voice.

"No. But his behavior is yet another example of how the Hawthorne curse ruins lives. I can't escape it."

"Of course you can." She covered his lips when he tried to protest. "I know your family history as well as you do. Perhaps better."

"How—"

"Your aunt. It is her favorite subject." One Emily encouraged. "You say obsession is a family curse, but I don't believe it."

"My great-grandfather and the South Seas Bubble."

"Dozens of men lost fortunes in that debacle, but only one Winters did so—the seventh earl. Look at the rest of his generation. His cousin Jeremy Winters was an explorer who longed to discover new lands. He even participated in several expeditions to South America."

"I know. The family often laughs at his obsession."

"Yet he turned down an invitation to join a South Seas voyage because he didn't want to leave his new wife and child alone, even though there were plenty of family members who could have looked after them while he was gone."

His lips pursed, but he said nothing.

"And what about the seventh earl's brother, Thomas? He was known for deep gaming before his marriage. It was said that a man need only rattle dice in the next room to entice him to the table. Yet he turned his back on games after his marriage, handing his wife's dowry to a banker who multiplied it through sound investments. When he died without issue, his fortune rescued the earldom."

"It is not the same."

"Isn't it? I don't believe obsession is a trait one can inherit. I do believe the members of your family are passionate about their interests, but that is something else entirely. Some use the so-called Winters curse to justify following their own selfish whims, then disclaim responsibility for the consequences. That may have been your father's excuse, but you have already demonstrated that you prefer duty. Why else did you try to do right by Harriet?"

"None of my ancestors ignored duty, but they were locked into obsessive behavior despite their responsibilities."

"No. The ones who came to grief never paid more than lip service to duty. They were stubborn, arrogant men who never admitted fault and continued down their destructive paths even when it was obvious that they must come to grief. But you are not that stubborn. I've seen you backtrack when wrong."

Maybe. Jacob shook his head. God knew he'd made too many mistakes in recent weeks to consider himself infallible. Kissing Emily had been yet another in a long line of—

He stared. Emily had broken off that kiss because she didn't want him to betray Harriet. But she herself was betraying Charles.

"Why did you let me kiss you?" he demanded.

She blushed. "I wasn't thinking and—"

"That isn't like you. Nor is it like you to be furious that I might betray Harriet when you were betraying Charles—and don't tell me that your betrothal is a lie. I was there when he announced it."

Her blush deepened. "It was a mistake. Much of what I just told you mirrors what I'd realized about myself. Making a good match is a goal drummed into girls' heads from the moment of birth. It is a duty for which we train for years, a duty so essential that our entire lives are judged on whether we achieve it. But success in the eyes of the world is not worth tying a decent man to a life of regret. I was trying to decide how to tell him when you fell into the river."

"You are breaking your betrothal?" He had to have heard wrong. He wanted it too much.

She nodded. "It is awful of me, and it will embroil him in scandal, but remaining together would hurt worse."

"It would." He raised a hand to trace her jawline, reveling in the softness of her skin. "It would," he sighed, sliding an arm around her shoulders.

His mouth covered hers, softly this time, tasting, savoring, licking slowly around her lips. He inhaled her soft sigh as he laid her gently on the grass. This was what he wanted, what he needed, the only thing that could make him complete.

"Jacob?" she asked as his hand moved to her breast to find the nipple puckered from her damp gown.

"I love you," he said, deepening the kiss. By the time he pulled back, he was panting.

"You do?"

Her heart raced beneath his palm. "You're my obsession, Emily. Or my passion, if you prefer. I chose not to pursue it once you accepted Charles, because acting on it would dishonor us both."

"I can't—"

"What I hated was my slowness to accept the truth. I've loved you for ten years, but I convinced myself that I was too young to know my mind. And you were certainly too young to know yours. So I passed it off as gratitude for your friendship. When you came to London, I was so used to that idiocy, that I didn't think—until the night in Lady Debenham's garden. I meant to tell you, to court you properly. But Charles—" He clenched his fists.

"I love you, Jacob. I always have." She smiled up at him.

Her smile put the sun to shame. Happiness bubbled up, bringing a lightness he'd never felt before. He kissed her again, covering her from head to toe, aching as his hips flexed against her. Heat rose until their clothes steamed.

She moaned his name, rolling until she was on top. Her hands framed his face as she stared down at him—and laughed.

"You look like a highwayman, Jacob. Disheveled hair, muddy clothes, scraped face. How can I love you so much?"

"Practice." He took her mouth, his hands hovering over her ties, itching to open her gown.

Voices brought him to his senses.

"We need to stop before we do something we'll regret," he panted, jumping to his feet. A tug brought her to hers. "Where is Cha—"

His voice died as Charles entered the dell, accompanied by a smiling Richard.

Charles examined them from head to foot, missing none of the grass clinging to their damp clothes. "I trust you have an explanation, Em?"

Jacob speared his friend with a piercing glare, then snapped his mouth shut. Satisfaction burned in those green eyes, not anger. Charles knew. And arriving with Richard meant he'd planned this.

He laid a reassuring hand on Emily's shoulder, then followed Richard into the trees, growling, "You'll pay for this, Richard."

Emily wanted to crawl into a hole, but that was cowardly. It was bad enough that she must jilt Charles. Having him find her with Jacob might destroy their long friendship. His face was grimmer than ever.

Yet his eyes weren't.

"Charles." She stopped, groping for words.

"Spit it out, Em." He stroked her hand. "We both know the truth."

"We do?" She shook her head. "I should not have accepted your offer. It was unfair, for I will never be the wife you deserve."

"You don't love me?"

She drew a deep breath. "No."

"I'm glad."

She stared.

"Let's both be honest. When you arrived in town, you dazzled me."

"What?"

"You are a lovely lady, and you had changed so much since I'd last seen you that I fell into an instant infatuation. But it was not truly love. When the flush waned, I was horrified to discover that I feel the same for you as I do for Sophie."

"Oh, my!"

"Exactly. I love her dearly, but not as a wife."

"I understand." She smiled. "You are more a brother than a husband."

He burst out laughing, draining tension away. She joined in, overcome with relief.

"Thank you, Em," he finally gasped, pulling her into an exuberant hug. "I hope we can remain friends, my dear, but I would have made you an abominable husband."

"And I would have driven you mad in a month. Thank you for being a gentleman." She met his gaze. "I hope you won't suffer from it."

"Never. I've enough credit to survive a jilt, especially if we remain friends."

"Always."

Releasing her, he raised her hand to his lips as the others returned.

"I trust you've settled your affairs," said Jacob coolly.

"I trust you've a betrothal to announce," added Richard, staring at Jacob.

"Of course. It would be best that she wed as arranged, only with a different groom. You'll stand up with me, of course."

"Of course."

Emily stared. He'd announced a wedding without even proposing! "Haven't you forgotten something?" she demanded, pulling Jacob around to face her.

"What?"

"Planning a wedding seems rather presumptuous when you've neglected to obtain a bride."

He snapped his mouth shut, shaking his head. "I assumed—"

"Assumptions are dangerous, for half of them are false. That is how we got into this mess to begin with."

"Very well." With an exaggerated sigh of vexation, he dropped onto one knee, pulling her hand to his lips. "My dear Miss Hughes. You are the loveliest creature alive, a diamond of the first water who must steal the heart of every man who sees those amber eyes or hears your melodious voice. The sun pales beside . . ."

Behind him, Richard and Charles rolled their eyes.

Emily paid them no heed. This was better than her best fantasy. Sunlight sparkled from his dark hair, obscuring traces of his recent mishap—or maybe it was the tears of happiness shimmering in her eyes. No one could ever have received a more perfect offer.

". . . so please accept my hand in marriage, Em," he finished, again kissing her fingers. "Let me cherish you as you deserve. Share your wisdom, your love, and your life with me. Forevermore."

She hesitated, one niggling doubt staying her tongue—probably because she'd used it so often to convince herself that he was unworthy. "Tell me about Lord Raymond Perigord, Jacob. The tales do not fit what I know of you," she added when his eyes darkened. "But they are pervasive."

Jacob sucked in a deep breath, relaxing the grip that was suddenly strangling her fingers. "The tales are a mixture of lies and truth, Em. Tell her about it, Charles."

Charles shook his head. "Lord Raymond is a cheat, Emily. Not because he needs to support himself by fleecing greenlings or bilking honest merchants or paying debts with counterfeit notes. His father is the Duke of Metcalf, and he receives a generous allowance. But Lord Raymond enjoys the excitement of risk."

"Then why is he free?" She'd met the man in several ballrooms.

"His father," said Richard shortly. "The man is as culpable as his son, if you ask me."

"No one did," said Jacob.

"The rumors have the tale topsy-turvy," said Charles. "Jacob found evidence that Lord Raymond used forged documents to sell land for ten times its

value. He was ready to speak to a magistrate about it
when Lord Raymond fled the country. We thought
that was the end of it, but Lord Raymond returned.
By then, the evidence was gone."

"Gone? You mean stolen?" Emily looked at Jacob.

He shook his head. "The evidence included the
forged documents and the testimony of the man who
had bought the land. He'd been furious at being
cheated. But when I returned to take him to the magistrate, he refused me entrance and claimed it had all
been a mistake."

"Why?"

"He'd resold the land to Metcalf for a tidy profit and
handed over the documents. The next day rumors swept
Mayfair that I had cheated Lord Raymond out of a
parcel of property. I had no way to counter them, especially since there *was* a parcel I'd recently bought."

Charles and Richard cursed under their breath.

"So you looked vindictive," said Emily, squeezing
his hand.

"It will pass in time." He met her gaze. "Why don't
you answer my question now? Will you marry me or
not?"

"Yes, Jacob." She gasped when he bounded to his
feet to draw her against his side.

"The kiss comes later, without the audience," he
growled into her ear, then glared at his friends.
"Satisfied?"

Richard nodded.

"Good, because I may have to call you out for en-
dangering Emily."

"She was perfectly safe," said Charles. "I've been
to that spot a dozen times. The bank only *looks* unstable. You could race horses along there without doing
any damage."

"What are you talking about?" demanded Emily.

"They set us up," Jacob explained. "Charles left
you in danger while Richard poured out his fears
about your inclination to suicide."

"What?" She glared at Richard.

"There was *no* danger!" snapped Charles.

"Then why did the bank collapse?" demanded Jacob. "Three steps, and it tossed me into the river."

"He nearly drowned," snarled Emily.

"How—" Richard stared.

"Em jumped in to fish me out."

"But she can't swim."

"Neither can I."

"What?" Charles stared from Emily to Jacob, then turned to Richard.

"I didn't know, either."

"Em did," said Jacob, pulling her closer.

Guilt sent both Richard and Charles back a step.

"No more plots," Jacob said bluntly. "You nearly killed us both, and for nothing. She was going to jilt you anyway."

Emily watched the Beaux rush into apologies as they reforged the friendship that had splintered in recent weeks. It was good to see them together again. She'd feared that Charles and Jacob would suffer from her brief betrothal.

"Come along, Richard," Charles said at last. "I'll give you a ride back to town." He turned to Jacob. "You can bring Emily."

"Gladly." The moment the others left, he pulled Emily into his arms. "Now you get your betrothal kiss."

This one was even better, Emily decided hazily as every bone in her body melted. Knowing that he loved her and acknowledging her love aloud banished the last doubt, allowing passion free rein. Sparks ignited fires that swelled to consume her flesh. Her heart raced, trying to batter its way out of her chest. Moans burst from her throat, begging for more, though she lacked the words to explain what she needed. His kiss was everything she had expected, everything promised in ten years of dreams, everything love should be.

"I love you," he murmured in her ear when he paused to catch his breath. "Never doubt my love. The last fortnight has been dreadful."

"And never doubt mine," she said, smiling as he pulled her against his side and headed toward his curricle. "You were right that I was too young ten years ago, but I *did* know my mind."

"I'll apologize for that charge, then." He paused before they left the trees to kiss her one last time, then brushed the grass from her gown. She smoothed the wrinkles from his jacket. Confident that they would appear proper from a distance, they stepped into the open.

"So tell me about our wedding," he said, offering his arm. "What do you have planned?"

"Small," she said, shaking her head. "But perhaps we should expand it. Gather every gossip in town so they get the facts straight. You don't need more twisted rumors."

He laughed. "Perfect, my love. With Richard and Charles at our side and Lady Inslip assisting your mother, we will nip any scandal in the bud. We'll hold the breakfast at Hawthorne House," he added as they reached his curricle.

"Perfect." Raising on tiptoe, she kissed him tenderly, then let him lift her onto the seat. The grinning groom leaped up behind as the team trotted toward the road, heading for the future Jacob had thought was forever out of reach.

A grin suddenly split his face. Challenging his friends was impossible, but he could still take his revenge.

Emily burst into laughter when he announced that they would go immediately into the matchmaking business. It was time *all* the Beaux retired from raking.